Tactical Lies

JANE BLYTHE

Cover designed by RBA Designs

❀ Created with Vellum

Acknowledgments

I'd like to thank everyone who played a part in bringing this story to life. Particularly my mom who is always there to share her thoughts and opinions with me. My wonderful cover designer Letitia who did an amazing job with this stunning cover. My fabulous editor Lisa for all the hard work she puts into polishing my work. My awesome team, Sophie, Robyn, and Clayr, without your help I'd never be able to run my street team. And my fantastic street team members who help share my books with every share, comment, and like!

And of course a big thank you to all of you, my readers! Without you I wouldn't be living my dreams of sharing the stories in my head with the world!

CHAPTER

One

August 16th
11:13 A.M.

What was she thinking?

Could she have picked a more dangerous country to move to?

Okay, so Connor Charleston knew he was slightly exaggerating. Cambodia was, in fact, a relatively safe country to visit and even live in. But there were still rumored to be a few remote pockets where remnants of the Khmer Rouge remained, renamed and revamped, but as dangerous as they had been years ago.

While he didn't have firsthand knowledge of how bad things had been in the country during that time his grandfather, who had been a Navy SEAL, had served during that era and had performed a rescue with his team of a group of aid workers who were captured.

After his dad's Delta Force team had been ambushed and slaughtered, and his mom remarried the only survivor just months later, then both of them were arrested and "committed suicide" he and his siblings had been raised by his grandparents.

Which meant he'd heard a lot of stories about what it was like to serve in special forces over the years. First from his dad when he was younger, and then from his grandfather when he was a little older.

The most chilling of those stories was the one that took place on the very land he was currently hiking across.

A place where a lot of innocent blood had been shed.

A place where his grandfather met the woman he would wind up marrying and having three children with when he saved her from what would have been a brutal death.

Now, fifty years later, Connor felt like he was following in his footsteps.

Was he going to wind up marrying the woman he'd come to Cambodia looking for?

Almost definitely not.

He'd blown that shot over a decade ago and regretted it ever since.

It wasn't even likely that Becca Marsden's life was in danger. There was going to be no saving her from bloodshed and being her hero like he should have been back when they were in college.

Back then, he'd flipped out and made a stupid mistake. When he should have been standing by her, supporting her in every way she needed him to, he'd run in a panic, and by the time he realized how stupid and selfish he was being, it was already too late.

There was no point in denying he'd love a second chance with the only woman he'd ever loved, but he knew holding out hope it would happen was ridiculous. Becca had every reason to hate him, and he couldn't even fault her for it.

Becca had needed him, and he wasn't there for her.

How could he ever make that right?

Knowing that he couldn't was the only reason it had taken him twelve years to get his head on straight and come to do what he should have found a way to do all those years ago. Instead, he'd been a coward, dropped out of college, joined the navy, made it onto a SEAL team, served, and then left to work for the world-renowned Prey Security. He'd hidden behind the shield of it would be impossible to fix things, so why even bother, for years longer than he should have, and now, as he hiked through Cambodian forests he was ashamed of himself.

Especially as he thought about how brave and strong Becca was. Everything she'd had to fight through. The struggles she would live with for the rest of her life. And all that she had accomplished.

After graduating, Becca founded an aid agency with a couple of her friends, and they had now grown to have bases in several Asian countries. They provided both medical and educational support for small, impoverished villages. She had dedicated her life to doing such an amazing thing and he was so proud of her.

Would she believe him when he told her that?

Just because Connor would love to believe that after twelve years and a lot of growing and maturing on both their parts the past could be laid to rest, he knew Becca wouldn't see things the same way. They would likely never be together in the way he wanted them to be but maybe they could at least become friends.

Hell, he'd take acquaintances who talked occasionally.

Whatever he could get.

Because it didn't matter how many years had passed, she still owned his heart.

As he approached the village where Becca lived, he fought against the urge to hold his breath, feeling like he was a kid all over again.

Wishing that he'd handled things differently, better, was pointless. The breakup of their relationship rested squarely on his shoulders, one hundred percent. He wasn't denying that, and he would tell Becca when he saw her.

But he *did* wish he hadn't wasted so many years getting his head on straight.

Why had it taken learning that his mom had been gang raped while on a mission for the CIA and had fallen pregnant from the assault, resulting in his baby sister, for him to realize he had to go to Becca?

It was stupid of him and only added to the shame he felt.

If his dad had been alive to see how he'd treated Becca in the aftermath of her own vicious assault he would have torn him to shreds. His dad had been a calm guy, who never raised his voice and always disciplined them fairly, taking time to ensure they actually learned something rather than just punishing them.

Connor had a feeling this would have been the exception.

When the woman his dad loved had been raped and wound up pregnant, he'd stood by her side, supported her, and raised that child as though it were his own. Because from all his memories of life before his parents' deaths, he couldn't remember a single time that their dad had treated Cassandra any differently from how he'd treated him and his brothers.

Yet when the woman he loved had been raped and wound up pregnant, he'd panicked and ran. The fact he'd barely been twenty at the time made no difference. If he was old enough to know he was in love with Becca and wanted to marry and spend the rest of his life with her, he was old enough to stand by her no matter what.

This was why shame was the dominant emotion inside him as he spied the small village where Becca lived and worked. Set amongst the trees, it was comprised of small huts where fifty or so families lived. There was also a clinic that Becca and her team had built and managed, and a schoolhouse where they taught the village's children, again built and managed by Becca and her team. There were no stores, what the people couldn't grow themselves, they bought from the nearest larger village about fifty or so miles away. There were no cars, electricity, sewage, or running water, but from what he'd learned, Becca's team had generators brought in. People walked or rode in small carts pulled by donkeys, and small farms littered the landscape.

It was like stepping back in time.

Knowing this was the life Becca had chosen for herself, that she wasn't just good at what she did but loved it and was making a difference doing it, filled him with so much pride it nudged a little of the shame out.

A burst of childish laughter suddenly filled the air, and as he watched, a group of children rushed out of what must be the school. They were all giggling and chattering, and as he got closer, he saw a woman step out the door, watching the little ones with a smile on her face.

He froze.

Long, inky black hair hung in a braid down the woman's back. Dressed in a white tank top that showed off her toned arms, and a simple pair of cotton pants that hung to her sneaker-covered feet, he didn't have to be close enough to see her face to know who it was.

Becca.

His Becca.

His moonlight.

Between her midnight blue eyes and her silky black locks, the pale skin of her face had always reminded him of the moon, and the nickname had popped into his head not long after they went on their first date when they were fourteen.

Now her pale skin was tanned, likely from spending most of her time outdoors, and as her head turned in his direction, he saw even from twenty-odd feet away the sudden tension in her body, the sweet smile he was used to seeing on her suddenly gone, he realized how little he knew about this woman.

This Becca. The one she'd turned into over the twelve long years since he'd broken her heart. He also realized how deeply he craved learning everything about who she was now. Connor wanted to know every single thing there was to know about her, all her secrets, all the things that made her sad, all the things that made her angry, and all the things that brought her joy.

He wanted it all.

But from the tension rolling off the woman watching him, he knew she wanted the complete opposite.

August 16th
   12:00 P.M.

Surely, she was seeing things.

Because there was no way *he* would be there.

Becca Marsden stared at the man standing not even twenty feet away from her and seriously pondered the possibility that she had died or was currently hallucinating.

Anything made more sense than the idea that Connor Charleston was in Cambodia.

What on earth would bring him here?

It certainly couldn't be her.

Of that she was certain.

Even though they had grown up together, her family living right across the street from his, playing together as small children, dating through high school, together through some of college, she knew that Connor was not the kind of man you trusted to be there when you needed him.

She'd thought he was.

Right after her assault, he'd been her rock. Staying by her side in the hospital, supporting her through surgeries, giving her everything she needed.

Until things got worse.

Then he bailed.

She would never forgive him for that.

But Connor was part of her past. It had been twelve years since they'd broken up, and in that last decade and a bit, she had grown and changed a lot. She'd banded together with a group of friends and started an aid agency that provided support to thousands of vulnerable people across Asia, something she was proud of. She'd fallen in love with another man and been engaged, only to lose him to a horrible car accident.

Becca had had a whole life without Connor, and she rarely thought of him anymore.

It was too painful.

Going back was the last thing she wanted to do, dredging up old memories she had worked so hard to deal with, it was too much. Already she'd lost the boy she thought she was going to spend her life with and the man who had captured the heart she'd thought was dead and brought it back to life.

As badly as she wanted to believe it wasn't really Connor closing the distance between them, she couldn't.

It was him.

The why didn't matter, all that did was that she wasn't going to talk to him. She knew her struggles, knew her strengths and weaknesses, knew her triggers, and Connor ticked all those boxes. He was her greatest struggle, her greatest weakness, and her greatest trigger.

Seeing him, talking to him, interacting with him in any way was too much for her.

Ducking back inside the schoolhouse, Becca did what her old therapist would have rebuked her for. Lived in denial. Connor wasn't there. Connor wasn't there for her. Connor wasn't her problem anymore. Connor was nothing to her.

It had been over for such a long time that he shouldn't hold any power over her anymore.

But he did.

Just a single glimpse of him told her he had way too much power over her despite the fact more than a decade had passed since they last saw one another.

Still, for now, denial it was. It was easier. Better for her blood pressure, too, than screaming at him. So, she went to work tidying up the small room. The kids did a good job of helping keep it clean, they were so excited about all their school supplies that they treated them like treasures. There were still things she could organize though, and that's what she started doing.

However, her hands faltered when she heard the unmistakable sound of boots against the floor.

Not only was Connor in Cambodia but he was here in her schoolhouse.

A space that was supposed to be a safe one for her.

While her parents and sister would love for her to return home, they understood that her work kept her sane. It helped still the storm inside her. Over the years, she had learned to calm and keep it under control, but it was always there, simmering under the surface.

There was one surefire way to send it into a rage.

And it was currently standing behind her.

Tears blurred her vision as she sorted and re-sorted the papers on her desk. They were already organized but her hands needed to do something. It was either this or she wrapped them around that man's neck and unleashed over a decade's worth of pain and pent-up rage on him.

Definitely better to occupy them with busy work than to strangle Connor Charleston.

The last thing she wanted was legal trouble on her hands.

Several minutes ticked by, and the tears continued to burn the backs of her eyes—angry tears not sad ones—Connor continued to stand there.

He didn't speak.

She pretended he wasn't there.

He didn't move.

She pretended he wasn't there.

Until she couldn't.

Spinning around at warp speed wasn't good for her prosthetic foot, and she stumbled a little.

Moving faster than the speed of light, Connor was there, his hand on her arm, steadying her.

Sucking in a shocked breath, Becca froze.

It had been so long since she'd felt his touch.

It used to ground her, but now it picked her up and threw her into the wind to be tossed about.

There had been a time when she needed it so badly, when she craved it more than her next breath of air. For so long it was the only thing keeping her going, and she'd had no idea how she was supposed to survive without it.

But she'd learned.

She'd learned how to survive without Connor and the last thing she wanted was for him to be back in her life in any way, shape, or form. Whatever reason he had for being in Cambodia had nothing to do with her and he could leave her the hell alone.

"Don't touch me," she hissed, jerking backward and almost losing her footing all over again. Learning to walk with a prosthetic foot had been one of the hardest things she'd ever had to do but it wasn't the hardest.

The hardest was learning to live without Connor. He was the man she had planned to spend her whole life with. He was her first love, and she'd expected them to marry, have kids, and grow old side by side.

But that wasn't what life had planned for them.

And she had learned to live without Connor.

She had been living without him just fine until he came intruding on the life she'd built.

Connor's blue eyes widened in shock at the tone of her voice, and even though she'd stumbled again he restrained from reaching out to steady her, his fingers curling into fists at his sides, knuckles white, indicating the tension in him and the level of restraint. The man before her reminded her of the boy she used to know in some ways, but in others he'd changed so much he was barely recognizable. He was still tall, a little over six feet, but instead of the long, gangly limbs she remembered, he was pure muscle, his black T-shirt straining to cover his chiseled torso and arms. His brown hair was a little longer than the last time she'd seen him, and back then, he hadn't had a scruffy beard.

"Becca."

Her name was all he said but it was all he needed to say. She had known this man her whole life, they'd been together as a couple from the time they were fourteen until they were twenty. They had been best friends, they'd done everything together, she knew Connor better than she knew anyone else.

Or at least she thought she had.

Turned out she hadn't known him at all. Because the man she had thought she loved wasn't one who would walk away from her when she needed him the most.

Now his voice was so full of pain, grief, guilt, and regret that it tore at the wounds his betrayal had caused. Wounds that she'd thought had scarred over, but in this moment, she realized had merely scabbed over and underneath were still raw and open. Infected and festering.

"Don't," she snapped. There was nothing he had to say that she wanted to hear. If he was there because of her, she wasn't interested. The past needed to stay where it belonged.

If she allowed it to creep into her future, all the hard work she'd done rebuilding herself and her life would be for nothing. In the blink of an eye, she would become that terrified and traumatized twenty-year-old girl all over again.

That couldn't happen.

She had work to do and people relying on her, there was no way she would let them down by reverting to who she'd been in the aftermath of her assault.

"I don't care why you're here, Connor. I don't care why, after twelve years, you felt the need to track me down and come back to torment me some more. Leave now. I don't want to talk to you, I don't want to see you, I just want to pretend you don't exist."

CHAPTER

Two

August 16th
12:09 P.M.

Connor had been unprepared to hear the venom in her tone. Hear her tell him that she wanted absolutely nothing to do with him. Hell, she couldn't even stand for him to touch her.

Stupid of him.

Of course, he should have expected Becca to hate him.

Why wouldn't she?

Panic coursed through his body. What if this wasn't fixable? What if the damage he'd caused ran too deep and there was no chance that Becca could forgive him? He could handle not being part of her life—barely—if she didn't want to become friends again, but he couldn't handle this.

Couldn't handle her hate.

As he watched her storm across the small schoolhouse it was hard to remember why he'd waited so long to track her down.

Only then she stumbled again as she reached the door, and it was all he could think of.

Shame.

That's what had held him back all these years. Facing Becca meant facing what he'd done head on, facing the deep running guilt and shame that consumed him. Over time, it had dulled a little, and there had been plenty to keep him busy, keep his mind occupied, but it was still there, and looking at Becca made him realize how far in denial he'd really been.

"Becca, wait. Please," he begged as her hand shoved open the door bathing her in a stream of light. She was so beautiful it hurt to look at her and know she was no longer his to touch, to pleasure, to worship.

Shockingly, she did stop, but he wasn't sure it was because she actually cared to hear anything he had to say, or she was merely so thrown by the fact that he was here in Cambodia standing in her school.

Whatever reason he'd take it.

He was not leaving until he had made things right with her. His family had things handled back home. With the threats hanging over their heads from the three other men involved in their mother's assault, Cassandra had gone to stay with Prey's Delta Team, a group of men with scarily unnatural abilities. Since she was the product of their mother's rape, they had to protect her because once they got a hit on her DNA or compared it to a suspect, they could bring the entire conspiracy surrounding his mom and stepdad's deaths tumbling down.

With Cassandra safely tucked away, Cooper was protecting his new girlfriend, Willow, and Cole was looking after his new girlfriend, Susanna, and helping her heal from her recent ordeal. Together, Cooper and Cole continued working with their oldest brother, Cade, and stepbrothers, Jake and Jax Holloway, to unravel the conspiracy.

His family had business at home handled so he could be there.

They knew he wasn't coming back until he'd made things right.

However long it took.

For the foreseeable future Becca was his priority.

Which was exactly what his parents would have wanted. While he'd lost his parents when he was thirteen, six months apart, and hadn't started officially dating Becca until he was fourteen, they'd been unofficially together since they started middle school, and both his mom and dad had loved her. Even back then, they'd seen the writing on the wall, knowing that she was the only woman for him.

No other woman could ever live up to Becca Marsden in his mind.

So even though he wasn't expecting a miracle, wasn't expecting her to take him back as her lover and partner, Connor already knew that it was reunite with Becca or remain single for the rest of his life.

"What are you doing here, Connor?" she asked, her voice hard, unyielding, but he caught the underlying threads of pain because he knew her better than he knew himself. "Are you here for work?"

Work was the furthest thing from his mind.

Eagle Oswald, founder and CEO of Prey, had been exceptionally patient and understanding with Charlie Team's need to prove their parents weren't traitors, and in between official ops for the company, he made sure all resources were available to them for their hunt for answers. Eagle had also been more than accommodating this past couple of months as dominos fell and answers appeared, and he had approved this time off for him to come to Cambodia.

"No. Not here for work," he answered.

"Why then?" She still hadn't turned to face him, but he didn't need to see her expression to know she one hundred percent believed there was no possible way he could be there for her.

But he was.

And he had to find a way to prove it to her.

"I'm here for you, moonlight."

Whirling around, once again almost losing her balance, it took everything Connor possessed not to run to her, steady her, and be ready to catch her when she fell. It was only remembering that he'd lost that right, and Becca loathed his touch, that kept him rooted to the spot, his hands still curled into fists tight enough his fingers ached.

"Do not call me that," Becca snarled at him.

Seeing her like this, so cold, so hard, so angry, it shook him. The Becca he remembered from childhood was a sweet, slightly shy girl, who was always smiling, always giggling, always such a free spirit. She loved music, loved to dance and paint, she was a creative who had so much imagination inside her it couldn't help but spill out around her, painting the world in bright colors.

Of course, things had changed after her assault, but back then she'd sought comfort and security from him, dragging him closer rather than shoving him away like she was now.

His fault.

He was the one who had messed this up.

What should have been the perfect love story, the kind that made up fairytales and romance novels, had been ruined by him and him alone.

"I'm sorry, I won't call you that," he agreed, he'd agree to anything if it could wipe the hatred out of those dark blue eyes he used to love staring into.

Becca said nothing.

Just stood there and glared at him.

"I came to do what I should have done all those years ago," he told her. If she was giving him an opportunity to talk, he had better hurry up and say what he needed to because he knew she could walk away at any second. "I'm here to apologize."

"To apologize?" she repeated like the words sounded ridiculous.

"I owe you the world's biggest apology," he acknowledged. Getting down on his hands and knees and crawling across shards of broken glass or hot coals was not out of the question. Nothing was out of the question.

"You think any amount of sorry can make up for you walking out on me when I learned I was pregnant?" Becca demanded, planting her hands on her hips and cocking her head. That was such a Becca move, one he'd seen hundreds of times before when they were arguing over something stupid, that he had to fight back a smile knowing she wouldn't understand it was because he missed her in all her wonderful shades of life.

"No, moo—, no, Becca," he replied, catching himself before the nickname that had always fallen so easily from his lips could slip out. "Nothing in the world can make up for what I did to you. For how stupidly I acted when I panicked. I've spent twelve years wishing someone would invent a time machine so I could go back and fix what I broke. But I'm here to make it right now. Shame kept me away for over a decade, I won't let it keep me away a second longer."

Tears shimmered in those deep blue depths of her eyes, but she didn't allow them to fall. "You should be ashamed, Connor. I'd only just gotten out of the hospital, was trying to learn to deal with my new reality, and I found out I was pregnant and didn't know if you or the man who raped me were the father. I needed you and instead of being there for me, you told me you didn't think you could raise my rapist's baby if you weren't the father and left."

Her voice broke on that last word and his heart cracked into a million pieces.

He had run that night. Driven for hours, panicked and crying, unable to hold it together any longer he'd let out all the pent-up emotions he'd felt seeing the girl he loved suffering. Emotions he'd kept locked away because he had to be there for Becca. The pregnancy had just been the straw that broke the camel's back, the last nail in the coffin, no longer had he been able to lock those emotions away and they'd burst out in the worst way possible.

By the time he pulled himself together and returned to their apartment, Becca had packed her things and left. All attempts to contact her had been blocked by her family, and eventually he'd given up.

Another failure.

How could he ever have given up on this woman?

"I don't accept your apology, Connor. You were what I needed back then, and you left. Now I don't need you anymore. Nor do I want you. Leave and don't ever come back."

With that, she turned and hurried out of the building, leaving him staring after her, his heart cracked wide open, wondering if this had been how she'd felt that night watching him walk away from her, taking her heart with him.

∿

August 16th
10:43 P.M.

Something soft feathered down her cheek.

Becca sighed and nuzzled into the touch.

She loved it when Connor crawled into bed after her and woke her with gentle touches to make love to her.

The hand on her cheek drifted down to grasp her breast, and she sighed again, thrusting her chest forward seeking more of Connor's sensual touches. After being together since they were young teenagers, he knew her body, knew how to make it come alive, how to make it burn so brightly she was sure she was going to explode into a fiery mass of brightly colored fireworks.

After kneading her breast for a moment, Connor suddenly grabbed her nipple and yanked.

Hard.

A startled squawk fell from her lips.

He knew she didn't like it rough.

She wasn't the most adventurous when it came to their sex life, they tried different positions and a few toys, but she never liked to be hurt during sex.

Another hard pinch on her nipple had her jerking awake and Becca realized she wasn't at home in her bed, and it wasn't Connor who had crawled under the covers to wake her for some beautiful love making.

She was in her car, and it was a guy from one of her classes who had his hand on her breast.

Now she remembered. She'd been at a late-night study group, she was supposed to head back to the apartment she shared with Connor after, but she'd been so tired from juggling a heavy course load and her job that she'd been afraid she might fall asleep at the wheel. A quick power nap had been her plan, but she must have fallen into a deeper sleep than she realized.

"Don't touch me," she growled, swatting at Dylan Sanders' hand as it continued to squeeze her nipple painfully tightly. "What are you doing?"

"Don't pretend you don't want this, Becca," Dylan snarled, grabbing a fistful of the breast he was already hurting and yanking her half out of her seat.

Fear uncurled throughout her as reality settled in.

It was late.

She was alone.

In her car with a man who was making his intentions clear.

Her mouth opened to scream, but an unexpected blow to the side of her head startled her into silence as pain exploded behind her eyes.

"Make a sound and I'll kill you," Dylan told her as he shoved at the hem of her skirt trying to yank it up over her hips.

The bulge in his pants was already obvious and she knew what was going to happen.

She just didn't know how to stop it.

"P-please," she begged, hating her voice's weak and terrified sound. "I-I don't want this."

"Course you do," Dylan said as he managed to pull at her dress enough to expose the lacy white panties she was wearing. "I see how you look at me."

She didn't look at him in any way.

They had some classes together and they'd spoken maybe a handful of times, but she was in a relationship, she was with a man she loved.

"I-I d-don't," she stammered. "N-no. S-stop."

"Did you tell me no?" Dylan snapped, grabbing hold of her panties and physically ripping them off her body, making her skin sting. "Nobody tells me no."

Outweighing her by a solid hundred pounds, Dylan dragged her over so she awkwardly straddled his legs, then unzipped his jeans and pulled free his already erect length.

When she struggled, desperate to stop this from happening, Dylan clamped a hand around her neck.

It felt like her body was being torn in two when he shoved himself inside her. She was so dry, it was nothing like when she made love to Connor. This was just pain. It wasn't just her body that hurt but her heart and soul as well.

He was stealing from her.

Taking something she would never willingly give.

Time lost all meaning. The world was filled with nothing but the sounds of Dylan grunting and her blood pounding in her ears as he squeezed her neck tight enough that the world dimmed around the edges.

Yes.

Take me.

End me.

Becca didn't want to live out the aftermath of this.

Death would be a blessing.

When he suddenly let out a curse and she felt him come inside her, she was disappointed that he pushed her to the side, and she was still breathing.

Why couldn't he have at least given her the gift of ending her life?

Shoving her off him, he all but threw her limp body back into the driver's seat. She flopped like a ragdoll, her mind seemed to float above her body like the two were no longer connected.

Muttering a curse, Dylan leaned over her and opened her door, pushing her out as he tried to get into her seat. She fell, landing on the rough asphalt of the road.

The sound of her engine roaring to life startled her a little.

Although she'd been pushed out of the car, her ankle had gotten tangled in the seatbelt.

Either he didn't notice or didn't care, but Dylan didn't lean over to disentangle it, he just started driving.

Dragging her along with him.

The last thing Becca remembered was the sound of her own screams as she was pulled along beside her moving vehicle before the world turned black around her and she mercifully fell unconscious.

Becca woke with a gasp.

Cold sweat coated her skin, and she shook all over.

Absently, she lifted a hand to brush against the scarred skin on the left side of her face. The plastic surgeons had done the best they could to minimize the damage, but there were still scars. Faint lines that were rough to the touch from the abrasions of her skin tearing along the road.

Those weren't the only scars she had.

Her nose and cheekbone had both been broken, as had her left arm which had also had the shoulder joint popped out of place. The bones had required surgery to fix. There were more road rash scars along most of the left side of her body.

But the worst injury was to her left ankle.

Being twisted as it was in the seatbelt as she was pulled down the road alongside her car, the break had been severe, her foot barely attached to her body by the time Dylan realized that he wasn't making a clean getaway in her car and dumped it and ran. Doctors had done all they could, but in the end, her foot hadn't been salvageable and after enduring eleven surgeries to try to save it, she'd wound up having to have it amputated.

None of those were the worst scars she had, though.

That would be the broken heart she'd been left with after Connor bailed.

He'd been her rock those first four months only to disappear when she received the news, she was pregnant.

Less than a month after he'd left, she miscarried the baby.

A DNA test she'd had performed showed Dylan Sanders hadn't fathered her child. The baby, a little boy, belonged to Connor. Despite her fury at the man she'd loved who had abandoned her when she needed him the most, she'd named her son after Connor's father. Carter Marsden-Charleston might never have gotten to take his first breath, but he was the reason she had pushed so hard to work through her trauma and build a life for herself. He was the reason she worked so hard, traveling the world, helping children living in poverty, because she wanted her son's name to carry on, for his death to mean something.

Shoving back the covers, no longer able to stand them touching her skin, Becca bypassed her prosthetic and instead reached for the crutches near her bed.

"Bec?" Isabella Baker's sleepy voice called out from the other side of the room.

Best friends since college, Izzy had stuck by her through thick and thin and was one of the co-founders of the CMC Project, named after her son. They'd worked together in four countries over the last seven years and shared the same small hut in Cambodia.

"I'm fine, Izzy, go back to sleep," she assured her friend even as she fought back the tears.

"You're not fine. He shouldn't have come. Want me to go find where he is and beat him up for you?" Izzy offered.

The image of tiny four foot eleven Isabella beating up six foot two Connor made her laugh. "Thanks for the offer, but I don't need him beaten up. I don't need him anything. He's nothing to me anymore."

Still as she hobbled toward the door to their hut, needing some fresh air, Becca knew that wasn't really true. Despite her anger toward Connor, a part of her heart and soul would always belong to him. He'd been such a big part of her life for too long to just amputate him and make it like he'd never existed.

Dropping to the ground once she was far enough away from the hut, Becca curled in on herself as the tears she'd tried to hold back ever since Connor had popped up flooded down her cheeks, and a sob broke free.

She did need something from Connor.

She needed him to disappear.

To stay out of her life.

To leave her alone.

Because his presence would destroy her.

CHAPTER

Three

August 17th
5:31 A.M.

Connor hadn't slept a wink.

It seemed the people in the village were protective of their schoolteacher and nobody he'd asked had allowed him to sleep on their property, not even in a barn. The weather was warm, and he'd found a reasonably comfortable spot close to the tiny house where Becca lived with her friend Isabella. It wasn't sleeping outdoors that had prevented him from sleeping, in his years as a SEAL and working for Prey he'd slept in plenty worse places.

Knowing that Becca was so close and yet he couldn't go to her was the cause.

For years, he'd dreamed of her, ached for her, beaten himself up for what he'd done, wished like he'd never wished before that he could go back and redo that night. The distance between them had always hurt him, but there had been nothing he could do about it.

Now she was so close.

It made it so much worse.

If he didn't know that going to her was only going to make things worse, he would be there, by her side, doing anything she required of him to earn back her heart.

Which was all he'd ever wanted.

One moment where stress had gotten the best of him had ruined everything. Not that he was making excuses for his behavior. Just because he'd been holding all his emotions about Becca's assault and trauma inside for four months and they'd suddenly exploded out when he'd been unable to hold them in a second longer, didn't make it okay.

Nothing made it okay to hurt the people you love.

And he hadn't just hurt Becca.

He'd destroyed something in her.

Something he was desperate to put back together. If she let him. And he was pretty sure she had no intention of giving him that chance.

As he watched, she left her small house, her head down and arms wrapped around her stomach. She looked so small and fragile, but he knew looks could be deceiving. His Becca had always had a big heart, sometimes too big, a dead baby bird, a worm trapped on the concrete in the sun, another child getting in trouble in class, and so many more hurt her heart. She included everyone, she was the kid who welcomed in the new child in class, who stood up for those being bullied, who was a friend to everyone.

Watching her curl in on herself after her assault had been painful.

But he'd also seen her strength, her determination to keep moving on. While she might look small and fragile, his moonlight was so much tougher than she looked. She was a warrior, she fought with everything she had, and he was in awe of her.

Connor was determined to convince her of that.

So, he headed off after her. All he needed was a chance, he had to believe that, because if he gave up hope, he'd have to go back home and accept that Becca would never be part of his life again.

It was only as he followed her into the Cambodian jungle that he admitted to himself that he'd spent the last twelve years with the secret hope that one day things would work out the way they were always supposed to.

Now he knew the chances of that were close to zero.

"Nuh-uh."

Just as he went to pass by Becca's house, a woman stepped out and blocked his path. She was a tiny little thing with a mess of wild curls and a glare that was sharp enough to slice through glass. This had to be Isabella Baker, Becca's best friend. He vaguely remembered the woman from college, and she'd been one of the few friends Becca hadn't completely managed to shove out of her life, even though she'd tried back in those early days when her trauma was too raw.

"You need to leave her alone, Connor Charleston," Isabella snapped at him. While she was well under a foot shorter than him and had to crane her head up to meet his gaze, she looked like she was ready and willing to rip him to shreds with her bare hands if he hurt her friend.

Even though she prevented him from going after Becca, he couldn't be more glad that his moonlight had someone so fierce in her corner.

"I just want to talk to her," he told Isabella.

"Your talking made her have nightmares," Isabella shot back, hands planted on her hips, glower set on her face. "I don't remember the last time she had bad dreams. She's doing well, she's happy, and she's moved on from what happened. Then you come back, and a couple of hours later she's having nightmares and crying. It's you. You brought it all back up. She doesn't deserve that. She's fought through hell to get where she is now, and I won't allow you to bring all that bad stuff up again."

Hearing that his presence was doing more harm than good, cut through his chest like a knife. In those first days and weeks, only his presence held her together. That wasn't him being arrogant or playing up his own importance, that was what Becca used to tell him.

"That's not why I came," he told Isabella.

"To be perfectly frank with you, I don't care why you came, Connor. I just want you gone. I don't want my best friend to hurt again. I don't want her to regress to waking up shaking and soaked in sweat from nightmares, to crying all the time, to jumping at every little noise. To live ruled by fear. She's moved on, Connor, I think it's time you do the same."

Isabella's words weighed heavily upon him.

It wasn't just that Becca didn't want to see him, didn't want to talk to him, didn't want anything to do with him. His presence was actually making things worse. Making her life harder. Bringing back all the things she'd been through.

Hanging his head, he had to fight against his instincts that screamed to go to Becca, fix this, make it right, earn back her trust and heart, or at least earn back her friendship.

But he couldn't do that.

Not if he was hurting her.

He'd done that enough.

"Fine," he said softly. "I'll go. But I need to say goodbye to her. Tell her one more time that I'm sorry."

When he looked up, Isabella's frown had faded and she seemed to be debating with herself. "Okay. You can go say goodbye. I don't think that could make things worse."

"I didn't come to make things worse," he murmured as he started walking in the direction Becca had gone.

"I believe that," Isabella called after him. "You're not a bad guy, Connor, but you let her down. I get it. It was a lot on top of what had already been a lot to handle. But she needed you, and you weren't there for her. I don't think I can forgive you for that."

"Won't ever forgive myself for that," he told her, then kept walking.

Expecting to find that Becca had gone to the schoolhouse, instead he found her standing beneath a tall tree, staring off into space. She was leaning back against it, idly tapping the line on her leg that he knew was where the top of her prosthetic was, and she didn't seem to notice his approach.

That was the old Becca he remembered from before, when she used to get lost in thought, living in her imagination and seeing the world through a colorful lens most of them didn't have access to. The Becca from after her assault noticed every little thing happening around her, hyper-aware of her surroundings, of what people were close, of gauging whether or not they were a threat.

Since the last thing he wanted to do was scare her, Connor made some noise as he approached, so she'd hear him and not get caught by surprise. At the sounds, her head snapped in his direction, and when she saw it was him, her brow furrowed.

"It's okay," he said, holding up his hands, palms out. "I got the message. I'm leaving, but before I go, I need to tell you one last time how sorry I am. I should have been there for you, Becca. I shouldn't have panicked, shouldn't have freaked out. You needed me, and I wasn't there for you, I won't forgive myself for that. Not ever, no matter how many years go by. Hurting you is my biggest regret, and I wish more than anything that I could make it right. But I'm respecting your wishes and leaving you alone."

"You're going to leave?"

"Yeah. I came to make things right, but I'm making them worse. I won't do that to you, Becca. Besides, I don't want Bella to beat me up," he joked.

A tiny smile quirked up one side of her mouth. "She's not your biggest fan that's for sure."

"I'm proud of you, Becca. What you've done, what you've built, how many people you're helping. I just wanted you to know."

Her stance softened a little. "Thank you. I'm happy, Connor. Life didn't turn out the way I had always planned but I'm happy."

While it hurt to know she could be happy without him when he could never be truly happy without her, Connor would never begrudge her that happiness. She deserved it. Deserved the entire world.

"I'm glad. I wish I'd handled things better, wish I'd never lost you, but I'm glad you're happy. I hope you get everything you want out of—"

The unmistakable sound of gunfire erupted in the village, and Connor didn't hesitate, he threw himself at Becca, and took her down with him, rolling so his body took the brunt of the fall and then rolling again so she was beneath him as the shooting continued.

∾

August 17th
5:45 A.M.

.   .   .

It wasn't until Becca was pressed into the ground, a rock or stick or something digging painfully into the small of her back and Connor's weight on top of her, crushing her to within an inch of her life, that it actually clicked.

Gunfire.

The loud rapping sound was actually someone shooting a gun.

Or multiple guns.

Here.

In her village.

Where she lived and worked.

Where she'd dedicated the last two years of her life to helping improve the lives of the people who lived there by giving them medical care and an education.

Now someone was ruining what was supposed to be a safe place.

She couldn't just lie there while the people she cared about were possibly being killed. Everybody in this village had become a part of her family, and her best friend was out there somewhere. What would she do without Isabella's support? Her friend had been a rock for her all these years, and she needed Izzy.

Only when she began to struggle to try to dislodge Connor's body so she could wriggle out from underneath it, he pressed down harder upon her.

Shockingly, it didn't instigate panic like someone lying on top of her usually would.

Probably because she knew that even though Connor had broken her heart, he would never physically hurt her. Never ever in a million—a billion—years use his superior size and strength to cause her pain and overpower her, making her do things she didn't want.

More than that, she actually felt safe having him with her.

Nothing would hurt her as long as Connor was there.

He wouldn't allow it.

That she believed even as she knew she would never trust him with her heart, that he would and had shredded to pieces.

But he would protect her from whoever was attacking her village. The problem was, who was out there protecting her people?

"Connor," she hissed, managing to get her hands up between their bodies and planting them on his massive chest.

"Shh," he urged. There was fear in the blue eyes that looked down at her when he slightly lifted his head.

No.

That was wrong.

It wasn't fear.

It was terror. The kind of terror she'd felt so many times since she was raped by a classmate and her entire world was tossed on its head.

"We have to do something," she whispered, trying to keep her voice as quiet as she could, but she doubted anyone could hear her over the sound of the gunfire.

"We are doing something."

"No, we're not. We're just lying here." Didn't he work for Prey Security? Hadn't he been a Navy SEAL? Just because he'd come here to talk to her and not because of his job didn't mean he would have come unarmed, surely there was something he could do.

"We're keeping you alive. That's what we're doing."

"But what about everybody else? Who's keeping them alive?"

Guilt and remorse filled his sky-blue eyes, and she knew it wasn't fair to put the weight of the couple of hundred people who lived in the village on his shoulders. "I can't save them all, Becca. Not on my own with only one weapon. If it were just a few assailants, or just a few people to save, then maybe, but not like this. I'm sorry."

"H-how do you know there isn't just one person sh-shooting?" she asked, hating that her voice trembled on a few words. Now was not the time to fall apart. She had to be strong, had to hold it together.

"Because I know what it sounds like when multiple weapons are firing simultaneously," Connor replied.

She didn't even want to think about him knowing things like that.

While she'd always known Connor would follow in his father and grandfather's footsteps and join the military no matter how many times he'd told her he wasn't going to enlist, she didn't like to think about him being in danger. Even now, over a decade after he'd shattered her fragile heart, she didn't like it.

"What are we going to do?" she whispered. How were they

going to survive this was what she really wanted to ask. If several men were shooting up her village, sooner or later they would find her and Connor even if they stayed there and were quiet. Besides, it was cowardly to hide with the only skilled, armed man there while everyone else died. "What about Izzy? What about the children?"

He was torn, she could see he was.

The thing was, even though she had so much anger still inside her, all directed at this man, and even though he'd hurt her so badly, she believed him when he said he was sorry for what had happened. At heart, Connor was a good man, she knew that, she even got why he'd panicked and ran. If she'd had the luxury of running from her life, she would have bailed, too.

And maybe that was why she was so furious. He'd done what she'd wanted to do but you couldn't run from yourself, no matter how badly you wanted to.

"I could ... hide?" she suggested. "Then you could go."

"Becca—"

"Please, Connor." While it irked her to ask this man for anything, much less beg, she wasn't above doing it for this. For the best friend who had stood by her no matter what, and for all those sweet little children who looked up to her. She had to do something to help them. There was no way to know who was attacking the village or why, but depending on their motives, they could slaughter everyone they found, old and young alike.

There were plenty of rumors that a leftover pocket of Khmer Rouge, now using a new name, lived and operated in the area. They trafficked anything they could get their hands on, drugs, weapons, and people. How could she just lie there and not try to do anything to protect the people she cared about?

"All right. I'll see what I can do, but I can't make you any promises. Do you understand that, Becca? Not because I don't want to, but because I can't. I'm outmanned and outgunned, and even if you hate me for it my priority is you and your safety."

"Okay," she agreed. Part of her wanted to argue with him about it, but in the end he was right. He was only one man and said he only had one weapon. No way could he take on a potential gang alone, and she didn't want him to get himself killed.

"You're going to head that way," he said, gesturing to their right. "You're going to keep walking—walking, not running, so you aren't as obvious—and you're not going to stop until I find you."

"How will you find me?"

"Trust me, I will."

Without waiting for a response, Connor stood, grabbing her hands and pulling her up with him. When he gave her a gentle nudge in the direction he'd told her to go she hesitated.

That moment of hesitation was the only reason she saw it.

Movement.

Two men, dressed in black, with assault rifles in their arms, heading right toward them.

Even though his back was to them she knew Connor sensed their presence.

"Go," he ordered as he spun in a fluid motion, bending down and coming up with a knife in his hand, which he threw at the two men. The blade of it buried itself in the neck of the closest man and he fell to the ground.

Connor had killed him.

By throwing a knife.

How did you even learn to do that?

And did she really want to know?

Actually part of her did. How empowering must it feel to be able to protect yourself like that? Of course, Connor wasn't infallible, there was every chance he could be shot and killed, or killed any number of other ways, but he could do things she could only dream about.

"Becca, go. Now," Connor ordered as he dodged low, and charged toward the remaining man aiming his weapon right at them.

Part of her that wanted to argue, she couldn't go running off and leave him to fend for himself. The other part knew staying was being a hindrance. If she stayed, Connor's attention would be split between her, himself, and trying to save the village.

She had to go.

Only she couldn't seem to go slow like Connor had told her to.

Becca took off in a mad run. Infinitely glad that she'd gone back to her hut the earlier this morning to swap out her crutches for her prosthetic.

She was making way too much noise.

Should slow down.

Should do as Connor instructed.

But she couldn't.

Couldn't stop running.

Now that she was moving away from the village any bravado she'd possessed seemed to disappear.

Leaving her just plain terrified.

A feeling she loathed.

It was only when two men appeared before her, weapons in their hands, slimy grins on their faces, that she slid to a stop.

CHAPTER Four

August 17th
   6:11 A.M.

A bloodbath.

That was all Connor could describe it as.

Over a dozen men dressed in black moved through the village. People screamed as they ran in the fields and along the one dirt road that ran the length of the village and then disappeared off into the jungle.

The assailants appeared to be striking at random. Passing by some farms and then hitting another. Shooting at random at the parents running through the fields with the children, seeming not to care who they hit.

This wasn't some targeted attack, and he wondered why this village had been chosen.

Was it odd that even though Becca had been living in Cambodia for several years, less than twenty-four hours after he showed up they were attacked?

That was crazy.

Wasn't it?

This whole conspiracy thing was really getting to him, and it was hard to tell these days what was real and what wasn't. The other men involved in his mom's rape had already proved they were willing to go to any lengths to try to get his family to back off. Everything Cole and Susanna had been through was proof of that.

Were they determined enough—or crazy enough—to try to target the village where his ex-girlfriend lived and worked?

As badly as he'd love to say no, Connor couldn't.

With his one handgun, he was no match for the well-armed attackers, and if he tried picking them off one by one, he'd only be signing his own death warrant. Which he would be more than prepared to do if it meant saving Becca's life, but right now, he was possibly the only thing standing between her and death.

So he had no choice but to slip soundlessly between the trees as he headed the way he'd told Becca to run. He knew she was going to be angry he hadn't been able to get to her friend and the children, but the kids were scattered throughout the town, and several men were standing around the house Becca shared with Isabella.

There was nothing he could do, and he hated it.

Hated knowing the tiny woman who hadn't hesitated to tell him to stay away from Becca was likely going to be murdered.

If she was lucky.

Because if Bella wasn't she was going to be wishing for death before it finally came for her. He knew what these kinds of men were like, knew the torture they delivered to beautiful young women like Isabella. She'd be raped for sure, possibly trafficked, so he had no option but to hope she was already dead.

Becca would no doubt blame him, which he would absolutely take if it meant he could get her out of this mess alive.

There wasn't anything he wouldn't shoulder so she didn't have to, anything he wouldn't take to make her load a little lighter. If she had to blame him for Isabella and the villagers' deaths to process them then she could.

After all, she might be right.

Had the people after his family followed him here? Had he brought this horror right to the doorstep of the woman he loved? As much as he didn't want it to be true it quite easily could be. After all, when he was off alone on the other side of the world, he was a much easier target than when at home surrounded by his brothers.

He moved faster than he'd advised Becca to go, partly because this was his job and he knew how to move making barely a sound, blending into whatever landscape he found himself in, but mostly because he ached with the need to get to her. Needed to see her with his own two eyes, needed to confirm that she wasn't streaked with blood like the villagers he'd seen lying dead in the fields.

Like she had been the night of her assault when he'd rushed to the hospital as soon as he received a call from a cop friend who'd been on the scene.

Nothing could erase those images of her from his mind.

So small, so broken, laid out on a gurney. Most of the skin on her left side torn from her body, her ankle hanging off, barely attached anymore. Machines and wires had been attached to her body, and she'd been unconscious.

The stuff of nightmares.

In fact, he'd had nightmares about it regularly those first several months. Even after their relationship ended, he had them. Even now he had them often enough.

Now he needed to know his girl was okay.

Even if she wasn't really his anymore.

Only a sudden change in the atmosphere had him freezing. His gut screamed at him and he wasn't going to ignore it. Something was wrong and he needed to know what.

He'd been following the trail Becca had made so he knew she had been going in the direction he'd told her, the direction he thought would give them the best chance at escaping unscathed. She was likely around here somewhere, he hadn't been gone that long and she was scared and in shock. Catching up to her should be easy.

"Such pretty girl," a voice said in a slimy tone he recognized as one some men used when talking to a woman they felt they held all the power over and could do to her whatever they chose.

There was no response, and his heart rate doubled.

If the man was talking to her then Becca had to be alive.

And there wasn't a doubt in his mind that Becca was indeed who the man was talking to.

Even though everything in him screamed to rush in and rescue his girl from whatever fate these men wanted to deliver, Connor forced himself to move forward slowly, creeping toward Becca rather than running headlong into danger and making things worse.

"Pretty girl," another voice crooned.

So there were at least two of them. Easy enough to eliminate so long as there weren't too many more. He'd strike before they were even aware he was there.

Footsteps sounded, moving in a slow, almost lazy pattern, and he wondered what the hell was going on. He needed eyes on Becca sooner rather than later.

Another few yards and he finally spotted her.

She was maybe twenty feet or so ahead of him. Two men dressed the same as the ones who were attacking the village and similarly armed were circling around her. Her gaze kept darting from one to the other as she was forced to spin in slow circles in an effort to not allow the men to get behind her.

There was fear on her face, but something else was there too.

Determination.

His girl wasn't going down without a fight.

Pride swelled inside him, and he palmed the knife he'd pulled free from the neck of the man he'd killed earlier.

Creeping closer, he watched as the men continued to circle Becca, their attention focused solely on her.

Their stupidity was going to be the death of them.

As soon as their backs were to him, he threw the knife, lodging the blade in the back of one of the men on his left side, where Connor knew he'd hit his target and pierced the man's heart.

The other one yelled and spun around, lifting his weapon to fire.

But before the man could get off a shot, something hit him in the side of the head.

Becca had snatched up a rock and thrown it at the man distracting him. Connor was laughing as he launched himself at the man, knocking him to the ground and landing on top of him.

"Shouldn't have looked at my girl," he told the man right before he snapped his neck.

When he stood, Becca stared at him, mouth hanging open, eyes wide. Did she see him differently now she'd seen him kill several men? Was she afraid of him on top of hating him?

"That was ..." Becca trailed off and he couldn't place her tone over his growing panic. Then a small smile lit her face. "Can you teach me to do that?"

"Do what?"

"The knife thing. You hit them both right where you aimed. It's very cool."

Her response had him chuckling, a little of the tension easing out of him. While her assault had changed her and she was no longer the sweet innocent girl he'd fallen in love with, he still loved her every bit as much. There were some sharper edges to her now, before she'd been all soft, so it was jarring in a way, but he was so proud of her for adapting and coming out the other side of her trauma still fighting. Still living.

Which reminded him that if he wanted to keep her alive, he had to be vigilant, had to be at the top of his game. Bending down, he scooped up both weapons and handed one to Becca.

"I can teach you, but for now I think this is going to be a more effective tool."

"I've never shot a gun before," Becca said tentatively.

"Point and shoot, only if I tell you to," he instructed. Hopefully she wouldn't need to, but it didn't hurt to be prepared.

"Could you ... save anyone?" Becca asked.

"I'm sorry, Becca. I would have if I could have, but there were too many of them." While he braced himself for her anger, especially when she found out about her friend, she didn't ask anything else, just gave a tight nod.

"I understand."

Wanting to get her as far away from the bloodshed as he could, Connor set a brisk pace, one he knew would be difficult for Becca to keep up with. But his need to get her safe was all-consuming.

And pointless as it turned out.

Because they made it only about a half mile away from the village before the sound of an approaching engine had him freezing.

A black jeep with half a dozen armed men in the back appeared through the trees.

Once again, he'd failed the woman he loved, only this time she would wind up paying for that mistake with her life.

∼

August 17th
  6:29 A.M.

Instinct had Becca inching closer to Connor as a vehicle carrying more armed men approached.

As badly as she wanted to turn and run in the opposite direction or lift the weapon Connor had thrust into her hands and fire at the car, she didn't do either of those things.

Because neither did Connor.

Tension emanated from him, his posture stiff, the weapon clutched tightly in his hands. She wished he would tell her what to do or start doing something so she could follow his lead.

But he didn't.

Just stood there, glaring at the jeep and the men in it.

"Connor," she hissed. "Shoot them."

"Can't, honey," he said, never taking his eyes off the vehicle.

"Why?" They should be doing something. Should be fighting. Already Connor hadn't been able to do anything to save Izzy and the villagers, but he could do something now. The odds were better, two of them to eight of the others, and this time they were both armed.

"Because they'll shoot back, and I won't stand here and watch you die."

The force behind his words rocked her. He meant that. Actually meant it. While her logical mind had always known Connor hadn't run that day because he didn't love her but because it was all just too much to handle, her heart hadn't been so convinced. There had been so many times she wondered if she'd been wrong about Connor all those years, if he'd never really loved her at all.

"They'll catch us," she whispered, the old, dirty taste of fear filling her mouth. Over time, she'd forgotten how foul it tasted, but now it was back, and with crystal clarity, she remembered the last time she'd been this afraid. The night of her assault.

Only this time she wasn't alone.

This time Connor was there.

Delusional or not, Becca knew she could trust Connor to protect her, to keep her safe, and maybe even find a way to keep them both alive. It was only her heart she would never again trust in his hands.

Even if Connor couldn't save her, at least she wouldn't die alone as she had truly believed she would the night she'd been raped. That made her selfish, she was aware of that. Connor had a family at home who loved him and needed him, so being glad he would die with her probably made her a terrible person, but she couldn't help it. Anything was better than dying alone.

The vehicle stopped in front of them and the men in the back jumped out. Becca pressed closer to Connor until her body touched his. Just an hour ago she would have sworn that his touch would have made her feel ill, that the last thing she wanted or needed was any physical contact between them, even the most casual of touches.

Now it was the only thing that grounded her.

"Put weapons down," one of the men ordered, gesturing at the rifles she and Connor held.

When Connor bent and laid his on the ground at his feet, Becca did the same thing. Connor could do the impossible, somehow, she believed that. He had always been her superhero, the man she loved, the one she wanted to give every part of herself to. He'd betrayed that trust in the worst possible way, but she still believed if anyone could get her out of this alive it was him.

"Get on knees," the man issued another order.

Hard as it was to watch when Becca knew if she wasn't there and he wasn't worried about her getting hurt or killed, Connor wouldn't have hesitated to take on these eight men, he got down on his knees.

"You too," the man yelled at her when she stood frozen in fear.

She couldn't do it.

Couldn't.

It was like agreeing to let these men do whatever they wanted to her.

No longer was she the sweet, innocent girl she'd been back when she was twenty and raped. Now she knew the world wasn't sunshine and roses, you couldn't just smile, offer support to someone, and make things better.

The real world was full of darkness and people hurt one another just because they could. Because they prioritized themselves and what they wanted above all else.

These men *would* hurt her.

Because they could.

No one would stop them.

And Connor had already given up their only chance to fight.

When she didn't comply with the order she'd been given, the man who was standing closest to her swung his assault rifle at her. It slammed into the side of her head hard enough that she saw stars, and with a groan, she swayed and fell to the ground.

"Touch her again and I will rip you to pieces," Connor growled in a low and dangerous tone she'd never heard him use before.

Stupidly, the man who had hit her laughed like Connor was joking.

Only he wasn't.

She could tell by his voice that he was deadly serious, and it sent a cold shiver through her.

The boy she once knew wasn't this man kneeling beside her, calmly staring down eight armed men. Her Connor had been sweet and supportive, she'd seen him angry plenty of times, over what happened to his mom and stepdad, and with Dylan after her rape, but he'd never sounded like this. Like a man perfectly capable of ripping another human being to pieces.

It would scare her if she hadn't been absolutely certain he would never lay a hand on her.

The idiot who hit her obviously wasn't very smart.

Because he didn't leave it at just laughing mockingly at Connor's threat.

Nope.

Instead, he rammed his weapon into her ribs, knocking the air from her lungs, and Becca crumpled, gasping as she tried to suck in air.

Vaguely, she was aware of a commotion happening around her, but it was taking all her effort just to breathe through the piercing agony in her chest.

Her vision cleared enough to process that the shouting was coming from the men and was directly aimed at Connor, who was no longer on his knees beside her. He'd moved and was proving he was good at following through on his threats because his arm was around the neck of the man who had hit her.

How he'd managed to pounce without anyone shooting him she had no idea, but fear for him flooded her system.

He was going to get himself killed.

While looking the man who appeared to be the leader directly in the eye, Connor snapped the man's neck.

"Connor, no!" she screamed, positive she was about to witness his death. No matter how she felt about him, all the hurt, anger, and betrayal, she didn't want him dead. Not ever. A part of her heart would always belong to Connor Charleston because he was her first love, possibly even her greatest love.

As though they'd forgotten she was even there, weapons spun in her direction until they were all aimed at her, and she curled in on herself, trying to make herself as small a target as possible. Although how that would help her if seven assault rifles all opened fire on her at the same time, she had no idea. Well, actually, she did, and it wouldn't help her at all.

Not looking the least bit concerned, Connor released the now-dead body of the man who had hit her twice. "Told you what would happen if you touched her," Connor said calmly, that same deadly undertone evident.

"You will pay for that," the man in charge snarled, but Connor merely shrugged like he didn't care. He'd made his point, and he seemed happy with that.

When two of the men jumped at Connor, swinging their fists, hitting him over and over again, he didn't make a sound. Didn't so much as grunt in pain.

Unlike her.

Becca screamed and begged and pleaded.

Not that it did any good.

The two men stepped back only when Connor lay limp and unmoving on the ground at their feet.

Even then, one delivered a final kick to his still body.

"Take them," the man in charge ordered, and the two men who had beaten Connor grabbed his arms and hauled him up. He still wasn't moving, and she worried it was because they'd either killed him or seriously injured him.

What was she supposed to do if that was the case?

How could she get herself out of this mess much less herself and an unconscious man double her size?

When another two men approached her, Becca whimpered and shrunk away from them. She didn't want them touching her. It had taken years for her to accept even the most innocent of touches from anyone. Connor's touch had always been okay, even in those early days when her rape was still so fresh and vivid, but anyone else's felt like spiders scurrying across her skin.

These men didn't care about that.

They reached down and grabbed her roughly, their grips around her upper arms hard enough to leave bruises. She was taken to the back of the jeep where Connor's still limp body already lay and was tossed in beside him. Then, the armed men climbed in with them and the vehicle began to drive.

Taking her away from the village that had been her home.

Taking her away from any chance at escape.

Taking her away from life and firmly toward death.

CHAPTER
Five

August 17th
    8:54 A.M.

Pain throbbed through his body, but it was the soft, sweeping fingers stroking his forehead that registered first.

While his mind was stuck in the haze that consumed him, Connor knew that touch.

Becca.

Something in him relaxed for the first time in twelve years.

That feeling turned out to be fleeting as his memories clicked back into place and the haze retreated. The village where Becca lived had been attacked and the two of them had been cornered. He remembered wanting to fire on the approaching vehicle full of men, but there was not a chance in hell that Becca would have survived. As soon as he started shooting, they would have shot back, and at least one of those bullets would have hit his moonlight.

Still, he'd killed the man who dared to strike her, and a rush of smug satisfaction had him lifting his hand to cover Becca's.

She sucked in a small breath when he moved and her hand stilled but didn't pull away. Knowing that he was on thinner-than-thin ice with her, he soaked up this moment when he clasped her hand between his palm and his head.

"You're awake," she said softly.

"Yeah," he groaned, doing his best to compartmentalize the pain still pulsing through his system. He had no idea what had happened while he'd been unconscious, but he had to figure it out because he needed to devise a plan sooner rather than later.

"I was scared," Becca whispered, and he could hear the strain in her tone. She was holding it together because she knew she had to, but he hated that she was once again in a position where her life was on the line.

Connor couldn't help but feel this was his fault.

So far, he had no evidence that the strike at her village had anything to do with him. His family suspected the people involved in his mom's rape, and her and his stepdad's arrests and deaths were powerful. They had to be to have enough intel to have a Delta Force team ambushed and then pull strings and have two people set up as traitors.

Did they have enough power to pull off an attack on a village in Cambodia?

For the moment, it didn't really matter. Whether this was because of him or a random assault, the end result was the same. He had to get Becca out of there before she got hurt. Well, hurt worse than she had already been.

Unsure if she had been scared for him or just in general, Connor reluctantly released his hold on her hand and shifted so he was sitting. Doing a visual once over of Becca before he did anything else, he noted the small trickle of blood running down one side of her face from a small gash about an inch long on her left temple. A bruise was forming around it, but her dark blue eyes were clear, so he didn't think she had a head injury he needed to be worried about.

The way she sat, slightly hunched, one arm braced around her stomach did concern him. She'd been hit in the ribs as well and the last thing they needed was for the blow to have cracked or broken them. That was an injury that could impede her ability to escape, and worst-case scenario, lead to a punctured lung and death.

"Are you all right?" he asked, maybe a little harsher than he had intended but fear for her made it hard to think.

"I'm okay," she said, and while they both knew it was a lie, she met his gaze squarely and gave a small nod. His girl had been through a lot and suffered more pain than he could ever imagine, and he knew she was telling him that she was hurting, but she could manage it.

"Did they put their hands on you again?" Anyone who touched her was going to die just like the man whose neck he'd snapped. If he could manage it, he'd make their deaths as slow and painful as possible, but getting Becca out of there alive was his number one priority, not revenge.

"No. Well, not really. They just put us both in the back of the jeep and drove us here."

Waving her hands around she indicated to what appeared to be a tent. It was about ten feet by ten feet, there looked like metal posts were in the corners making a frame. The floor was dirt, and he noticed a metal ring cemented in the middle of the ground, with two chains running from the ring to where he and Becca were sitting.

Looking down his body, he saw that his shoes had been removed, and a cuff had been placed around his ankle attached to the chain. A glance down Becca's body showed she was similarly bound.

"They didn't hurt you?" he asked again because he needed the reassurance of knowing that his need to kill the man who had hurt her, leading to him being beaten and passing out, hadn't wound up causing her pain.

"They didn't hurt me, Connor," she assured him. "They dragged me to the jeep and threw me in, then dragged me back out and into this tent. They took off my shoes and yours, then shackled us both to the ring in the middle of the floor. Then they just left us here. You were still unconscious, and I was worried about you, so I pulled your head into my lap and ..." she trailed off and her cheeks tinted pink.

She didn't need to finish her sentence.

He knew this woman inside and out.

When he was sick, she used to sit in the bed beside him, his head on her lap, and sing to him. Her sweet voice was like an angel's, and it always washed over him in a soothing wave, cocooning him in a blanket of warmth and security.

Today she'd been scared and even though she was angry with him, had every reason to hate him, she'd still sung to him like she used to.

While Connor would love to believe that meant something, indicating he still had the teeniest, tiniest chance of winning back her love and trust, he couldn't allow himself to believe that. Not yet. Maybe after they spent some time together, maybe when they weren't in danger, maybe then they could talk a little.

Still, he couldn't let her comment pass without responding to it. He needed to make her understand how deeply he regretted his freak out that day twelve years ago. Connor was perfectly prepared to apologize for his mistakes every day for the rest of his life, but in the end, whatever happened next was up to Becca.

She held all the power.

"You sang for me," he finished aloud what she hadn't been able to say.

"Doesn't mean anything," Becca muttered, shifting her gaze so it was fixed on her lap. Right where his head had been when he'd regained consciousness.

On the contrary, Connor thought it meant a lot.

Becca still loved him. At least part of her did. But she didn't trust him, which gutted him even as he knew he had no one else to blame for that but himself.

"I made a huge mistake that day, Becca," he told her. "I let the stress of the previous months and all my pent-up emotions burst out in the worst way possible. I will regret that for the rest of my life."

She sighed. A deep, weary sound, that spoke of pain and suffering. "Don't you think I would have liked to bail on my life back then, Connor? But unlike you, I didn't get that luxury. Unlike you, I didn't get to decide this latest trauma was too much and just walk away. You promised me you would always be there. That nothing could ever make you leave me. You lied. You left me."

Tears burned his eyes. "I know, baby. I'm so sorry. Sorrier than I can ever express."

"He was yours," she whispered, her voice a mere hint of sound.

But her words were powerful.

After he'd left that night and returned to their apartment to find her gone, no one had allowed him to contact her. Becca had blocked his number and blocked him on all social media, her family had shut him out, backing up their daughter and sister, as had their shared friends. He'd never known what happened to her pregnancy, if she'd had the baby or if she'd given it up for adoption, he just knew she wasn't raising a child now.

"H-he? It was a boy?" he asked.

"A boy. I lost him a month after you left. I needed to know ..." Finally, her gaze lifted to meet his and he saw the tears swimming in her midnight blue depths. "I needed to know if it had been my rapist's baby or if I'd lost you over nothing. My parents thought it was a bad idea and there was no good outcome either way. But they were wrong. When the DNA tests said he was yours, there was relief. I didn't want to be carrying that man's child inside me. But there was also pain. Because you left me over something that didn't even exist. You left me because I was pregnant with your son."

Those words pierced his heart, causing wounds that would never heal.

He'd lost the woman he loved and the life he'd wanted over nothing.

The baby had been his and he'd walked away not only from Becca but his own child.

There was no way she could ever forgive him for that.

And he didn't deserve to be forgiven.

August 18th
   2:16 A.M.

Things were awkward.

Becca hadn't meant to blurt out that her baby had been Connor's and that he'd wound up leaving her for nothing.

It wasn't something she'd ever envisioned telling him.

What would be the point?

He'd already left, knowing that they weren't aware of the baby's paternity and that she'd had sex with him a whole lot more times than she'd had it with the man who raped her. He'd already proven to her that he wasn't someone that she could trust through anything. And she'd already cut him out of her life.

Telling him would only dredge everything back up.

And the baby was already gone so it wasn't like she was keeping him from his child or anything.

If her son had lived, she would have swallowed down her pride, shoved aside her feelings, and done the right thing. She would have offered Connor joint custody and done her absolute best to co-parent the way her baby would have deserved.

But since she lost her son there hadn't seemed any point in saying anything. Felt like it would have just been rubbing in his face that he left her over a child that turned out to be his anyway.

So, she'd kept it to herself and asked her family to do the same.

There was never a time she would have anticipated coming face-to-face with Connor again. They were out of each other's lives, which was for the best, so the conversation would never happen.

Only now, she'd blurted it out in fear and anger and that revelation rested heavily between them.

They'd barely spoken in what had to be close to twenty-four hours. They'd been left alone in the little tent for the most part, but someone had thrown in a couple of bottles of water and some scraps of food.

Even though Becca had insisted she wasn't hungry, Connor had made her eat something, telling her she needed to keep her strength up so they could take any chance that presented itself to escape.

But she didn't believe that chance was coming.

Despite the early hour, neither she nor Connor were asleep. Becca knew she should be exhausted, but she was way too wired to close her eyes and allow herself the respite of slumber. Throughout the hours, he'd stayed glued to her side, close but not touching, and even though she was still angry with him, she couldn't deny if he offered her his touch, she'd soak it right up.

A couple of times, his hands had clenched into fists, and she could have sworn he was going to reach for her, but he never did. Every one of those times, her own hands ached to reach out to him, entwine their fingers, allow his presence and his touch to comfort her like it had in the days following her assault.

They could never go back to those days though.

She no longer trusted Connor.

One bad decision on his part, even though intellectually she understood it, had ruined all the years they'd shared, and nothing could ever be the same again.

A shuffling sound outside their tent had them tensing, and this time Connor didn't hesitate to touch her, shifting her so she was partly hidden behind his body. While it was still early morning, the men in camp remained out there drinking. Their rowdy shenanigans echoed through the tent.

Now one of them was there.

What did he want?

The flap shifted, and the light from outside illuminated a large, shadowy figure.

Scared, Becca pressed closer to Connor's back, her fingers curling into his T-shirt as she clung to him. One of his hands moved behind him to sweep across her bent knee, even as she could tell his focus was on the approaching figure.

"Thought we'd have a little fun," the man sneered as he bent down and unlocked the chain binding one of them to the ring in the middle of the floor.

She wasn't sure which of them had been unlocked, but Becca knew what men like this thought was a fun way to pass away the time and she had a ball of terrified anxiety sitting like a rock in her stomach.

Were they going to rape her?

Could she survive that again?

There was part of her that would love to believe she could handle anything, survive anything. If she'd been raped once and managed to work through it and come out the other side, building a life for herself, then surely, she could do it again.

The bigger part knew there was every chance it would destroy her.

Especially if Connor had to watch.

But it turned out she wasn't what they wanted.

When the man tugged on the chain it was Connor's leg that jerked. And when two more men filled the doorway to the tent it was Connor that their gazes went to.

Another tug on his chain, and Connor went to stand, but Becca tightened her grip on his T-shirt. She couldn't let him go. What if they hurt him? What if they killed him? Just because she hadn't asked him to come to Cambodia didn't mean he wasn't there because of her. And if he died in this camp in the middle of nowhere, she would blame herself. Being angry with Connor and no longer trusting him did not equate to wanting him dead. She just didn't want him in her life.

"It's okay, moonlight," he whispered, softly enough for only her to hear. "I'm glad it's me they want and not you."

Reluctantly, she uncurled her fingers only because she was worried if she didn't, and she delayed Connor from doing what the men wanted him to do, it would only make them angrier with him, and he'd be punished.

So she twisted her hands into fists and pressed them into her lap as she watched Connor stroll out of the tent like he wasn't a prisoner and well outnumbered. She wished she could bottle his confidence and drink a little of it. She so badly needed some.

Only when the tent flap fell closed, enclosing her in the dark, loneliness overwhelmed her.

She wanted to beg Connor to come back, to offer to stand beside him and endure whatever horrible thing it was those men were going to do to him. Anything so long as she wasn't alone.

People might think, given she'd been raped, that touch might be her biggest fear. It was something she feared, something that still had the power to make her skin crawl and her insides clench.

But it wasn't her biggest fear.

Her biggest fear was being alone.

Just like she'd been that night.

Just like she'd been when Connor walked away.

This time, it might not be his fault. She knew he'd walked out of the tent without a fuss only so that their captors' attentions were focused on him and not her, but he'd still walked away. It was still the same result. She was still alone, and she still wished he was there.

No matter what he did, what changed between them, her soul still craved his.

After her assault, they'd had what she was sure everyone else would think was a weird way of him comforting her. But it had worked for them. It was a way for Connor to return her control over herself and what happened to her, a way for her to seek his comfort in the way she needed it.

What she wouldn't give to have that comfort right now.

To have his steady, warm, strong presence beside her.

But you didn't always get what you wanted.

That was something she knew all too well.

A shift at the door of her tent had her straightening. Were they done with Connor already? Was he coming back?

If he was, she was going to have the conversation with him that they both needed. They both needed to feel free to move forward with their lives without the chains of the past binding them to it. She'd tried and assumed Connor had, too, but now looking back, she knew that she'd only been pretending. Trying to convince the world—and even herself—that she could conquer her trauma and still have a life.

It wasn't Connor who slipped through the flap.

It was one of their captors.

Obviously, he knew he wasn't supposed to be in there because he snuck in, reminding her of a slithering snake.

As soon as the tent flap closed behind him, plunging her into darkness, her panic ramped up. Memories of the past blended with her terror in the present, overwhelming her and rendering her powerless.

There was no escape.

Her ankle was still bound to the ring in the floor.

The presence in the room grew stronger.

Closer.

Then it was there.

Above her.

A hand clamped around her neck and another fumbled at her pants.

In this second, Becca knew that this time she wouldn't be able to rebuild her life, this time, she would be left in tatters. A broken soul. Beyond repair. Ruined.

CHAPTER
Six

August 18th
   3:04 A.M.

Dodging the fist that came his way was easy.

Too easy.

Connor felt he might as well be play-wrestling with his four-year-old niece, Essie.

The men in the camp were drunk. Not just the rowdy kind, but the falling down, barely able to function kind of drunk.

Apparently, in this drunk state, they thought it would be funny to drag him out of the tent and make him fight them. He had no idea if they were aware of who he was and that he'd been a SEAL before he retired and went to join Prey. These men had to be the rumored Khmer Rouge group that lived in this area, they had some skills, but it wasn't anything comparable to his own.

And he was proving that even if the men were drunk.

It would be so easy to incapacitate as many as he could then get his hands on a weapon. But even though they were drunk many of them were still conscious. Sitting around the fire, watching as man after man tried to take him on, hollering and cheering, their weapons at their sides.

He could not get close enough to those weapons to secure one before the men could pick them up and start firing. The tent where he and Becca had been held, where his moonlight was still chained up, was close enough that it would be sprayed with bullets.

Risking Becca's life was not an option.

Not when he owed her so much more than he'd ever realized.

Of course, over the years he'd wondered about the baby. Wondered if it was a boy or a girl, if she'd had it and kept it, or given it up for adoption, and if she knew who the child's father was. But he'd been a coward and never tried too hard to find out.

Because he was afraid of this very thing.

Finding out that the baby he'd freaked out over was his all along was a vicious blow. One he would never recover from. He'd thrown away everything he'd ever wanted over his own son.

Son.

He'd had a son.

One he should have loved and protected in the same way he should have loved and protected its mother.

Blocking another blow, he delivered one of his own and dropped the man in front of him. The others cheered and laughed at their unconscious friend, and he prepared himself for the next one to take his turn.

Seemed like these men were slow learners.

Instead, the one who appeared to be in charge waved a hand at the others. "Put him away."

Good.

He was glad to be done with this stupid game. Connor was anxious to get back to Becca and tell her all the things he'd been trying to find the words to express in the hours since she'd confessed that her baby was his.

Something prickled against his skin as he was shoved back toward the tent where Becca was still waiting, alone and afraid. A sense of unease. One he'd felt many times before over his career, and one that always spelled only one thing.

Trouble.

There was not a doubt in his mind that something was wrong. He just didn't know what.

As soon as the two men dragging him back to the tent lifted the flap, he knew what it was. There were two moving shadows inside and there should only be one.

Connor didn't hesitate.

In one smooth move, he slammed his elbow back into the gut of one of the men behind him, shoving the air from his lungs. While he dropped, Connor spun and grabbed the head of the second man, snapping his neck. Without pausing, he did the same to the gagging man hunched over beside the body of his friend.

With both of those men dead, he rushed into the tent.

A man was shoving to his feet, fumbling with his belt and Connor saw red. All the rage he'd felt toward Dylan who had stolen so much from Becca that he hadn't been able to find an outlet for since he'd never had a chance to get his hands on the man, now zeroed in on this target.

The scream he couldn't allow out since it would bring every man not passed out drunk rushing right toward the tent echoed through his head as he lunged for the man who had dared to put his hands on Becca.

Death.

The man had to die.

There was no other option.

Nothing else would satiate the fury burning inside him.

Everything else in the world faded into a mess of blood and torn flesh as Connor rained down blow after blow. It was only when he felt a gentle hand on his shoulder that he finally stilled.

"It's okay, Connor. He didn't rape me. You stopped him before he could," Becca's soft voice penetrated his anger.

"He touched you," he growled, breathing heavily, so much anger still in his body that he was vibrating with it.

"He did. But he didn't rape me. Because of you. Because you stopped him before he got a chance. He's not Dylan."

"Not Dylan," he echoed. Not that the man deserved any less punishment than the man who had raped and almost killed Becca. The man who had been sentenced to only fifteen years in prison even though he'd destroyed Becca's future as surely as if he'd ended her life. The man who would be getting out in just a few short years and Becca would be forced to live the rest of her life knowing her rapist was a free man.

"Not Dylan," Becca repeated.

"I should have killed him for you," he said, spinning to drag Becca into his arms. While she came willingly, she didn't lift her arms and hold on to him. That didn't stop him from crushing her against him, unable to let her go. Needing to feel her small frame tucked against his for reassurance that she was still alive. She might hate him, but she wasn't dead, and that was all that mattered to him.

"I didn't need you to kill him, Connor. I never needed that. All I needed was you," Becca's muffled voice spoke, her face pressed against his chest.

"And I failed you. I left. I'm so sorry, Becca." He willed her to understand how deeply he regretted that one moment when he'd lost control. If he could take his regret and shove it inside her, she could see how honestly he felt those emotions. It was desperation, he needed her to understand, to know just how sorry he was.

"I know you are, Connor."

"Everything I felt bubbled over that night, and I didn't think I could take on another blow. I should have been there. I never should have walked away, not even for a second. I should have been there for you and our son. For your son even if he wasn't mine."

"Connor." Her hands pressed against his chest and pushed until he loosened his hold enough that she could look up at him. "I get it. I always did. You held all your emotions in because you were prioritizing mine, it was one blow too many. Asking you to raise my rapist's child would have been a lot. That all makes sense. I never resented you for having a breakdown. You were overdue because you held it all in for four months. I've been angry, yes, but beneath that, it's damaged trust and resentment. You got to do what I couldn't. You got to run. Even for a little while. I never got that luxury, and that you did, that's what cuts the deepest because it felt like you took something else from me, that once again I didn't get to be in control of my own life."

Dropping to his knees before her, Connor pressed his face to her stomach. So flat and smooth. A reminder of what he'd missed out on. If the baby had survived, he had no doubt Becca would have raised it on her own and he would have missed out on twelve years of his son's life.

There would have been no one to blame but himself.

"If he'd lived, I would have told you, Connor," Becca said as though reading his mind. "I wouldn't have kept your son from you no matter how angry I was with you."

Wrapping his arms around her waist he kept his face to her stomach and touched soft kisses there. Willing them to travel back through time to the tiny baby boy that had once called it home.

"I'm never going to be good enough for you," he whispered.

"It's not about being good enough or not good enough. I just don't trust you anymore, Connor. I still needed you, and even though I get why you lost it and left that night it doesn't mean it didn't hurt. Doesn't mean that now I won't always wonder if it will happen again."

Always sounded so definitive.

So hopeless.

"I never stopped loving you, Becca. I never stopped wanting you. Never stopped regretting leaving that night instead of staying and talking it through with you." It was time to lay himself bare, lay out all his cards and place them on the table so there was nothing more between them. "I never stopped wishing for another chance. Is it too late, Becca, or can you give me a chance to prove to you I can be the man you always deserved?"

∿

August 18th
3:27 A.M.

Her heart hammered so hard in her chest, it felt like a hammer knocking against her aching ribs.

Becca knew what Connor was really asking even if he couldn't outright say the words.

A second chance.

Connor was asking if she'd date him again and see if they could reclaim what they'd lost.

Never had she expected that to be on the table.

The night he ran out of their apartment, claiming there was no way he could raise her rapist's baby, she had resigned herself to the fact that the dreams she'd had about her future were never going to become a reality. All these years, she'd done whatever she had to do to move on including dating other men and accepting a marriage proposal from one of them.

It was now, in this moment, when her blood-covered warrior knelt before her, bruises evident on the parts of his face she could see that weren't pressed against her stomach, that she realized marrying another man would have been a mistake. It wouldn't have been fair to him when she still had unresolved feelings for Connor.

But could she give him a second chance?

Honestly, she wasn't sure.

Before she could say anything, the body of the man who had come so close to raping her groaned, and her fingers quickly curled into Connor's T-shirt.

"H-he's still a-alive," she stammered. By the time she'd finally snapped out of the haze of watching the man she'd loved beating on her would-be assailant and managed to get him to stop, Becca had been fairly certain the man was already dead.

Giving her one last squeeze, she could have sworn he dragged in a deep breath of her scent—which could not be considered pleasant after two full days since she last bathed—he pushed to his feet.

For a moment, she wondered if he was angry with her for not answering, but his gaze was soft and full of emotions, and she refused to allow herself to accept for fear of getting hurt again. Pressing a kiss to her forehead that had her lips tingling, begging for one more reminder of what Connor tasted like, he then moved to crouch beside her attacker.

"I should try to get some answers from him before I kill him," Connor said, so matter of fact, her mouth dropped open in surprise. She'd seen him kill several times now, and it didn't make her afraid of him in any way, although it did make her aware of how strong and powerful he was, it was just this was a side of Connor she'd never seen before.

It highlighted how much of one another's lives they'd missed out on.

That made her sad.

This man had been part of her entire life. She was only a few months younger than his thirty-two years, so they'd been in the same grade at school, played together nearly every day, and dated for years. He'd been her everything, and then he'd just been gone, and she was quickly realizing how not over him she truly was.

Best to keep that to herself for now, though.

They were still in danger, and getting back to the village alive, getting help for Isabella and the villagers was their priority. Not her relationship with Connor or lack thereof.

"How are you going to do that?" she asked, hovering close enough to Connor to feed off the sense of security he infused into her, but not close enough that her attacker could reach out and grab her if he tried to.

"I don't think you want to know the answer to that, moonlight."

Not bothering to correct him on the use of the old nickname, Becca kept her mouth shut. He was right, she didn't want to know how he was able to make injured men that he planned on killing talk.

"Now would be a good time to close your eyes if you can't handle this, Becca," Connor warned.

Part of her wanted to, part of her wanted no part of this. But closing her eyes would be taking the coward's way out. For better or worse, in this situation, she and Connor were partners, and partners had one another's backs.

"I'm okay, Connor. Do what you need to do. I won't think differently of you," she added in a whisper because she sensed that was what Connor's biggest concern was.

Without saying anything, Connor reached out and placed his thumb on what was obviously a broken bone in her assailant's cheek. "Why did you raid the village?" he asked, using that low and deadly tone that made her shiver.

The man said nothing, although even in the dim light of the tent

Becca could see that his eyes were open and fixed on Connor. He gave a slight curl of his lips into a sneer, that quickly vanished from sight when Connor covered the man's mouth with his other hand and pressed down with his thumb.

Jerking and bucking the man's scream was cut off by Connor's hand. Her ex didn't let up, pressing against the broken bone for several long seconds before he finally released the pressure.

After another few moments, he removed his hand. "Ready to tell me why you attacked the village and took Becca and me?" Connor asked.

Breathing hard the man shot him a venomous snarl.

"Easy way or hard way," Connor reminded him. "I'd prefer the easy way since I want to get my girl out of here and someplace safe, but we can go the hard way if you choose. The ball is in your court, buddy."

Weighing his options, the man slumped in defeat as he realized he could either cough up the intel Connor wanted or suffer more pain and then die anyway. "Boss got orders to go for the girl," the man muttered.

"Go for Becca? Why?" There was something about how Connor asked the question that told her he already knew the answer.

What did he know that he hadn't shared with her during the hours they'd been chained up in this tent?

If he knew why they'd been abducted, why wouldn't he tell her?

"She's important to you. You came here for her. They want to keep you silent. Said we could do whatever we wanted to the girl, but we had to set you free alive when we were done with her."

Becca gasped. One hand flew to her mouth, the other pressed to her stomach where nausea churned relentlessly.

Someone had attacked her village on purpose.

Had planned on abducting her.

On raping her and then killing her.

Because of Connor.

To keep him silent.

Although she had no idea who "they" were or what they wanted Connor to keep quiet about.

Connor didn't say anything. Apparently, since he had the answer he'd been seeking and expecting, if the grim look on his face was anything to go by, he had no reason to keep the man alive any longer.

The snap of her would-be rapist's neck echoed through the small tent.

Patting down the dead man, Connor must have found the set of keys to free her, because he knelt at her feet, unlocked the cuff, then stood in front of her. One of his hands hovered near her cheek for a moment before dropping to his side. Then he was moving again. Snatching up the weapons of the men escorting him back to the tent, he thrust one of them into her hands.

"I'm sorry, Becca. For everything. We need to get out of here. Back to the village. I want you to shoot only if you have to, but if you do have to, your aim is for one thing only. Protect yourself and get out of here. You don't worry about anything else," Connor commanded, his voice harsh.

She knew what he was saying, and her head shook in denial.

"I can't just leave—"

"You can and you will leave me behind if it means you live," Connor cut her off and spoke in a voice that brokered no arguments.

Despite what he said she couldn't do that.

Unresolved or not, she still had feelings for Connor even if she wasn't one hundred percent certain exactly what those feelings were. No way would she leave him behind.

No way.

"I failed you, Becca," Connor said, his voice tortured now, losing the control it had possessed just a moment ago. "Do you know how much I hate myself for that? How much I want to go back in time and rewrite the past to have the future I always dreamed of? I let down the only woman I will ever love, and even if you could ever forgive me for it, I will never forgive myself. I will not fail you again. I. Will. Not," he vowed fiercely. "My own life means nothing to me if you're not alive. Nothing."

What could she say to that?

The emotion pouring off Connor filled the tent, seeping inside her and soothing a little of her past hurts, healing some of those old wounds.

Still, she wouldn't agree to prioritize her life over his.

Snapping his control back in place, Connor headed for the tent flap. "You stay behind me, do what I say when I say it, and let me protect you however I have to. Because one thing is for sure, Becca, I am getting you home alive."

As she followed him out into the warm night, Becca realized that in this moment she'd never, not even in all the years they'd spent apart, felt so much distance between herself and Connor.

And she didn't like it.

CHAPTER
Seven

August 18th
   3:38 A.M.

If it was the last thing he ever did, Connor would get Becca home alive.

That was all that ran through his mind as he swept up the tent flap and stepped through it.

Okay, it wasn't *all* that was on his mind.

In reality, his mind was running in a million different directions, covering everything from his fear for Becca to his regret over the past, to the knowledge that she'd been going to say no when he asked if she could give him another chance.

Maybe he should have begged for one.

He absolutely wasn't too proud to do anything that would allow him to keep Becca in his life.

It didn't matter that he'd told himself when he decided to come to Cambodia that he had no expectations, that he just needed to apologize, and he could handle just being friends, it was all a lie.

Because he wanted it all.

He wanted the future he'd cheated all three of them out of.

Even though he knew the miscarriage likely had nothing to do with him leaving Becca that night and making the worst mistake of his life, he couldn't help but wonder if their son would have lived if he'd stuck around.

Which was not a productive road to be running down when they were trapped in the middle of a camp full of men who wouldn't hesitate to rape and kill Becca. Not him though, because apparently, this whole ordeal was meant to push him into convincing his family to back off on their hunt for answers.

Not that it would work.

Just like targeting Susanna to hurt Cole hadn't worked.

He and his family would do anything to protect Becca and make sure she wasn't hurt again but they wouldn't give up.

If anything, this was more fuel added to the fire.

Becca stayed close to his back as they slipped through the night. The fire that was still burning brightly when he'd been out there fighting against the men had mostly burned itself out. While there were still a few men passed out drunk around it, most seemed to have taken themselves off to their tents and put themselves to bed.

As much as he wanted to kill every single man there because all of them would have participated in torturing Becca, he couldn't do that. It was too great a risk, and in the end, keeping Becca safe and alive mattered more to him than empty revenge.

Empty because when it came down to it, *he* was the one who had hurt Becca the worst.

Too bad he couldn't kill himself and offer his own heart on a platter as an offering and proof of how deeply he regretted his actions that fateful day twelve years ago.

They made it past two tents before he saw a man stumbling about. Using the weapon he clutched in his hand was a last resort, the noise would wake everyone, even those who had passed out drunk, and put Becca in greater danger.

"Stay here," he whispered to Becca, then sprung at the man.

Just before he reached him, the other man noticed his approach and reached for his weapon.

Thankfully, years of training meant Connor knew how to be both quick and efficient and the man was dead and dropping to the ground before he had a chance to grab his weapon or alert his friends.

Without pausing, he had taken the man's weapons—a handgun and a knife—and was back at Becca's side, urging her on. There was no time to worry about how watching him kill man after man was going to affect how she saw him, make her think he was more monster than human, to see how different he was from the boy she had once known, because they had to keep moving.

Whatever it took.

Even if that was killing hundreds of men and shattering her perception of him.

Becca would always come first. Never again would he make the mistake of allowing anything to sneak in ahead of her, not even his own fears and emotions.

They made it another two tents over when he heard voices. At least three. Too many to kill without one of them alerting the entire camp.

"Stay here," he whispered to Becca, gently pushing her behind the closest tent and down onto the ground. "Use this first, gun second," he added as he pushed the handle of the knife he'd just procured into her trembling hand.

"Where are you going?"

"To separate them. I'll be right back," he promised.

A small smile quirked up one side of her mouth. "You broke the rules."

"The rules?"

"Horror movie rules. You never say I'll be right back," she explained, and he almost choked on a laugh in his attempt not to make a sound.

Even though Becca had always had such a big and loving heart, so caring and compassionate to everyone who entered her orbit, she was a horror movie junkie, and they'd spent many hours watching them together when they were a couple. She could handle more blood and gore than he'd been able to as a kid, and she loved to tease him about it.

"I live to break the rules," he told her with a grin, so proud of his Becca—and there would never be a time when he didn't think of her as his—for being able to hold it together as well as she had.

"No you don't, you were always a goody-two-shoes," she teased.

There was a smile on his face as he dropped a kiss to the top of her head and then circled the tent toward where he'd heard the voices. He'd missed her so much. More as each year passed by. How had he managed to wait this long before tracking her down? Guilt and shame weren't good enough excuses. This is what he should have done in the beginning.

He hadn't fought for his girl like he should have. Like she deserved.

Now it might be too late.

When he peered around the tent, he could make out the three figures he'd heard. Two of them appeared to be engaged in a secret make-out session, and the third looked like he was playing lookout.

Bending down, his hands ran over the ground, stopping when they touched a stick large enough to make a sound when he threw it. Picking it up, he pulled his arm back and hurled it with all his might out into the surrounding jungle.

It landed with a small thud that caught all three men's attention.

"What was that?" one of the make-out partners asked, sounding scared. Afraid because he didn't want to get caught in the middle of a sex act with another man when what he should be afraid of was his impending death.

"I'll check it out," the lookout assured them and took off in Connor's direction.

Once the man was within striking distance, Connor pounced.

A snap of his neck, and another dead body dropped.

Dragging the man further behind the tent so he wouldn't be immediately noticeable, he moved closer to where the other two men were likely still making out, secure in the false belief that their lookout had things handled.

Well, he didn't.

And they were both about to die.

"Oof," he called out, trying to match the tone and cadence to that of the man he'd just killed.

"Did you hear that?" one of the men asked.

"Sounds like Dior needs help," the other replied.

"Think someone saw us?" the first asked.

The second didn't answer but the two men split up as they searched for their friend. One headed in his direction, the other back the way he'd come.

In Becca's direction.

Right as he was approaching his prey, about to pounce and take out another threat to Becca's life, the man who had headed toward where his girl was hiding spoke.

"What are you doing out here?"

The voice made his target turn, catching sight of him just as he was about to strike.

"Hey! You shouldn't be free," the man snapped, managing to dodge a blow Connor aimed at his head.

With no time to waste, fear for Becca, fear that the entire camp would be woken and their chance at escape thwarted, Connor launched at the man, aiming low this time and managing to tackle the man to the ground. His opponent put up a fight, and a few blows were exchanged before Connor managed to lock a hand around the man's neck. Aiming to cut off blood supply not his breath, it didn't take long for the man to pass out. Then it was a simple snap of his neck and he was on his feet and heading toward Becca.

There were no other sounds, and he didn't like that.

Why hadn't the man alerted the camp to the escaping woman in their midst?

Why had there been no sounds of a struggle?

Orders were to kill Becca, but surely the man wouldn't decide to do it on his own without all of them getting to play with her first.

When he rounded the tent, he saw the answers to his questions.

Becca was right where he'd left her, huddled on the ground, but the man who had found her lay at her feet in the middle of a growing puddle of blood. In her hand, Becca clutched the knife he'd given her.

The knife that had saved her life.

Because his girl had just killed to protect herself.

Pride and sorrow warred within him. Connor was so proud that his girl had been able to do what she needed to do, no matter how afraid she must be, but his heart also broke with the knowledge that she had just changed in a way that was irrevocable.

There was no time to dwell on it though. They were far from safe and if they wanted to stand a chance, they had to get out of there.

"Moonlight, it's me," he said softly as he approached, not wanting to startle her. "You did so good, Becca, but let me take the knife now."

She didn't stop him when he pried it from her white-knuckled grip, and she allowed him to tug her to her feet.

"I didn't think, just did it," she whispered, her gaze locked on the dead man.

"You did amazing, honey. I'm so proud of you," he told her as he gripped her shoulders and squeezed just enough to draw her attention to him. "Now we have to get out of here. In a few hours, everyone will wake up and realize we're gone. We have to get back to the village, find someplace to hide out, or hope that the survivors have called in help and the gang can't get to us again. You with me, moonlight?"

It was a lot to ask of her, especially since those villagers were her friends and she hadn't had time to process their deaths. But he knew his girl had it in her to conquer the entire world if she set her mind to it.

"I'm with you," she answered softly.

As he grabbed her hand and they took off into the trees, Connor could only wish she meant she would be with him forever.

~

August 18th
3:52 P.M.

Exhaustion coated every cell in her body.

But Becca wouldn't give up.

It didn't matter how loud her muscles screamed for a break or how badly her stump ached since she hadn't been able to tend to it in several days or given it a break from the prosthetic. A headache pounded between her temples and her ribs, likely cracked but probably not broken, protested each breath she took.

After hours of walking through the jungle, her breathing was harsh and labored, adding to the pain.

As anxious as she was to get back to the village and find out how much damage had been done, she was equally scared. How many people had been killed? Had Isabella survived? Was she going to get back there to find that it had been a complete bloody massacre and there were no survivors?

Since she and Connor still weren't really on speaking terms—although she couldn't say that the silence was uncomfortable—she had no idea what the man back at the camp had meant about wanting to silence him. Even though she definitely wanted answers and would make sure she got them before they parted ways, Becca sensed she wasn't going to like what she heard.

It had to be something about Connor's mom and stepdad. After all these years, had he and his brothers finally managed to prove their mom was innocent and never betrayed her country or her husband?

She hoped they had, Connor deserved closure. But if that closure had come at the price of the lives of her best friend and the villagers she loved like family, that seemed so high.

Still, she couldn't begrudge him answers. They'd been best friends back when his dad had died and then his mom had immediately remarried. She'd been there for him when he was consumed with anger about what he perceived as his mom's betrayal, and when he learned that the remarriage was in name only since his mom and stepdad didn't share a bed. That revelation had come too late, after his mom was arrested, and he and his siblings never got to see her again and make amends for the months of anger that had simmered between them.

Just like he'd been there for her after her rape, she'd been there for him during that difficult time. Held him while he cried over the loss of his dad, soothed the rough edges of his anger when he didn't understand his mom's actions, and tried to shoulder as much of his guilt as she could when he realized his mom had never stopped loving his dad. She'd promised to help in any way she could to prove that neither his mom nor stepdad were traitors.

A hand on her arm stopped her, and Becca had to lock her knees to keep from sinking to the ground. Connor had frozen and she wondered if he'd sensed something dangerous up ahead.

While she knew this area well, they'd taken a long route back to the village because Connor was worried that since they had vehicles the men who had taken them would get their first, and she was a little turned around. His plan had been to circle around and approach the village from a different angle, one they wouldn't expect, so that he could scope the place out first. It had meant walking for hours longer than it would have taken them to work backward from the camp to the village, but she had agreed it was a good plan.

"Village is only a quarter mile ahead," Connor said softly.

He seemed to have learned how to speak without his voice carrying very far, it was a great skill to have in the world he lived in now, but she couldn't copy the skill, so she merely nodded.

"I want you to stay here and I'll make sure it's safe," he whispered.

Again, she just nodded. This was Connor's area of expertise, not hers. If he had a plan she was going to listen to it. Too many things filled her head for her to worry about the past right now. Being kidnapped, almost being raped, killing a man, fear for her friend and the villagers had pushed her anger at Connor right out of her. Well, at least pushed it right into the background.

"You have the knife and the gun, you use either to protect yourself," Connor ordered.

Then he turned and walked away. There was no hesitation to his steps, he moved soundlessly and looked so strong and confident. But he could be walking into danger alone just so he could try to protect her.

That was the Connor she remembered, the one she'd grown up with, the one she'd loved. There wasn't a single thing he wouldn't do for the people he loved, and ... maybe he still loved her.

She just wasn't sure that could change anything, even though ... maybe she still loved him, too.

"Connor," she hissed, trying to make her voice soft like he did but failing.

Immediately, he hurried toward her, concern in his eyes. "What's wrong? Are you okay?"

Although they'd walked mostly in silence, he'd stopped her regularly to check in and ensure she was physically and emotionally capable of continuing. She was struggling on both fronts, but neither were going to get the best of her.

"I'm okay, I just wanted to say, be careful."

His entire face softened at her words. "I'll be careful. Promise."

Despite his promise, that rock of fear continued to sit heavily in her stomach as she watched him walk away again. This time she didn't call him back even though she wanted to stick close to him.

Just a few days in his presence, and she could already feel herself being pulled back into his orbit.

Something she couldn't allow to happen.

Trust.

It all boiled down to trust.

Theirs had been shattered, and she wasn't sure it could be rebuilt. Even if it could be, there were sure to be pieces missing. Things could never go back to the way they had been before, and she wasn't sure there were enough pieces left to put together to make something that would even resemble trust.

Seconds ticked by.

Fear grew inside her.

Her fingers curled tightly around the handle of the knife in her right hand and the butt of the gun in her left. She wouldn't hesitate to use either to save herself if she had to, but she didn't want to have to.

Had the men who had been ordered to abduct and kill her to try to keep Connor and his family silent made it to the camp before them? Had they killed any survivors of the first assault? Had they killed Connor too?

Finally, just when she thought she couldn't handle another single second of waiting, she saw him. Moving through the trees toward her. Coming fast. Was that a good sign or a bad one?

Unable to stand still, she hurried toward him, meeting him halfway. "What happened? What did you find?" she asked, forgetting to try to keep quiet in her need to find out just how bad things were.

The expression on his face was one she didn't like.

One that sparked more fear inside her.

"Connor? Are they all dead?" she asked her greatest fear. If everyone was dead there was no way she wouldn't blame herself even if the village had been attacked because of Connor and his family. Connor was only there because of her. That made it her fault.

"No, honey," he assured her, reaching out to take the weapons from her hands. What did that mean?

"You're scaring me, Connor. Something is wrong. Your face ... it's the one you always make when you have bad news you don't want to tell me."

A half smile wiped away a little of his anxiety. "I forgot how easily you can read me. I promise you not everyone is dead. In fact, there are fewer dead than I originally thought. I spoke with the leader of the village. He said the death toll is standing at six, but there are a couple of people in critical condition and a lot in serious condition."

Her chest eased a little at those words.

Those six dead would eat away at her, but it wasn't as bad as she'd feared.

"They were able to get help?"

"Yes. They got to the nearest town, and there are cops and military in the village now."

"So those men that took us, they're not there?" The last thing she wanted was to set off a second assault on the village by being there.

"No. My guess is when they realized we were gone, they packed up their camp and fled back to wherever they came from. That camp wasn't a permanent one, and it was close enough to the village that they were probably keeping tabs on it so they knew that the military had already moved in, and it wasn't safe for them."

"Okay, okay, that's ... good ... I'm glad not too many died." Her voice wobbled a little on those last words because even one death was one too many. Things were better than she could have hoped for, better than she'd believed these last few days. But ... Connor had that look she knew meant something was wrong.

Something he hadn't told her yet.

Something she dreaded hearing.

"What aren't you telling me?" she demanded, directly meeting Connor's blue gaze.

One of his hands rubbed the back of his neck, the other dragged down his face. "I don't know how to tell you this, Becca. But your friend Isabella is gone."

CHAPTER
Eight

August 18th
    4:15 P.M.

All the color drained from Becca's face.

Her knees buckled.

Connor snapped out an arm to catch her before she hit the ground.

She hung limply in his grasp for a moment as shock rampaged through her body, but his girl was too strong to stay down for long. In the aftermath of her assault, Connor had quickly realized that the soft, sweet girl he'd always known had a spine of steel, one he wouldn't have immediately assumed she possessed.

But she did.

In the darkest of times, her strength had shone through, blinding everyone who came into contact with her, amazing them all, leaving them in awe of the tiny woman who refused to be knocked down and stay down.

When she lifted her head to look up at him there was grief swimming in her midnight blue eyes. Grief that had the potential to drown her if she let it. All Connor could do was pray that she wouldn't. That she would fight through this like she'd fought twelve years ago and come out victorious.

Then he wanted to lock her away someplace where nothing could ever hurt her again. Because as much as he admired her strength and determination, he hated that she had to fight through pain and trauma just to survive.

"Izzy is ... dead?" Becca asked, her voice breaking on that last word.

Part of him wished he could tell her yes.

In a lot of ways, death could be easier to deal with.

It was final, it had a clearly defined definition.

What had happened was not.

"I spoke to the leader of the village and the leader of the military unit deployed here," he told her. Once he'd put his weapons down and walked into the village, explaining who he was and what had happened, the first thing he'd done was ask about the death toll and Becca's best friend. As much as he didn't want to say this, he didn't have a choice. She had to know. "Honey, Bella is gone."

"Can I see her body? I just ... I need to say goodbye."

When Becca went to pull out of his embrace, he gripped her biceps, holding her in place. "No, Becca. There is no body."

"I ... don't understand. You said she was gone." Those big blue eyes of hers stared up at him so full of confusion he wished he could wipe it away without shattering her heart in the process.

"She's gone, Becca, but she's not dead. She was taken."

Becca gulped. "Taken?"

"Some of the villagers witnessed her being manhandled into the back of a jeep and taken away," he explained.

"She was ... kidnapped?"

From the tone of her voice, Becca knew exactly what that meant for a young, attractive woman in any part of the world, but especially there.

Isabella hadn't just been abducted, she'd been trafficked.

There was not a doubt in his mind that the poor woman was already out of the country or deep in the clutches of someone who would sell her to the highest bidder and not lose a moment's sleep over it.

"Yeah, honey. I'm so sorry. Apparently, she fought hard. Witnesses said she was swinging and screaming, and managed to get a few hits in, but in the end, she was knocked unconscious, loaded up, and taken away."

"Taken away," Becca echoed, her voice faint. But then it came back with a vengeance, and she struggled against his hold. "We have to find her. They probably took her to the same camp where we were being held. We left her behind, Connor. We should have checked the camp before leaving. We have to get back there. We have to. We have to find her before it's too late."

Telling her it was already too late would be cruel even if deep down she already knew it. Becca wasn't ready to acknowledge that reality just yet.

There was one thing he could put her mind at ease about though.

"Listen to me, Becca. She wasn't at the camp. If she was there ... if she was there we would have seen her, the men would have been using her."

"Using her," Becca repeated, tears forming in her eyes. "You mean raping her."

"That's what I mean."

"If you don't think she's at the camp then where is she?"

"It's been more than forty-eight hours, she could be anywhere."

"Anywhere," Becca echoed again like she was his shadow. "Then maybe she is at the camp. We should go back there, Connor. Maybe they're still there. Maybe they don't know about the police and the military. Maybe she is at the camp."

"I'll give directions to the police and military so they can check out the camp, but she's not there, honey."

"You can't know that, Connor," she shrieked, her voice cracking with despair, anger, and grief. "She could be. Let me go." She fought against his hold, but he tightened his grip as much as he dared without outright hurting her. "I want to look for her."

"There's nothing you can do for her," he said gently.

"There has to be. I have to try, have to do something. She's my best friend. I love her like a sister. She's always been there for me. Always. I won't leave her behind, I have to find her."

Finishing with a sob, Becca collapsed against him, grabbing onto fistfuls of his T-shirt as she wept. Hating that there was no way for him to take this pain from her, Connor did the only thing he could. Wrapped her up in his arms and held her.

Eventually, her cries diminished, and she rested heavily against him.

Not willing to let her go while she was allowing him to hold her, Connor rubbed small circles on her back. "As soon as we talk to the cops and give our statements, I'll call Prey. I'll tell them everything we have on Isabella, and they'll look for her. I'm not giving up on her, Becca. We're not giving up on her."

It didn't matter what the odds were they'd search for Isabella with every resource Prey had. Becca needed closure and even if he had to deliver the news to her that her best friend was dead, he'd bring it to her.

"Okay," she whispered wearily.

There was one more thing they needed to address. One he was pretty sure Becca was going to fight him on.

"You heard the man at the camp, Becca. They targeted your village because of me, because they knew hurting you would hurt me, and that threatening you was an effective way to get to me. That means you're not safe. Not out here alone in Cambodia."

Lifting her head she shot him a suspicious frown. "What are you saying?"

"I'm saying I think you should fly back home with me. If you insist on staying, I'll stay here, too, I won't allow you to be hurt again, especially not because of me and my family. It will be harder to protect you here, but I won't force you to do something you're uncomfortable with. Still, I think it would be best if you came home with me. We'll find you a safe house to stay in until we have the proof we need to take these people down and make sure they pay for killing Mom, and hurting you, Willow, and Susanna."

Her forehead furrowed. "Who are Willow and Susanna?"

Was that a hint of jealousy in her voice or was he merely imagining it? "Willow is a woman Cooper met in Egypt, they're dating now. And Susanna was Cole's neighbor who he hated, but we all knew was secretly obsessed with. They cleared the air, and she was able to forgive him and they just got together as well."

"They were hurt by these same people that framed your mom?"

"They were. These people have to be stopped, Becca. But more than that, I can't let them hurt you. Please, I'm prepared to beg if that's what it will take, please let me protect you. I owe you so much more but please at least let me do this for you. Let me protect you, it's my fault you're in danger anyway. I have the skills and the ability to get you somewhere safe, and cameras can monitor the location, so you won't even have to spend time with me."

The last was harder to say because he ached to be in Becca's presence again. But in the end, her life was more important than his needs, wants, and desires.

"Connor—"

"I know you don't trust me anymore," he said, cutting her off. "But I can do this, Becca. I *will* do this. Because whether you spend the rest of your life hating me or not, you're going to live a long and happy life. I won't accept anything less. The world needs you in it, Becca. My world needs you in it."

~

August 19th
1:27 A.M.

She had to be crazy to have agreed to this.

Even as she thought that, Becca knew there was no other option.

Someone was after her because of her past connection to Connor, and even though it might seem like the smartest option was to put as much distance as possible between herself and her former boyfriend, she believed the opposite was true.

Who better to protect her from his enemies than Connor himself?

Already he'd killed for her, protected her, and got her out of the camp where she would have been gang raped and killed. He could keep her safe, that wasn't the issue, the issue was protecting her heart.

There was no way she could allow herself to put it on the line again.

What if Connor broke it all over again?

"Why don't you go lie down, there's a bed in the back," Connor suggested when she shifted uncomfortably in her seat again.

They were in a private jet that belonged to Prey Security, heading back home. The plane was nice, so much fancier than anything she'd ever been in, than she'd ever be in again, but she couldn't enjoy it. Her emotions were all jumbled together in a tangled mess inside her chest, and she didn't have the energy to work on untangling them.

Being near Connor hurt more than the bruised ribs and lump on her head, but being away from him hurt more.

She was so tired of hurting.

If a genie came out of a lamp and offered her three wishes, her first would be to make it so she never met Dylan Sanders. Because then she never would have been raped, lost her foot, and got left with ugly scars, or lost Connor in the first place.

But longing for wishes was childish.

If there was one thing she'd been forced to learn over the last twelve years, it was that bad things happened and you had to learn how to accept them and keep moving forward.

"Yeah, maybe I'll do that," she agreed, shoving to her feet. The future was too uncertain for her to allow Connor to become her safe place again. They'd been there and done that and he'd bailed. Letting herself fall into old patterns could wind up yielding the same outcome.

"Hey." Connor caught her hand as she moved past his seat heading for the bedroom at the back of the plane. "I've already contacted Prey, and they've started looking for Bella. If anyone can find her, we can."

While she appreciated that the company he worked for was going to look for Izzy, she wasn't naïve enough to think that finding her would be easy.

It wouldn't.

In fact, it would be next to impossible.

"I appreciate it," she assured him, gently tugging her arm free. If she let him touch her, she would end up throwing herself into his arms and begging him to never leave her side again, and that wouldn't be good for either of them.

Connor let her go, and she hurried down into the back room. There was a nice, big, comfortable-looking bed in there, and she climbed onto it and curled up in a ball in the center. It was much harder to be around Connor than she would have guessed if you'd asked her a week ago.

He'd been right there beside her while they answered questions, supporting her, watching over her, ensuring she was checked out by a doctor, and that she ate and drank water.

He was taking care of her like he used to and every cell in her body screamed at her to give in and let things go back to how they used to be.

But they couldn't.

You couldn't go back in life only forward.

Despite her whirring mind, exhaustion quickly took over now that she was lying down and drifted off into a restless sleep.

"Pretty girl."

Becca looked over her shoulder to see the man from the tent approaching.

She screamed.

Or she thought she did.

Only she didn't hear a sound.

Run.

She had to run.

Had to get away from him or he'd rape her.

But when she tried to run, she couldn't.

Looking down, she saw a metal cuff locked around her ankle attached to the ground, and because of it, she couldn't move.

"Let him touch you, Becca. You know you want it. Just like you wanted me," Dylan said, appearing at her side beside tent man.

"No! I never wanted you to touch me!" she screamed, this time her voice was so loud it hurt her ears.

How could he say that?

Didn't Dylan know that what he did to her ruined her life?

"Pretty girl," tent man crooned again as his hands ripped at her clothing, baring her body to him.

His hands touched her.

Dylan's hands as well.

She couldn't make them stop.

Couldn't move at all.

She was stuck.

Trapped.

Helpless.

When tent man and Dylan both shoved inside her simultaneously, she screamed and thrashed with everything she had. Desperate to get them out of her. Desperate to get rid of the feel of them. Desperate to erase their despicable acts from her mind.

"Becca."

Something was shaking her.

"Wake up, moonlight."

More shaking as the tent she was trapped in began to fade.

"Good girl, come on, honey, wake up."

Eyes snapping open, Becca bolted upright to find herself on the plane still in the middle of the bed she'd curled up on to try to get some rest.

Now she wasn't alone. Connor was there knelt on the bed beside her, his hands on her shoulders, panic in his sky blue eyes.

He'd ripped her from a nightmare just like he'd done so many times before in the months following her assault.

It wasn't all he'd done for her.

They'd quickly discovered there was something that helped to calm her when her fears were getting the best of her.

Not that it would be appropriate to do that now that they weren't a couple.

Still, her gaze dropped a little then her cheeks heated when she saw his head dip, his gaze following her own.

"Do you need to do it?" he asked without hesitation, making her gaze snap back up to meet his.

How could he ask her that?

Didn't he know it would be inappropriate?

It had always been a weird way for her to deal with her trauma, but it had worked. It had made her feel like she had control over her body, who touched her, when, and how.

Even now, with twelve years between this moment and the last time they'd been together, there was no fear like there would be with another man. With her fiancé, it had taken months for her to allow him to even hold her hand, more months before she would let him kiss her, and over a year before she'd been ready to have sex with him.

Connor was just different.

He was part of her and that hadn't changed even though so many years had passed.

"We can't," she whispered.

"Why?"

"Because we're not a couple anymore."

There was no way she couldn't miss his wince at her words. Still his voice was even when he spoke. "So?"

"What do you mean so?"

"Would it help?"

"Yes," she somewhat reluctantly answered.

"If we were still a couple would you do it without thinking?"

"You know I would."

"Then do it. I don't mind. Becca, all I want is to help you, to make up for letting you down, and find a way to fix things between us. I know this isn't that, but it is something. It's something I can do to help you now when you're scared and hurting. Please, let me give you this at least."

It felt wrong but her hands seemed to move of their own accord. Connor was offering and he wasn't trying to attach any strings to it.

The truth was, couple or not, this *would* help to calm her racing heart, it would help still the voices in her head, it would remind her that she was still a person, still a woman, and not just a rape victim.

He didn't stop her as she unzipped and pushed down his jeans. In fact, there was a tender smile on his face as she reached into his boxers and pulled his length free. At her touch, it hardened a little, but they both knew this wasn't about sex.

Shifting back so he was resting against the bed's headboard, Connor guided her head to his lap, and she took his length into her mouth.

As soon as the familiar taste hit her tongue, she felt every muscle in her body relax.

Home.

Connor tasted like home. Like safety, love, and protection.

Nestling her head on his massive thigh, she sucked gently on his length, almost like a baby would on a pacifier. Which was, in essence, what she was doing. Using the tactile feel of his penis to soothe herself while reminding herself that she was in charge. Connor would never turn this into a sexual thing, he wouldn't steal her power, he wouldn't take anything from her that she wouldn't willingly give him.

So when his hand began to stroke her hair, she let her eyes drift closed. She was safe with Connor, she didn't have to worry, didn't have to be on alert.

Even though she knew wishes were pointless, Becca couldn't help but wish there was a way that she could hold onto this feeling and make it her reality again.

But that was kidding herself.

It could never be her reality.

Could it?

CHAPTER
Nine

August 19th
3:01 P.M.

Bringing Becca here felt both weird and right.

The kind of right you felt down to your bones, that settling feeling inside you that said everything would be okay.

And for the first time in twelve years, Connor actually thought it was.

So far, Becca hadn't committed to any sort of future with him, not even as friends. Neither of them had raised his earlier question of whether she could give him a second chance. For her, he was sure it was because she was feeling conflicted, for him, it was because he didn't want to push too hard too soon.

The question was still out there, and she could give him an answer when she was ready.

Whether she realized it or not, she'd already taken a step toward giving him the chance he wanted when she allowed him to comfort her the way he used to.

Connor completely got that it was probably odd to most people, but after her assault, Becca had felt powerless, and she'd been so afraid. One day when she'd been crying and shaking, begging him to dump her because she might never be able to have sex again, he'd just whipped out his length and told her that it belonged to her. Never to another woman, and if she didn't want it then no one else would touch it.

He'd meant every word.

Becca had doubted him, but he'd told her she was in control of it, it was hers to do with what she wanted. If that was sex when she was ready then so be it, and if not, he was okay with that because he loved her way more than any cheap orgasm.

Determined to prove him wrong, she'd grabbed it, ran her hands over it, and told him he was lying, he could never give up sex indefinitely. He'd insisted that he could. So, she'd dragged him over to stand before her and taken him in her mouth. Almost immediately she'd calmed, and they'd both realized that using his penis like a pacifier was helpful to her, soothed her, and it had become their thing.

One she'd accepted on the plane, allowing him to comfort her.

"This house ... it reminds me ..." Becca cast him a confused look as she hobbled on her crutches down the front path toward the porch.

"Reminds you of what?" he asked, hoping she knew exactly what the old farmhouse reminded her of and was just uneasy about saying it out loud.

"Did you pick this house because of me?" she asked. "Because it looks exactly like the kind of place we talked about buying when we mapped out our future."

"Yep. I absolutely did."

"Why?" she whispered.

"Because there hasn't been a day that went past in the last twelve years that I haven't thought of you. Ached for you. Regretted what I did and wished I could make it up to you somehow," he answered honestly. This was no time for stubborn pride or a macho need to hide his emotions. Connor knew he was fighting for his future and that required honesty and vulnerability. Both of which Becca deserved from him.

For a moment she was silent, something flitted through her eyes, and then she blurted out words that stopped his heart. "Connor, I was engaged."

She was engaged?

Was, as in not anymore?

Did it matter?

She'd fallen in love with another man.

Moved on.

Before he could say anything, the door to his house was thrown open and his brothers spilled out.

"You going to bring the pipsqueak in to see us or not?" Cooper demanded with a grin. All his brothers had loved Becca. She'd been part of their childhood, and they'd all assumed she would be part of the rest of their lives. None of them understood how he'd managed to mess up a sure thing, and honestly, he wasn't either.

"Coop!" A genuine smile lit Becca's face as his twin brother came down the porch steps and swung her into his arms, making her giggle.

"Missed you, pip," he said, kissing her cheek.

Sadness tugged the edges of her smile down. "Missed you, too. I'm sorry. I should have made an effort to keep in touch. With all of you," she added, looking over to where Cole, Cade, Jake, and Jax were still on the porch. Even though his stepbrothers had entered the picture once they were all teens, they'd come to love Becca as much as his biological brothers had and they all considered her family.

"No need to be sorry, pipsqueak," Cooper assured her as he set her down on her feet, and Becca reached out to grab the crutches he'd automatically grabbed when his brother swept her off her feet.

Something he might have been tempted to be jealous about if he didn't know Cooper was madly in love with his new girlfriend, Willow.

"You know I hate that nickname, Coop," Becca grumbled as she shot him a glare.

"I know, that's what makes it a fun name," Coop teased, ignoring her frown and ruffling her silky black locks.

"We all understood why you needed space, Becca," Cade assured her as she hopped up the porch steps using her crutches.

"Thank you, Cade," she said, reaching out to rest a hand on his forearm. Unlike when most people touched him, his oldest brother didn't pull away. "Still, I missed out on a lot. I heard about your wife, I'm so sorry for your loss. I understand what it feels like. I'd love to meet your little girl one day, if you're comfortable with that, of course."

Surprisingly, Cade reached out and covered Becca's small hand, which still sat on his arm with one of his own. "I appreciate that, Becca, and I'm sorry for whatever loss you had. If anyone deserves happiness it's you, and I hope you find it one day."

As he said the words, Cade looked directly at him, but Connor was still stuck on the engaged part.

Pressure in his chest made it almost impossible to breathe.

He'd waited too long, and Becca had moved on.

It seemed like maybe her fiancé had passed away from what she said to Cade but knowing that she'd pledged her life to another man meant that she'd left the past behind her.

Left him behind.

Too late.

He'd come for her too late.

"Come on in," Cooper urged her after she'd greeted Cole, Jake, and Jax.

"You'll meet Essie today, she's right inside," Cade told Becca as they all headed into his house.

Connor trailed along behind, watching as the tiny tornado that was his little niece barreled over to Becca.

"Hi, I'm Essie, who are you?"

"I'm Becca. Nice to meet you, Essie." Becca held out her hand, and the little girl preened as she shook it, Essie loved anything that made her feel grown up.

"What happened to your foot? Why do you gots only one?" Essie asked.

"Esther," Gabriella Sadler, who was Essie's nanny, rebuked. "That's not polite to ask when you just met someone. Sorry," the woman said to Becca who brushed off the apology.

"It's okay, I'm fine with talking about it. I actually prefer questions rather than stares and whispers behind my back." Becca sat in the chair at the table that Jax pulled out for her and turned back to the little girl. "A long time ago somebody tried to hurt me. They pushed me out of a car, but my foot got all tangled in the seatbelt, and it got broken when they drove the car away. The doctors did everything they could, but my foot was too badly hurt so they had to take it off."

Essie gasped. "Doctors took away your foot."

"Not something you have to worry about happening to you," Becca assured the child. "But yes. They had to or I could have gotten very sick and died."

"I'm glad you didn't died," Essie said seriously.

"We all are," Cole said, placing his hand on Becca's shoulder and squeezing.

"Are you hurt?" Becca asked, pointing to the bandage peeking out of the neckline of his T-shirt, then glancing over to the bandage covering Susanna Zangari's arm.

"Nope, we got tattoos," Cole replied, tugging Susanna to his side. "Matching tattoos. Becca, this is Susanna, my girlfriend. Susanna, this is Becca. She's an old friend of the family, grew up across the street from us."

"Nice to meet you," Becca said, and even though Susanna struggled with letting people get close to her she offered a genuine smile at Becca. The two women had more in common than Becca was aware of.

"Nice to meet you, too," Susanna returned.

"And this is Willow," Cooper added.

"I'm glad you're home safe and sound," Willow said as she came to stand before Becca.

"Me too," Becca agreed. "For a while, I wasn't sure we were going to get out of there alive. Where's Cassandra? I thought she'd be here with all of you."

"Cassandra had to go someplace safe for now," Cade informed her.

Although it was clear Becca wanted to ask more questions, she didn't push, instead falling into easy conversation with his brothers like over a decade hadn't passed since she last saw them.

However, he was still stuck on her revelation.

Engaged.

His brain couldn't seem to comprehend what should be an easy enough concept. But it wasn't easy. Nothing about his reunion with Becca had gone like he'd hoped it would, and worse than that, he had no idea how to get things back on track.

Or if it was even possible.

~

August 19th
  3:32 P.M.

Trying her best to keep her concentration on the conversation she was trying to engage in, Becca found it next to impossible.

Her attention kept sneaking over to the man standing in the doorway to the kitchen. Connor hadn't come in to join the rest of them around the table, and she knew that was her fault.

Why had she blurted out that she'd been engaged?

That was a conversation they should have had when it was just the two of them. To be fair, she hadn't realized that his brothers and their girlfriends and families were there, but still, she shouldn't have blurted it out on the garden path.

Now she was wishing she'd kept her mouth shut.

Did Connor really need to know that she'd been engaged?

Reluctantly, Becca admitted to herself that he did, which was why she'd told him. He'd asked for a second chance, and while she wasn't sure whether she could give him one, she did know that for both of their peace of mind, they had to talk everything through so they could finally set down the burdens of the past.

"You okay, Becca?" Susanna asked, her green eyes full of empathy and something else she couldn't quite place.

"I'm hanging in there," she answered, that seemed to be the most truthful response she could give. Her ribs pulsed with pain when she breathed, although the painkillers she'd been taking helped. A headache throbbed behind her eyes, but it wasn't as vicious as it had been, and although her stump ached, it was nothing like the pain she'd experienced just after the amputation.

"Sometimes that's all you can ask of yourself," Susanna said, more like she was reminding herself than Becca. While she didn't know all the details of what had happened to the other woman, she knew that

Susanna had been targeted because the same men who had ordered her village to be attacked thought she was dating Cole.

"What's your tattoo?" she asked.

Absently, Susanna brushed her fingers along the bandage. "It's a quote. Something Cole said to me. Something I desperately needed to hear. It says, I believe you."

"It's always important to be believed," she agreed. How much harder would her own ordeal have been if she'd been called a liar? Told that she wanted what Dylan had done to her. He'd tried to claim that during the trial, but the fact he'd shoved her out of the car door and driven off with her still tangled in the seatbelt helped prove her case. "I'm sorry someone didn't believe you. You deserved better than that. Telling your story is brave and to have someone shove that back in your face sucks."

A beat passed then a wide smile lit up Susanna's face. "It definitely does. Thank you for saying that, I needed to hear it."

Becca smiled back at the other woman. Susanna seemed like someone she could become friends with, and she got the feeling that perhaps they shared a few things in common when it came to being hurt.

From the way Cole kept darting glances at Susanna, Becca knew the younger woman was in good hands. Cole was a great guy, and she was glad he'd found someone to spend his life with.

Her gaze darted once again to where Connor leaned against the doorjamb. There was a hint of despair in his eyes that hadn't been there before.

She'd put it there.

By blurting out that she'd been engaged.

"Cole said you and Connor used to be a couple," Susanna said gently.

"For a long time. He was my first love." Turning back to face the other woman, she read the expression on her face. "I'm guessing he told you that I was raped while in college. Connor was there through all of it, right by my side, giving me whatever I needed. Then I found out I was pregnant. We didn't know if Connor or my rapist was the baby's father, and Connor freaked, told me he couldn't raise another man's child, especially not a man who hurt me. He left our apartment, and I was heartbroken. I packed my stuff, called my parents, and went back home. I refused to talk to him and hadn't seen him until he turned up in Cambodia."

"I know it's absolutely none of my business, we don't know each other, and you have no reason to trust me, so you can tell me to mind my own business if you want."

Susanna's sincerity made her chuckle. "I would never do that. Cole was a good friend to me when we were kids. If you're with him then that makes us friends because I'd like to keep Cole and the others in my life."

"Do you still love Connor?"

"Yes." The word fell from her lips without thought, an automatic answer to a question that had played in her mind a lot in the first few years after they broke up.

Nothing could ever change that.

Not him leaving her.

Not her inability to let it go.

Not twelve years of him being absent from her life.

Loving Connor Charleston was as natural to her as breathing.

"I know that doesn't fix everything ... doesn't fix anything really ... but at least you know that. It's something to hold onto," Susanna said.

"Something to hold onto," Becca echoed. The other woman was right, it was something to hold onto, something solid when her world had once again been tossed upside down.

Glancing over, she saw that Connor still hadn't moved, and she didn't like the distance between them. She'd survived twelve years without him, but for some reason, it seemed next to impossible to face the next minute with him on the other side of the room.

"The guys and I were talking," Cade announced as he and Jake handed out cups of coffee.

"About me?" Becca asked, assuming it was since he was looking right at her. She'd missed these guys, they'd been such a big part of her childhood and adolescence. Looking back with hindsight she knew she shouldn't have cut all the Charleston and Holloway brothers out of her life along with Connor. They'd just been a painful reminder of what she'd lost, and it was easier to not deal with it than face it headlong.

Which is what she should have done with Connor back then.

Instead of running because he'd hurt her, she should have done the mature thing and stayed and talked it out. Even if she'd decided she needed to break up with him she'd owed him at least a conversation instead of running like a coward.

"Yeah, about you, pipsqueak," Cooper answered, earning him a scowl, which he merely laughed at.

"We need you to stay someplace safe while we sort this mess out," Cade continued. "Going home to your family is exactly where they'll look for you, and now they know that you are, in fact, a good way to target Connor."

Connor didn't say anything, and his silence and distance were making her uneasy.

Did she want a second chance with him?

Honestly, she wasn't sure. But she did know she didn't want Connor to hate her for trying to move on with her life.

"That makes sense, I won't go home," she agreed. While she would have liked to go home and see her parents and sister, it had been too long since she'd last been in the same room as them, she absolutely did not want to put them in danger. "I can go and stay at a hotel or something."

"Hotel is a terrible security risk," Jake told her.

"So, we came up with a better solution," Jax added.

"I have a cabin I don't use very often. It's still in my wife's family name so nobody should immediately connect it to us," Cade told her.

"I can't stay in your cabin, Cade," she protested.

"Why not?" he asked.

"Because ..." she trailed off not really sure what the answer was. It just didn't feel right. That cabin had probably been a special place for him and his family, she didn't want to intrude.

"It's not up for debate, Becca," Connor said, straightening and striding across his kitchen toward her.

There was determination burning in his eyes and she felt a little of the pressure in her chest subside. Connor still cared even if he was angry with her and maybe even regretted asking for a second chance.

"You're in danger because of us, because of me, the absolute least we can do is give you a safe place to stay. The cabin is remote, it'll give you peace and quiet. It has a good security system, I'll make sure you're armed, and we'll be monitoring the system. You'll be safe there, Becca, and I need you to be safe."

She needed to not be alone.

The thought surprised her, coming out of nowhere, along with it a deep sense of who she wanted for company.

Connor.

The ex who had been her everything, then taken it all away, only to return and bring with him a sense of security she knew she couldn't allow herself to trust in but didn't know how to stop it from happening.

CHAPTER

Ten

August 19th
    6:18 P.M.

"So?"

"So, what?" Connor asked Cooper as his twin dropped down onto the couch beside him.

The last thing he was in the mood for right now was some sort of lecture from one of his brothers.

Or all of them.

Since every single one of them was lounging around his living room looking at him expectantly.

What did they want him to say?

That he'd messed up with Becca to the point where she had literally moved on and planned to spend the rest of her life with another man?

He knew that already.

Talking about it wasn't going to change anything.

At least talking about it with these guys wasn't going to change anything.

The person he needed to talk things through with was currently being driven out to Cade's cabin by Cade. Becca was the only one who could give him the answers he needed. Who was the man she'd been engaged to? Had he passed away or had one of them ended things? If one of them had ended things, was it her or him? Had she truly loved this person the way she used to love him? How long after they'd broken up had she met this man? How long had he been out of her life?

All of those questions raced around his head along with a hundred others, tormenting him, mocking him, driving him crazy.

Had he lost any chance with her?

Was it already too late?

Everything that he'd told Becca all those years ago was still true. She was his, she owned every part of his body, heart, and soul. There was no other woman for him, he wasn't interested in anyone else. Never had been. She was the other half of him, no one else would ever fit him like she did.

But he couldn't force her to forgive him and want to be with him again.

Which meant he might have to accept the possibility that it was over.

Truly over.

Not the kind of in-between purgatory that, to him, their relationship had been languishing in these past twelve years. Part of him had always known he was going to go back to her at some point. All he had to do was manage his guilt and shame before he could face her again.

"You don't have anything to say?" Cole asked. "Because you all had plenty to say a couple of weeks ago when my relationship with Susanna was just getting started."

"That was different," Connor protested.

"Why? Because I acted like the world's worst jerk for three years with a bunch of completely unfounded accusations that I kept throwing at her because I wouldn't let go of the damage my ex caused?" Cole asked. "We all know that when it comes to jerkiness you're the one who treated their partner way worse than I ever did."

Even though he knew that, accepted it, Connor still flinched at the words.

"We know you left her, Connor," Jake reminded him. "We all know what went down, you never lied about it, never hid it from us."

That was true.

His worst actions and words had never been ones he kept to himself.

After driving around for hours that night before realizing he could absolutely support the woman he loved and raise her rapist's baby with her if that was what she chose to do, he'd returned to their apartment to find her gone. When calling her family confirmed Becca was with them but that she refused to have any contact with him, he'd gone right to his own family.

At the time, they'd been spread throughout the world. He'd been the only one to go to college, the others had all jumped right into military careers, which is what he'd done after losing Becca. But despite the physical distances between them, every one of his brothers and his baby sister had all been there for him. They'd called him out, expressed their disappointment, and told him that he had to go and fix things.

Advice he'd ignored.

And now it was too late.

"She told me the baby was mine," he admitted. Saying those words out loud made them feel so much more real. He'd had a son, a little boy he never got to hold, never got to tell that he loved. Knowing Becca had been without him when she lost their child was a pain that lodged in his chest and he was pretty sure he could never dislodge.

Didn't deserve to dislodge it.

What he deserved was to suffer the same pain Becca must have suffered in those moments when she realized she was losing her baby for the rest of eternity.

"She lost it," he added. The pain in his chest was too much, and he lifted a hand and pressed it above his heart as though that could ease it. But it couldn't. Nothing could.

"I'm sorry, Connor," Cooper said gently, reaching out to clasp his shoulder and squeezing it.

"That sucks, man," Jax said. "I'm sorry you both lost your baby."

"A boy," he said softly. "A son. I walked away from her because I didn't think I could handle raising her rapist's baby. I walked away for nothing. I walked away from the woman I love and our child."

"That's not true," Jake told him.

"Pretty sure it is."

"You walked away because you never took a breath that whole four months. You kept everything in, refused to allow yourself a single feeling or emotion because you were so focused on Becca," Jake said.

"She'd been raped. She had physical injuries and her foot amputated because the doctors couldn't save it. Of course my focus was on her, she needed me. Was I supposed to prioritize myself over her?" What was he supposed to do? Leave her alone and go and have his own little pity party?

"No, that's not what you were supposed to do," Jake said in a voice that sounded exactly like Cade's would have. Both Cade and Jake were a lot alike, both gruff, both intimidating, both told it like it was without holding back. "You were supposed to make sure you were taking care of yourself so you could keep taking care of Becca. You loved her, we all know that, she knew that. You were there for her one hundred percent. She needed you and you didn't shy away from giving her whatever she needed. But you didn't do the same for yourself. You bottled everything up when you could have spoken to me, Jax, Cade, Cooper, or Cole. Could have spoken to Cassandra. Could have let out the emotions that were eating you alive."

It was easy to say in hindsight that he could have—should have—done exactly that. But, in that moment, all he'd been able to think about was Becca. He hadn't just come a distant second or even last, he hadn't even been in contention, nothing had. Just her.

"He's right," Cooper agreed. "You weren't taking care of yourself, and that was just the straw that broke the camel's back. You realized you were wrong and went back."

"Too late. I went back too late."

"Is it really too late?" Jax asked. "I saw how she was while she was here. She kept sneaking glances over at you like she needed to check you were still there."

"Looked at you like she wanted to glue herself to your side," Cole added.

"Wishful thinking there, bro," Connor said, sure both were wrong. He'd asked Becca if she could give him another chance and she hadn't said she could or would. It was hard not to believe that what happened on the plane, her letting him comfort her, was anything but a fluke.

"I don't think so," Jax contradicted.

A weary sigh heaved its way out of his chest, and Connor let his head dip until it rested in his hands. It had taken everything left in him not to demand to be the one to drive Becca out to the cabin and spend that last little bit of time with her. But she hadn't asked him to, and she seemed comfortable with Susanna and Willow, so when the two women had offered to go along for the drive he hadn't spoken up.

Neither had Becca.

"Look, she told me she'd been engaged, okay? I think it's pretty clear that she's moved on, and honestly, I don't deserve a second chance anyway." It sucked saying that, but it was absolutely the truth.

"Did I deserve a chance with Susanna after how badly I treated her?" Cole asked. If there was one thing you could say about the Charleston brothers, it was that none of them shied away from admitting when they'd done the wrong thing.

"What Cole is saying is that love isn't always logical," Cooper said. "I fell for Willow quicker than I could ever have believed you could develop feelings for another person. But when it's right, it's right, and whatever obstacles get in the way, no matter how big and seemingly insurmountable they are, you can find a way over them, or through them."

Normally he would agree with that.

But the obstacles he'd placed between himself and Becca were so big that he didn't believe there was space to squeeze anywhere around them, over them, beneath them, or even through them.

~

August 20th
    8:54 A.M.

It was beautiful out there.

Becca knew she'd made the right choice in agreeing to stay at Cade's cabin.

It would have been so easy to keep her distance from the entire Charleston Holloway family, to insist that while she agreed she might be in danger and needed protection, someone else could do it.

There wasn't a doubt in her mind that if she had insisted she wanted nothing to do with any of them, they would have set her up with someone else from Prey to play bodyguard. No one in the family would ever seek to control her or force her to do something she wasn't comfortable with.

But that was the thing.

She *was* comfortable with the family.

For most of her life, she'd thought that one day they would be her family.

It had always seemed like a foregone conclusion because she'd loved Connor, and he'd loved her back. Why wouldn't they wind up happily living out the rest of their lives side by side? There was no way she could have guessed what the future held for her.

Despite the ... uneasiness ... between her and Connor, as soon as she saw his brothers, it felt like no time had passed. They'd all slipped back so easily into the relationships they'd had back then. They were like more siblings, they made her life better, and she truly wished she hadn't cut them out of her life along with Connor.

Maybe at first, she'd needed the distance, but once the pain of betrayal had dulled she could have reached out and re-established contact. It wouldn't have been fair to Connor though. It would have been asking his own family to choose between the two of them, and she would never have done anything to take away his support system. He loved his family, and he'd needed them because even in the darkest days of her pain, she'd known that her rape had affected him, too. She'd had a support system, and he'd had his own. Back then, it had been best to keep them separate, but now ...

Now she wasn't sure.

Now she didn't want to let any of those men go again. She wanted their friendship back and she already liked Willow, Susanna, and little Essie's nanny, Gabriella. They were all women she could see herself being friends with, and they loved the Charleston Holloway family as much as she did.

Would it be fair to keep in contact with Connor's family regardless of what happened between the two of them?

Did she even know what she wanted to happen?

Scooping up her cup of coffee, Becca stood and headed out the kitchen door to the wraparound porch. Immediately, warm air wrapped around her like a soothing blanket. It was the perfect temperature, not too hot, but cozily warm. Later this afternoon she might rethink that once the temperature heated up, but for now, it was lovely out.

A gentle breeze sent her loose hair fluttering around her face as she headed for a huge porch swing and cuddled into it. She tucked her legs up beneath her and looked out into the trees surrounding the cabin, birds chattered, and she'd spotted a deer while eating breakfast. Butterflies and dragonflies danced about, and she could see bees buzzing around the flowers that dotted the landscape, turning it into a colorful living painting.

Tears blurred her eyes.

Here she was, sitting safe and sound in an adorable little cabin, in the middle of a picture-perfect landscape, knowing that people she trusted were monitoring the security systems in case anyone found out where she was staying.

All while her best friend in the whole world was out there somewhere hurting.

Where was Isabella?

Had she been hurt physically?

Raped?

What were the plans of the men who had taken her?

Were they going to traffic her to someone who would keep her prisoner and abuse her until they eventually killed her?

Of course, they were.

Becca didn't make a move to stop the tears that tumbled free, rolling down her cheeks.

There would be no point in abducting Izzy if they were going to let her go. They weren't. They'd taken her to traffic her, there was no other plausible reason.

And Isabella would fight them.

Her best friend was a four foot eleven tornado of energy. She was strong, loyal, and determined. Nothing fazed her, she would give anything a try once, and she was fearless.

Fighting the people who took her sounded like it would be a good thing, but in the end, it wouldn't be.

It would only make her captors more determined to break her.

A broken Izzy sounded like an abomination. It went against nature. But that was what would happen. Those men would destroy her, and even if Prey Security were able to find her and rescue her—and she wasn't kidding herself, she knew that was unlikely—Izzy would never be the same again.

That wasn't right.

It wasn't fair.

The only reason the village had been attacked in the first place was because these people Connor and his family were hunting had come after her. If either of them should have been taken it should have been her, not Isabella.

How could she be sitting there worrying about her love life, trying to decide what her answer to Connor's question would be, when her best friend, who had stood beside her through everything, was out there suffering an unimaginable traumatic ordeal?

What was wrong with her?

Priorities, Becca.

Get them straight.

Did it really matter what her future held, whether Connor would be part of it or not, and if he was in what way, when Izzy was out there suffering?

No, it didn't.

Yet it seemed almost impossible to tear her thoughts away from the man who had always been destined to be hers. Connor hovered constantly at the back of her mind like he'd been there all along, only she couldn't remember the last time before he showed up in Cambodia that she'd consciously thought of him.

Mostly she'd just shoved him out of her mind because thinking about him was too painful. But these last few days he'd taken up permanent residence inside her head. He'd filled her dreams, and she felt an ache in her chest that had nothing to do with the bruised ribs because he wasn't there with her.

Crazy.

If Izzy could see her all hung up on Connor, her best friend would freak out. Isabella had been such a rock for her throughout everything, and she'd hated Connor for hurting her.

Only ... that wasn't quite true. Izzy hadn't really hated anyone, and the only reason she'd been angry with Connor was because Becca herself was. One thing she knew for certain about her best friend was that if she wanted to give Connor another chance, Izzy would be her biggest cheerleader.

Because in the end, that's what friends did. They supported you, guided you, offered their opinion, and did their best to ensure you didn't make mistakes, but whatever you did, they were there for you. Isabella was the very best friend in the entire world, and she would have supported whatever decision Becca made.

"I'll find you, Izzy. I swear I'll keep on those guys at Prey, make sure they don't give up, anything I have to do, whatever it takes, I promise you, Iz, I won't give up. Not ever. Not for anything," she vowed.

It didn't matter what the odds were because there was one thing she knew for certain.

Nothing on this earth would have made Isabella give up on her.

Nothing.

If their positions had been reversed, Izzy would do everything in her power to try to find her, even though it was obviously well outside her skillset as a nurse.

She owed her friend the same.

Over the years, Izzy had put into practice the dedication of her friendship. She'd been the support system Becca needed, and when— because her sanity depended on her believing there was hope even if it was only a teeny tiny amount—Izzy came home, she'd do the same.

For now, she was going to have to find a way to deal with being safe while her friend wasn't. There was nothing practical she could do for Isabella except keep checking in with Prey to see if they had updates and offer any information they might need that she might have.

Alone out there all she had was time.

Time to heal and recover.

Time to process what had almost happened in Cambodia.

Time to think about her future and what came next.

And time to think about the man who had stolen her heart the first time she ever met him, long before she even understood what it meant to fall in love and what part he was going to play, if any, in whatever her future looked like.

CHAPTER

Eleven

August 20th
  12:32 P.M.

Finally, he was alone with his thoughts.

While he loved his siblings with everything he had, they weren't just his family, they weren't just his team, they were his best friends as well, they hadn't given him a moment's peace since he got back from Cambodia with Becca.

And Connor needed some peace.

Needed time and space to figure out the mess of thoughts and emotions raging inside his head.

It had taken a lot of convincing, but he'd finally got all five of his brothers and two one-day sisters-in-law to leave. They'd been gone only about thirty minutes, and while he did admit it left his house feeling empty, that wasn't necessarily a bad thing.

Well, it was, but the emptiness that clawed at his insides wasn't because his brothers had left, it was because Becca wasn't there.

There had always been an emptiness. Ever since he realized he'd lost Becca twelve years ago it had existed. It was an ache he'd done his best to ignore over the years, but never once tried to fill. How could he even think about filling a hole that was Becca-sized when there wasn't another person who was that same exact size?

He'd only ever wanted one woman, and he would only ever have one woman.

While he doubted Becca would believe him, he'd never had sex with anyone other than her. There'd been plenty of offers, he knew he had a good body, worked hard for it, and he'd been a SEAL, there were plenty of women who would try to sleep with him for that alone, but he didn't want another woman.

Only Becca.

Always only Becca.

So, he'd had to make do with his hand and his memories.

Not enough.

Never enough.

And now his Becca was back in his life, possibly temporarily, but at least she was close by, within reaching distance and it was tearing him up that he couldn't just go to her. Couldn't just pull her onto his lap like he used to, and wrap his arms around her, hold her, rock her, soothe her, touch her, kiss her, make love to her.

None of those things were appropriate anymore and he had no idea how he was supposed to survive the rest of his life without her if she decided she couldn't give him a second chance. It would help if he at least knew more about this fiancé. If her love for him had truly died because she'd found someone to take his place, it was a lost cause.

When his phone, which he'd tossed onto the couch beside him, began to ring, he looked at it only because Becca had his number and she might call if something was wrong. Might. Because if something was wrong there was every chance she'd rather call one of his brothers than him.

It wasn't Becca, but it was Cassandra.

Not knowing where their baby sister was sucked, but they all agreed it was for the best. If he or one of his brothers were captured by the men trying to silence them, there was no way they could give up her location. Couldn't tell someone what you didn't know. And they all believed there was no safer place in the world for Cassandra than with Prey's elusive Delta Team. Those men didn't exist in any legal sense of the word, and they had skills that were distinctly nonhuman even though he knew they were, in fact, human beings and couldn't be anything else. Still, they kept their secrets locked down tighter than anyone could hope to loosen, and nobody tried anyway. Delta Team deserved their privacy.

Cassandra was in the perfect place, but he missed having her around. If it had been any of his brothers calling, he wouldn't have picked up, but for his little sister, he absolutely would.

"Hey, squirt," he said when he answered.

"Hey, jerk," Cassandra shot back in her sassy way that lifted his mood. When they'd said goodbye to her, and she'd left with Delta Team she'd seemed like a shell of her former self. The revelation of her true parentage had knocked her about, as it would anyone, but it was great to hear her sounding more like her old self.

"Hey, is that any way to talk to the big brother you love and adore? Your favorite brother?" It was a running joke in their family that they all pretended to be Cassandra's favorite, even though they all knew she loved them equally. Given that she'd only been five when they lost their parents and the rest of them had been teens and preteens, they'd all stepped in to help raise her since their grandparents were old and in poor health.

"You're not my favorite." She huffed.

"Yeah? So which one of us is?"

"Today it's Cade since he called and clued me in on what's going on."

Since when did Cade become Mr. Chattypants? That wasn't like his older brother at all. Yet Cade had always had a soft spot for Becca, and it didn't take a genius to figure out why he'd think it would be a good idea for Cassandra to know she was back.

Just like the son he'd never known existed could have been conceived through rape, Cassandra had been.

In his own roundabout way, Cade was attempting to play matchmaker.

None of his brothers had been able to talk him into going out to the cabin to see Becca—something he wasn't prepared to do unless she expressly invited him—Cade thought that maybe their little sister would have better luck.

"He shouldn't have done that," Connor said softly.

"Why not? Just because I'm eight years younger than you and Becca doesn't mean she wasn't my friend too."

Her little sister tone made him smile. "Becca used to babysit you," he reminded her.

"And she was the best sitter I ever had. Brothers included." Cassandra huffed. "I know she was raped, Connor. That's why you two broke up."

He probably shouldn't be surprised that Cassandra knew, even though back then, he'd tried to shield her from the truth. She'd known that Becca had been hurt, but none of them had ever mentioned rape, and while his brothers knew about the pregnancy he'd never told Cassandra.

"That's not why we broke up, Cass," he told her.

"Then why *did* you break up?"

There was no point in keeping it from her any longer. Cassandra knew about the rape, and given what she'd just learned it wasn't fair to lie to her. Especially if Becca decided to give him the chance he didn't deserve because sooner or later it would come up.

"Four months after her rape Becca found out she was pregnant," he said the words he knew would pierce his sister's heart.

Cassandra's gasp made him wish they were having this conversation face-to-face so he could pull her into his arms and try to soothe her pain.

"She was raped, wound up pregnant, and you left her?" Cassandra screeched, sounding borderline hysterical. "How could you do that, Connor? You are definitely not my favorite brother."

Her words hit him hard.

Harder than any physical blows could.

"I know," he agreed because anything else would be lies.

"Do you know how badly I'm struggling right now? Knowing that dad wasn't really my dad, that mom only got pregnant with me because she was raped, that I wasn't planned or wanted?"

"You were always wanted," he hissed.

"Even though I wasn't his, Dad stayed. He accepted me, raised me, and never let on that I wasn't one hundred percent part of our family. I don't have many memories of them, but those I do have, I think he even loved me."

"No thinking involved, Cassandra. He did love you. Adored you. You were his daughter in every sense of the word. He loved you because you were a part of Mom and he loved her with everything he had. Never ever doubt that he loved you."

"Didn't you love Becca that way?"

Those words fueled the guilt and shame that had plagued him for over a decade. "She's my other half. I love her more than life itself."

"Then how could you leave her when she was suffering through that?"

A deep sigh rattled through his chest. "I messed up, Cassandra. I freaked out that day, thought I couldn't raise her rapist's baby even though we weren't sure who the father was. I fell apart, something I hadn't done since I found out what happened to the girl I loved. It all piled up on me and I crashed. I'm not proud of myself, actually, I'm ashamed of myself. But I panicked and destroyed my relationship with the only woman I'll ever love in the process."

"Twelve years, Connor. That's how long I'd been alive at the time and that's how long it's been before you finally went to her. She must have felt so alone, so scared. Mom had Dad, but Becca had ..."

"No one," he finished for her when she trailed off.

"You aren't giving up on her again, are you?"

"I asked her for a second chance, but she never answered." But she did let him comfort her on the plane. And she did tell him she'd been engaged. And his brothers said they believed she wanted him to take her to the cabin.

Was it Becca standing between them now or was it his own fears that he wasn't good enough for her?

"You can't give up on her," Cassandra insisted. "Even if she doesn't take you back, you still have to make it up to her. Right now, she's scared and alone all over again, and you're not there to make things better. Go to her, Connor. Now. Talk things through. Work them out. Figure out whether there's anything to salvage, and if there's not, at least be her friend. Don't let her be alone again."

~

August 20th
   6:49 P.M.

Was that a car?

Becca jerked upright from where she'd been lazing on the porch, where she'd spent most of the day, when she spotted what she was positive was an approaching car on the long, winding driveway that led from the remote road to the cabin.

Someone was coming.

Who?

How?

The alarm hadn't triggered, she would have known if it did. Becca hadn't gone anywhere without her phone just so she would know if anything had set off the alarm.

So, whoever it was had to have the skills to bypass the system.

That couldn't be good for her.

Scooping up her phone, she hopped back inside the cabin as quickly as she could. It wasn't large, there was a bedroom to the left of the front door, beside it was the bathroom, then the middle and right side of the cabin was the living area. At the back was the kitchen, a huge fireplace was on the side wall with a couple of couches around it. Two rocking chairs were by the front window and a solid oak dining table in the middle of the room. A small set of stairs led up to two attic bedrooms and another bathroom.

Not a lot of places to hide.

Since she hadn't put her prosthetic on after lunch because she'd wanted to give her leg a chance to recover a bit from all those hours of walking through the jungle in Cambodia after they escaped, she could hardly hop her way to freedom.

Which meant flight was out.

Leaving fight as her only option.

When Cade brought her to his cabin, he and the other brothers had insisted that she be armed just in case.

Luckily.

Otherwise, she wouldn't stand a chance.

Retrieving the weapon from the lockbox in the nightstand drawer where she'd put it, Becca quickly scooped it up. The gun felt heavy in her hand, wrong. She'd chosen her path in life to help people not to hurt them.

But this was about protecting herself.

No time to be squeamish.

Besides, she'd killed in Cambodia to save herself. If she could do it then, she could do it now, too.

Still clutching her phone, Becca hesitated and then pulled up the contacts list. Connor's number was in there. Should she call him?

It felt weird, both right and wrong. She'd learned not to rely on him for anything, but this wasn't about them, it was about her not getting herself killed or abducted. The last thing she wanted was to die *or* to be used to manipulate Connor and his family. They deserved answers and she didn't want to be part of the reason they didn't get them.

Stupid.

That's what it would be not to call Connor or one of his brothers.

And if she was going to call one of them it may as well be Connor.

Because he's the only one who makes you feel truly safe.

Ignoring the whisper in her head, she quickly touched on Connor's name just as she caught sight of the car she'd spotted coming closer to the house. Ducking down behind the bed, she held the phone to her ear and counted the rings.

"Becca?" Connor's voice came down the line moments later.

"There's a car outside the cabin," she said in a harsh whisper without any preamble. "I can hear it." If she could hear it then it wasn't just close, it was pretty much right on the other side of the wall.

"Becca—"

"The alarm didn't go off," she added, hurrying to get all the information she had out before it was too late. "Whoever it is managed to bypass it. They just turned the engine off."

Her heart hammered so hard in her chest.

Was this how it was going to end?

Would these men hurt her before killing her like the men in Cambodia had been going to do?

If they were, she'd rather kill herself now and not allow them the chance.

"Becca—"

"I have the gun and I'm in the bedroom. I'll do my best to shoot whoever it is, but if I don't and they take me I'm sorry, Connor. I wish things had worked out the way we'd always planned."

"Becca, if you would just let me get a word in," Connor said in a rush before she could cut him off again and keep rambling.

This time she didn't.

She'd said what she needed to. If these were going to be the last words they exchanged, she wanted him to have his turn, too.

"It's me. My car. I'm the one outside the cabin, so please don't shoot," he said, his voice a mixture of amused and reproached.

"Y-you?" she asked, hardly daring to believe that was true.

"I should have called, but if I asked if I could come and see you I was afraid you'd say no," Connor explained.

Which she probably would have.

Because she was finding it increasingly difficult to think logically around him.

The desire to just curl up on his lap and let him take care of her, make everything okay, was too strong.

Just as strong was the fear of him letting her down again.

"It's really you?" She was hesitant to believe it even though it would mean she wasn't in danger. The fear of being alone out there with Connor and what that would do to her was almost as bad as the fear of what those men would do to her. They could destroy her body but only Connor had the power to destroy her heart.

"I'm going to knock on the cabin door five times so you know it's me."

Five slow, loud, deliberate knocks echoed through to her in the bedroom.

It was Connor.

And she didn't know if she wanted to throw her arms around his neck or tear into him for scaring her like that.

Anger won out as she carefully stood and hopped to the living room, throwing open the front door.

"You scared the life out of me," she grumbled, taking a half-hearted swing at him, her knuckles glancing off his muscled shoulder and causing him no damage at all. "What were you thinking?"

"That I had to see you," he answered, looking appropriately chastised for scaring her. "I should have texted at the gate, I was going to surprise you."

"Some surprise, you terrified me, I could have shot you." Although now that she knew she wasn't in danger, and her heart rate was calming, she wasn't as mad as she felt she ought to be.

"In my defense, I did bring you these." He held up a box of her favorite chocolates, a bouquet of her favorite flowers, and a funny-looking little penis-shaped plushie. It was a running joke between them ever since they first started doing ... stuff ... when they were teenagers.

Laughing, she reached out and took the little penis stuffy. "Don't think this is going to get you out of trouble," she warned. It should be weird holding this in her hand, knowing she'd had the real thing in her mouth just days ago, but for some reason, given their long history it wasn't weird at all.

"Noted. Can I come in?"

"What are you really doing here, Connor? You didn't come all this way just to give me a silly plushie and some chocolates."

"And the flowers."

"Right, and the flowers, because there's not an entire wildflower meadow out there. Why are you here?"

"Because someone talked some sense into me. Told me that I'd left you alone once when you were vulnerable, and I couldn't do it again." Pain filled those sky-blue eyes she knew so well. "We found out just before I came to find you in Cambodia that Mom was raped. There was proof, that's why they had Dad and his team killed and set Mom up to look like a traitor."

Her heart went out to the woman who had been a second mom to her growing up. "I'm so sorry, Connor. I hate that your mom went through that. Is this proof why they're trying to silence you all? So you can't find it and expose them and the conspiracy?"

"Yeah."

"I hope you have this proof tucked away somewhere safe."

"The proof is Cassandra."

It took a second for his words to sink in, for their meaning to click. "Your mom was raped, and Cassandra is the product of that rape," she said, pain and sorrow filling her heart for the girl she remembered. "That's why you were vague about Cass not being there yesterday. You have her tucked away someplace safe."

"No one can get to her where she is," Connor told her. "She called and I told her about the baby, about how I reacted when I found out, and she told me that I had to find a way to make it up to you. I already knew that, but maybe I needed to hear someone give me permission to come to you before I could allow myself to do it."

"Why would you need permission?"

"Because I hurt you, Becca. I freaked out, I left you alone, I didn't fight for you."

Remembering his question, her chest tightened. She wasn't ready yet to decide one way or the other. "Connor, I can't ..."

"I'm not asking you for anything more than to let me stay here with you," he told her. "That's it."

"That's it?" she asked skeptically. "Because I can't make any promises about the future right now."

"I'm not asking you to, I swear. Just please, can I stay here with you?"

Saying yes was a bad idea. It opened the door to letting him back in and she wasn't sure she wanted to do that. Right now, it was a battle between her head, desperate to protect the rest of her from more pain, and her soul which couldn't stand to be apart from its soulmate a single second longer.

Praying she wasn't making the biggest mistake of her life, Becca nodded and hopped backward, opening the door wider to let him in.

She just had to hope she was strong enough to keep the door to her heart firmly closed.

CHAPTER
Twelve

His game had to be on point if he wanted to even stand a chance.

Which was why he was going all out for the breakfast he was preparing for Becca.

Connor knew he was lucky Becca had agreed to let him stay. Especially after he'd scared her when she'd spotted his car approaching. If he'd been thinking clearly, he would have stopped at the gate and texted to let her know he was there, but by the time he'd reached the ten-acre plot where Cade's cabin sat he was so eager to see Becca that he couldn't focus on anything else.

As bad as he'd felt knowing he'd scared her, there was also relief that he'd managed to make her laugh. The plush penis gift was a stupid one, but after his call to Cassandra, when he'd realized she was right and he had to fight for what he wanted, fight for his girl, instead of waiting for her to tell him he could jump into the game, he knew he couldn't come empty-handed.

So, he'd grabbed her favorite chocolates and flowers, then dug into a box buried at the back of his closet of things he'd packed up from their shared apartment after he realized Becca wasn't going to come back. One of those things had been a seven-inch penis plushie he'd intended to give her the day she'd gone for her first prosthetic fitting. Unfortunately, he'd been out of her life by then but kept the toy.

Something he was grateful for.

Because seeing Becca laugh like she had when he'd given her the toy reminded him of the woman he used to know. They'd both changed a lot over the years, grown up, matured, and been shaped by everything that had happened, but underneath they were still the same boy and girl who had grown up and known well before they were old enough to understand that they were two halves of the same whole.

Now all he had to do was remind Becca of that.

Prove to her that he could earn back her trust, and hopefully her heart, and get back to what they'd shared when they were young.

If nothing else, he wanted to be her friend again and be there to support her after what they went through in Cambodia. Support her as she worried about her friend and whether Prey would be able to find Isabella before she was lost to the human trafficking network forever.

Step one was coming to the cabin so she wouldn't be alone.

Step two was to get to work on wooing her.

Everything was perfect, the table was set, the flowers he'd brought her that she'd put in a bright ceramic vase sat at the center of the table, and he'd added some candles. Not subtle but he wasn't going for subtle. He'd cooked way more food than two people could eat, but he'd made everything Becca loved. There was fresh fruit salad, pancakes, waffles, scrambled eggs, piles of toast, and oatmeal. Personally, he hated oatmeal, but Becca loved it with cinnamon and a drizzle of honey, so he'd made it for her, and it was sitting in a pot on the stove, steam pouring off it.

All that was missing now was Becca herself.

She always used to start her day with a steamy hot shower regardless of the weather. If she still got up at the same time she should be finishing up, braiding her long black locks, and getting dressed right about now.

Like she'd read his mind, the soft pad of footsteps on the stairs had him wiping his hands on his apron and turning around. Although he'd offered to let her stay in the bigger downstairs bedroom, she'd insisted he could have it and she'd stay upstairs. When Becca came into sight, his heart about beat its way right out of his chest. Denim cut-offs left almost all of her long, toned legs visible, and she wore a loose T-shirt that still managed to hint at the soft curves he knew were hidden underneath. She'd twisted her hair into two braids, and freshly scrubbed from the shower she looked young, sweet, and innocent.

Well, all except for the penis plushie she still held in her hands.

A groan rumbled through his chest at the sight of it, pulling Becca's attention. All night while they'd watched TV, sitting on separate sofas because he hadn't wanted to push too hard too fast and make her uncomfortable, she'd held the toy in her lap, fiddling with it. There was no way he could watch her nimble fingers stroke along the soft fabric and not feel the echo of that touch in his own penis.

A small smirk tugged at the corners of her mouth, and he wondered if she'd brought the plushie down with her this morning just to taunt him. If she had, he wasn't angry with her about it. If anything, it filled him with hope because the old Becca, the one he'd grown up with, loved to tease him.

Things had always been so simple between them, so natural, they'd just clicked from the moment they were toddlers, and their connection had only grown over time. Even if he could win back Becca's heart and her love, he would never forgive himself for letting her down.

She'd needed him and he hadn't been there.

Never again.

"Breakfast is served," he told her, sweeping out his arms to indicate the table and the counters filled with plates of food.

"Is your whole family coming to join us?" Becca asked, a hint of amusement in her tone as she finished coming down the stairs.

"Nope, just the two of us."

"And do you figure we can eat all of that?"

"Probably unlikely."

"Then why make so much?" she asked as she reached the kitchen counters.

"Because I wanted you to have anything you felt like. You've been through a lot these last few days, and with what happened to Bella, I know you have to be struggling. When we're stressed, we don't always take care of ourselves the way we should. I want to make sure that I made you something that will appeal to you even while I'm sure you have a knot of anxiety sitting in your stomach."

Her dark blue eyes softened, and she gave him a hint of a smile. "It's hard to do anything knowing what Izzy is likely suffering through right at this moment."

Taking a step forward, Connor hesitated for a moment before trusting his gut and grasping Becca's shoulder, squeezing lightly. "I don't know Isabella as well as you do, but one thing I do remember about her is that she's a fighter. She won't give up. That means you can't either."

"I won't," Becca said softly.

"Part of not giving up means that you keep living. You do everything you're supposed to do, like eat, and sleep, and you do the things that make you happy. That's what Bella would want you to do."

"I hate that you're right," Becca said with a sigh.

"I'm always right," he teased, reluctantly releasing his hold on her.

"Arrogant much?" Becca huffed, but good-naturedly, and she picked up a plate and piled it up with more food than he would have thought she'd take.

It wasn't until he'd also filled his plate and they'd both taken seats at the table, that her eyes widened, obviously taking in what he was wearing. Her glass of sparkling water paused halfway to her mouth, and when she quickly went to set it down before spilling it, she almost knocked over the glass of apple juice he'd also poured. There was a mug of coffee as well, just so he covered his bases.

"You kept it," she said, partly in awe, partly amused. "I always hated that apron."

"You loved it," he corrected. "You smiled every time I put it on."

"It has a giant penis on it." She snorted, genuine joy sparkling in her midnight-blue eyes. "What is it with you and penises?"

He laughed. It felt like the first real laugh he'd given since that fateful night, even though he knew in reality it wasn't. There had been plenty of times he'd laughed over the last twelve years, but he'd never once felt this light.

"After I saw how much you laughed the first time I gave you one, I just wanted to keep recapturing that moment," he answered honestly.

That softness he'd seen in her earlier was back. "I remember you gave me the first one the morning after we had sex for the first time."

"Your sixteenth birthday." Every second of that night was etched into his memory. He'd done everything his teenage self had thought was romantic, wanting their first time to be utterly perfect. And it was. Every moment with Becca had been.

"I don't think I ever told you this, but my mom found it and asked me if the two of us were having sex," Becca informed him. "It was highly embarrassing. I tried to lie but—"

"You're a terrible liar," he finished for her, laughing at the thought of poor, sweet sixteen-year-old Becca and her mom talking about their sex life.

"Hey," she exclaimed, tossing the penis plushie at him, hitting him square in the forehead. "It's your fault. You bought me the silly toy."

"Silly, maybe, but I bet you still own every single one I bought you over the years." Connor arched a challenging eyebrow. He was taking a big gamble there because there was a chance she'd tossed them all after they broke up. But he knew Becca, knew how sentimental she was.

The smile fell from her lips, but no frown or sadness was taking its place. Instead, she looked almost thoughtful, like he was making her think of something she hadn't before. "I do. I still have them all," she acknowledged, making his heart soar.

Hope.

There was still hope for them, and he would cling to that because he couldn't accept that Becca would never be his again.

August 21st
11:55 A.M.

Maybe she shouldn't have told him she'd kept all the penis plushies.

But lying would have felt like playing games and they were both too old, had been through too much, and meant too much to each other for that.

Because Becca knew she was lying to herself if she pretended Connor didn't still mean something to her.

He did.

That had never been the problem.

Never once had she doubted that Connor Charleston loved her. The problem had always been a combination of her lack of trust in him and her anger that he got to have a choice in whether or not he bailed from the mess her life had been back then.

The more time she spent around Connor now, the more she realized what a mistake it had been getting engaged. Not that she hadn't loved Toby because she had. It was just the love she'd had for him didn't even come close to comparable to what she felt for Connor.

With Toby it was more like a comfortable companionship that she'd allowed to go further than she had initially planned because she felt safe around him. Toby had been a bit of a geek. He loved numbers and had become an accountant, he never pressured her to do anything she was uncomfortable with, supported her passion and drive to start her charity and travel the globe, and had been willing to work as the charity's finance guy. He was sweet and funny, and she knew he loved her, and while she'd loved him back, now she could acknowledge that she hadn't been *in* love with him.

How could she be when one man already owned every piece of her heart?

Glancing over at where Connor was lying sprawled on the steps, his nose buried in a book he'd found on the bookshelves inside, Becca found her fingers almost compulsively stroking the silly penis plushie she couldn't seem to put down. Not only had she held onto it while they watched TV last night, but she'd taken it to bed with her as well.

It was a poor comparison to what she really wanted to be touching but it was better than nothing.

Wait.

Did she just think that it was Connor's penis she wanted to be playing with?

Her cheeks blushed what she was sure was a dark pink and Connor chose that particular moment to set his book down and look over at her.

The blush deepened.

Did he know what she was thinking?

If she went to him and asked if she could take him in her mouth, would he say yes?

Of course, he would.

This was Connor and he had made it clear he wanted her back and was prepared to fight for her. That's why he'd come out there, to be with her, to watch out for her, take care of her, just like he always did.

One failure didn't have to change what should have been their happy ever after.

It had but it didn't always have to be that way.

Over the last decade, Becca had done a lot of healing, a lot over these last few days as well.

Maybe she was ready to consider what her future looked like and if the man before her was going to be part of it.

"Want to go for a walk?" Connor asked, pushing to his feet. He was all muscle and power and strength as he strode toward her. Dressed in nothing but a pair of shorts and a T-shirt, he looked so handsome that it was hard to focus on what he was saying when she was overpowered by how he made her feel.

Like the center of the world.

That was how Connor had always made her feel.

When they were little kids playing in the neighborhood and when they'd been a couple. He respected her, cared for her, cared about her, and always made her feel like she was the sun that his life revolved around, even though his nickname for her was moonlight.

Had she spent enough time telling him how much that meant to her?

Had she made him feel the same way?

Those last few months they'd been together had been rough, and she'd been a mess, maybe she hadn't communicated how deeply grateful she was that he had been her rock.

"Becca?"

Right.

He'd asked her a question.

"A walk ... yeah ... that would be nice."

The bright smile he gave her had an answering smile curling her own lips. How had she gone so many years without seeing that smile? Even on the darkest of days, it had bathed her in light and warmth.

When he held out his hand to help her out of the porch swing, she hesitated for barely a second before reaching out and placing her hand in his. His fingers closed around hers and something settled inside her.

Whatever had happened between them, she couldn't help but feel this was where she belonged.

Connor tugged her to her feet but didn't release her hand as he helped her down the porch steps, and she found that she didn't want him to let go.

Maybe she needed to see him fight for her, for them. He was the one who had broken what they had, shattered their foundations, and before she could think about rebuilding them, she had to know he was all in. That no matter what life threw at them, he wouldn't bail again. That if he started feeling like it was too much, he'd talk to her rather than screaming, ranting, and then running.

For a while they wandered in silence. The air was warm again today without being too hot, the sky was a bright, vivid blue, and dappled light bathed them as they walked amongst the trees. With the chirping birds and fluttering butterflies, it was like walking through paradise.

Or maybe it was who she was walking with that made the woods feel so special.

"I met him about three years after we broke up," she said, breaking the spell. As much as she didn't want to have this conversation, she knew it had to be done. They had to clear the air, get everything out in the open, and then go from there.

"The man you were engaged to?" Although Connor's voice was even, his fingers tightened ever so slightly around hers and she knew he wasn't unaffected by her words.

"His name was Toby. He was a good man, and he was what I needed at that time in my life. He helped ease me out of the protective cocoon I'd locked myself in. He was sweet and shy, he never pushed me, always treated me with respect, and was supportive of what I wanted to do with my life."

"You loved him?" The thread of jealousy in Connor's voice was impossible to miss even though his words came out without the heat she knew was bubbling inside him.

"I loved him, but I didn't love him the way I should have to say yes to his proposal," she added. "It wasn't fair to him. He deserved to be loved the way I loved you."

Connor froze.

Slowly he turned so he looked down at her.

"Loved or love?" he asked, his voice shaking slightly.

How could he even ask her that?

Was there any doubt?

"Love, Connor. Always love. It was never about not loving you, that's not why I left. I was angry and I didn't trust you. I don't know if I overreacted, it's hard to tell. Now, looking back, I think I should have waited for you to come back and talked it through, but at the time my emotions were too raw, and I did what I felt was best," she explained.

"Oh, moonlight. I'm not mad at you for doing what you had to do. I messed up. Me. It's all on me."

"Toby and I were together for about two years, engaged for about a month when he was killed. Hit by a drunk driver. Died instantly."

"If he hadn't died, would you have married him?"

Would she?

"I ... don't think so. He was safe because I think deep down, I knew I wasn't really in love with him. Izzy always told me I was settling, picking the easy option so I didn't have to push through my fears of being with men, letting them in, and trusting them. I said yes to the proposal because it seemed like the logical next step, but I think when the wedding became real, and I started thinking of all the things I'd been planning for our wedding since I was ten, I would have realized it was the wrong thing to do."

A slow smile spread across Connor's face. "Picked out for our wedding?"

She chuckled. "Don't pretend like you didn't know I was planning our wedding from before we were even a couple. I used to ask you all the time what you thought about different ideas."

"I remember." He reached out and tucked a stray wisp of hair behind her ear. "I just like hearing you say it."

"You always used to tell me you didn't care one way or the other, that so long as I was happy, you were happy."

Leaning in, he feathered his lips across hers. "That's still true, moonlight. Still true."

Becca was smiling, her lips tingling, her fingers curled around the penis plushie, still wishing it was Connor's length in her hand, as they started walking again. Spending time together like this, just the two of them, made it feel like old times.

Times that seemed closer within reach than they had this time yesterday.

CHAPTER
Thirteen

August 21st
    6:51 P.M.

"I forgot how bad a cook you were," Connor teased Becca as he pulled her loaf of bread out of the oven.

Well, it was supposed to be a loaf of bread, but in reality, it was a lumpy, burned, hunk of ... nothing.

Because this thing was not edible.

Not in any way.

"Hey!" she protested, tossing him a glare. But then her gaze fell on the tin in his hands and her nose scrunched. "Okay, well baking home-made bread obviously isn't my strong suit, but I can cook."

"Sure you can," he said indulgently. They both knew differently.

"I *can*," she insisted.

"You can boil or steam vegetables," he agreed. She'd learned to after they first moved in together, and she ruined four pots by boiling them dry. After that, she realized she had to pay attention and keep an eye on the pots so you didn't both boil them dry and turn the vegetables inside into mush.

"I can cook pasta, too."

"Yes, that's a very challenging meal."

Becca poked her tongue out at him. "I make a great macaroni and cheese from scratch, and you love it. That involves cooking the pasta, making the sauce, getting the amount of cheese just right, and baking it."

"You do cook a mean mac and cheese," he agreed, but that was about as complicated as Becca could do. It hadn't taken them long to realize that he would be the cook in their family. It wasn't that she didn't try, she just had an uncanny knack of ruining pretty much any food she touched. He'd seen her ruin cereal, basically the easiest food to prepare, because she always poured in way too much milk, making it seem like you had a few grains swimming in an ocean of milk.

"And I make a great tomato pasta sauce," she added as she gave the loaf of bread he'd set on the counter one last disgusted look then began to make a burger with the meat he'd just finished grilling. Luckily, they had some buns he'd bought from the supermarket, otherwise, they'd be eating them as salad and burger patties.

"Agreed." It was really good, she didn't even add anything beyond some onion and herbs, but it was amazing.

"So I think we both agree I *can* cook then," she said with a triumphant smile as she carried her plate over to the sofa and dropped down onto it.

"We don't agree on that, babe," he told her as he plopped beside her and held out the cutlery she'd forgotten to grab before leaving the kitchen. Becca always ate her burgers with a knife and fork no matter how many times he told her to just pick it up with her hands and take a bite.

"You're just being difficult." She huffed as she took the cutlery from his hand.

"You're just being stubborn," he shot back, enjoying their casual banter. The more time they spent together, the more relaxed Becca seemed to become in his presence.

Not that he was expecting any miracles.

Every bit of trust he got from her had to be earned. But he felt like he was making progress. She'd told him about her ex and the relief he'd felt when she admitted that she most likely wouldn't have gone through with the wedding was topped only by the fact that she'd also told him that she still loved him and always had.

While he was doing his best not to count his chickens before they were hatched, Connor couldn't help but believe that he was going to get a second chance with the woman he loved that he craved. Becca was still yet to answer that question he'd asked back in the tent they were held captive in in Cambodia, but he sensed the reason.

She was being cautious, moving slowly, he got that, and agreed. They had a lot of catching up to do and were such different people than they'd been when they were twenty. There was a lot to learn about each other and he was enjoying every second of finding out who Becca was now.

It was like getting the gift of falling in love with her all over again even though there had never been a second since he was old enough to understand his feelings that he hadn't loved this woman.

Becca was his everything, but as he glanced down at her, wondering why she hadn't shot back a sassy remark after he'd called her stubborn, the smile slid off his face.

Something was wrong.

Becca was no longer relaxed, her smile was gone, the twinkle that had been in her eyes all afternoon had disappeared, and she was staring at the cutlery in her hand as though it was going to grow fangs and bite her.

"Moonlight?" he asked, setting his plate down on the coffee table and then lifting hers off her lap and putting it beside his.

When she didn't respond, he captured her chin between his thumb and forefinger and nudged her face up so she was looking at him. There was fear in her eyes, and pain, and he could see her pulse fluttering wildly in the hollow of her neck.

"What's wrong, Becca?" he asked gently, sweeping the pad of his thumb across her bottom lip.

After a slow blink, her gaze met his. "Sorry," she said in a tiny voice, not at all the same as the sassy one she'd just been using as they bantered back and forth. "I just ... the knife ... I hadn't touched one since ... and I guess ... what happened in Cambodia ... in the tent almost being ..."

A shudder rippled through her body and Connor didn't hesitate to wrap his arms around her and haul her onto his lap. So far, she'd held up so well, and he had to remind himself that while his focus was rebuilding trust and earning his way back into Becca's life, she'd also been through a major trauma. Just because she was holding it together didn't mean she wasn't struggling.

If anyone was an expert on dealing with trauma it was Becca.

Already in her life, she'd been through so much, and he hated that she was suffering all over again because of him and his family. It just served to highlight all the ways he'd messed up. If he'd gone to Becca years ago and sorted things out, she would have been protected and safe with him rather than him leading danger right to her doorstep.

"Honey, do you need …" The question wasn't even fully out of his mouth before Becca was nodding and shifting off his lap to curl up beside him on the couch. Shoving down the waistband of his shorts and boxers, he pulled himself free and offered his length to Becca, who immediately took him into her mouth.

Nestling her head on his knees, a soft sigh rumbled through her, and he felt some of the tension ease out of her as she relaxed.

They sat like that for a while, his hand stroking the length of Becca's spine, his length tucked inside the warmth of her mouth. Honestly, he could stay like this forever. There was no better feeling in the world than knowing he was helping his woman. It was a headier high than sex because an orgasm was fleeting, here one second, gone the next. This feeling lasted forever.

Eventually, Becca lifted a hand to stroke the base of his length that wasn't in her mouth, a sign that she was ready for more than just sucking on him.

At least it had been.

What did it mean now?

Her eyes lifted to meet his and she pulled back, letting his tip fall out from between her lips. There was a fire burning there, one he used to know well. They'd had a great sex life, waiting until they were sixteen before having sex for the first time. For about a year before that, they'd done other stuff, fooled around, and in the years after, they'd experimented with a few different things.

Now, though, he couldn't just reach for her like he would have a decade ago.

"Becca?"

"I told you about Toby, there weren't any other men. How ..." she paused as though drawing on reserves of courage. "How many women have you been with?"

"None," he answered honestly.

"None?" Becca repeated, scrambling onto her knees, staring at him in shock. "What do you mean none? How could you not have been with anyone else for twelve years? What did you do? Men have needs."

"I took care of them myself. I have hands, moonlight," he said, quirking up one side of his mouth into a half smile as he held up his hands and wriggled his fingers. "I didn't want to touch anyone else. It's only ever been you for me. Only you, my beautiful, bright, brave moonlight."

"I ... I don't ... but I ... I was with ..."

"It's not the same thing, Becca. I broke what we had, you had no reason not to try to move on with your life. I hate that another man touched you, but I don't begrudge you that, not after everything you've been through. I'm glad you were strong enough to go on and forge a new life for yourself. All I ever wanted was your happiness and I hate that I was ever a reason you were unhappy."

"Connor—"

"Don't apologize," he warned. Every word he'd spoken was true. It made him sick thinking of this Toby guy touching Becca, but she deserved to move on, and he was the one who had ruined what they shared.

"I think I'm going to go to bed," Becca said, shoving off the couch and scurrying over to the stairs.

He ached to call her back, to explore what she'd been willing to offer tonight, but he didn't. Instead, he let her go. Because he'd seen the look in her eyes before she bolted.

Relief.

She was glad no other woman had touched him.

And he'd just taken one step closer to regaining her trust.

~

August 22nd
    10:07 A.M.

"Are you sure about this?" Becca asked doubtfully.

"Course. What could possibly go wrong?" Connor asked, looking over his shoulder with a mischievous grin.

"Uh ... I can think of plenty of things," she replied, glancing around the river. "Starting with I've never been in a canoe before and don't know how to row."

"The worst that can happen is we capsize." Connor shrugged, making the canoe wobble wildly, and Becca clung to the sides of the barely water-worthy little boat.

Despite her reservations about Connor's let's go canoeing plan, she was glad he had dragged her out of her room this morning. Okay, so he hadn't really had to drag her out. She'd skipped dinner last night since she'd run upstairs after Connor's revelation, so sooner or later, her stomach would have led her down to the kitchen, but Connor had come for her before she'd had a chance.

When he'd asked her to spend the day with him, she'd said yes without hesitation.

It wasn't just that they were alone out there, and what else were they going to do if they didn't spend the day together, it was because she actually wanted to.

Somewhere along the way, the anger that had burned so brightly inside her these last twelve years had been snuffed out. Maybe it was when he'd issued one of his many apologies, maybe it was when he killed people to save her life, maybe it was when he'd offered her comfort without asking for anything in return, maybe it was when he told her he hadn't touched a woman since they broke up.

Or maybe it was just because she was ready.

Because she was ready.

Ready to move forward, stop living in the past, and break the final chain that connected her to Dylan Sanders.

Did that mean she was ready to jump right into a relationship with Connor?

No.

Not yet.

There was still trust to be rebuilt even if the anger was gone. After all, he had walked out on her when she needed him despite her begging and pleading with him to stay and talk it out with her. So, it was going to take time before she was ready to see Connor as anything other than a friend.

But she was ready to see him as her friend again, and that felt nice.

Better than nice it felt ... right.

"All you have to do is follow my lead," Connor told her as he pushed the canoe away from the small wooden dock that came out into the river behind Cade's cabin.

"Follow your lead," she echoed. That sounded easier said than done. She wasn't the most coordinated of people. She'd been okay at sports when she was in school, but she was never going to be great. While she loved the water and loved swimming, she'd never been in a boat this tiny, and she was pretty sure she was never going to be able to get her oars moving through the water as smoothly as Connor was making his move.

"Easy-peasy, even for you," Connor teased.

"Hey!" Flicking the oar in her hand, she sent a spray of water all over Connor then gave the back of his head a smug smile.

"You little monster." Connor dropped his oars into the bottom of the canoe and turned, holding up his hands and wriggling his fingers. "You know what my favorite monster has always been?"

"You wouldn't dare," she said, a warning in her tone even though she knew he was more than likely going to do it anyway.

"Aww, tickle monster is your favorite, too," he said, amusement glimmering in his eyes that matched the bright summer sky above them.

"Maybe when I was five," she shot back. She was ticklish. There were patches of scarred skin that weren't ticklish, they felt more numb than anything else, but the rest of her? Ticklish to the extreme.

"Nah, well past five, I remember we used to have lots of fun when I'd tickle you," he said, almost wistfully.

"You were having fun, I was laughing too hard to be having fun."

"Laughing is having fun," he contradicted. His hands were still held up, fingers wriggling, and she couldn't stop staring at them. As much as her skin was ticklish to most touches, Connor seemed to have the power to turn those touches from ticklish to sensual and she had no idea how he did it. When they were in bed making out and he touched her, giggling had always been the furthest thing from her mind because her body was too busy burning from the inside out with a desire that only one man could quench.

"Connor," she warned as he advanced on her, but even to her own ears, her voice sounded breathy and needy. Like she wanted his touch, and ... she did.

Last night she'd been going to ask him for more. Going to ask him to touch her, to let her touch him, to make love to her like he used to because she'd needed something to bridge the gap.

Didn't matter that her brain said it couldn't be sex.

That sex wasn't the foundation you built a life on.

Becca knew better than most that sex could be pleasurable or it could be used as a weapon. It could be fickle and switch from one side to the other in a heartbeat.

If she wanted to be able to say yes to giving Connor a second chance, they had to do this right. They were different people now and they'd lived half a lifetime since they'd last been together. Rebuilding trust was the only way to answer his question with a yes, and yet seeing the fire in his eyes that she knew echoed what was in her own, staring at his fingers that she knew were capable of making her feel indescribable pleasure, it was hard to think with her head.

"Becca," Connor shot back as he reached for her, hesitating before his fingers made contact, giving her an out if she truly wanted one.

But she didn't.

She craved his touch with an intensity she would never have believed if she wasn't living it right this second.

The moment his fingers touched her sides she couldn't think at all. He was going easy on her, she knew that, in deference to her bruised ribs, but still he knew just which parts of her were the most ticklish, and he attacked them with an amused laugh that joined her own, adding to the joyful cacophony of the peaceful woods.

The more he tickled the more she squiggled.

The more she squiggled the more the canoe rocked.

The more the canoe rocked the more she realized they were going to capsize.

"Connor, we're going to sink," she spluttered out through bouts of giggling.

"Then we sink," he said, his face close enough to hers that if she wanted to, she could lean up and kiss him.

She did want to.

Badly.

Whether it was a good idea or not, she wanted all of Connor. Every single part of him. Everything that used to be hers, that used to be so easy, that she had taken for granted because she'd just assumed he would always be there.

"You know how to swim so I don't see what the big deal is," he added, swiping his fingertips across her stomach and drawing another round of giggles from her.

What would the big deal be?

The day was warm, the water looked inviting, and Connor was right, they both knew how to swim.

She had to let go and stop trying to control every aspect of her life because the truth was she couldn't. The last few days had drilled that into her. The answer to dealing with her trauma wasn't trying to micro-manage every part of her life so it remained under her control, it was accepting that life was never under control. That made it terrifying, but it also made it beautiful because unpredictability could bring fun and playfulness. Without both, what was the point of living?

Giving in to the moment, she stopped holding back and let her laugh ring free as Connor's fingers continued to tickle her. Their laughs seemed to dance together, joining as one, and when the inevitable happened and they both landed with a splash in the cool water, it only drew another laugh from her lips as the river enveloped her.

Before she even had a chance to think about swimming up to the surface, just a foot or two above her head, Connor's arms were around her, bringing her up alongside him.

He'd been there for her.

Without her asking, without her even thinking about it.

He was just there.

Could she break down the walls still erected between them and allow herself to believe that he would always be there? That no matter what troubles life threw at them he wouldn't be going anywhere?

CHAPTER

Fourteen

August 22nd
10:19 A.M.

This wasn't what he'd had in mind when he decided to take Becca out canoeing this morning.

Not that Connor was complaining.

All he'd wanted was to spend time with her and put her at ease like she always used to be when they were together. He'd thought a canoe ride along the peaceful little river that flowed through Cade's property would be romantic. The sunshine, the soft breeze, the gentle sounds of the water combined with everything nature had to offer. What could be more perfect?

Turned out this could.

Kicking his feet in the water to keep them both afloat, one of his arms locked around Becca's waist, holding her anchored against his body, water streaming down both of their faces. There was a look in her eyes that he remembered so well. This was happy Becca, relaxed Becca, content Becca.

Even though it wasn't how he'd envisioned it turning out, this was exactly what he'd hoped would happen today. They'd take another step closer toward healing and reuniting.

No longer was Becca fighting against that.

Just because she still hadn't offered him an answer to his question about whether she could give him a second chance, she didn't really need to. He could feel her answer. She was working through her issues, learning to forgive him, learning to trust him again, and he'd know when she was successful because that's when she'd give him the yes he craved.

All he had to do was show her that he would always put her first.

"Guess we did wind up capsizing," he said, his gaze drifting to her lips. How badly he wanted to kiss them.

"I think that was inevitable from the moment you decided to tickle me just because I splashed a little water on you," Becca said wryly.

"If I got wet it was only fair we both did."

Because he was holding her against his body, her legs wrapped around his hips, he felt the way she shifted at the mention of getting wet.

Was his girl wet for him?

Did she long to feel him inside her as desperately as he longed to shove those cute little, short shorts down her legs, pull her panties off with his teeth, and then plunge inside her tight, wet heat?

Now it was his turn to shift as his body responded to the beautiful woman wrapped around him. This was different than when he offered her the comfort of taking his length into her mouth. That was about soothing her, reassuring her, offering her the power over him to do whatever she wanted, to make sure she knew she was in control when it came to them and their relationship.

This was about need and desire, warring inside him with his brain's knowledge that Becca wasn't ready yet for this step even if she was thinking about it.

Because he would never do anything to her without her express consent, he started swimming them back toward the pier. That had been their rules after her assault. Two months after she'd decided she was ready to try being intimate, he'd been uncertain if enough time had passed. They'd decided together that so long as Becca clearly articulated what she was and wasn't comfortable with, he gave it to her.

If she wanted his mouth on her, she asked for it, and he gave it to her.

If she wanted his fingers roaming her body, she asked for it, and he gave it to her.

If she wanted sex, she asked for it, and he gave it to her.

So long as she asked with words, he knew she was sure it was what she wanted.

Today she wasn't asking with her words. The look in her eyes said she wanted more than him just holding her. The way her hips rocked ever so slightly against his hardening length also said she wanted more.

But until she used her words, he wouldn't do anything.

Violating her trust like that would be something he could never take back.

When he reached the dock, only about a dozen yards from where they'd capsized, he shifted his hands to circle Becca's hips and lifted her up and onto the wood. Then, placing his hands on the dock, he hoisted himself out and up onto the pier beside her.

She'd flopped onto her back, her knees bent over the side of the dock, toes dipped into the water, staring up at the vast expanse of sky above them. He stretched out alongside her, also with his feet in the water, keeping just enough space between them that he wouldn't be tempted to do something like haul her over so she was straddling his legs and let her do what her eyes had been begging for.

Taking things slow might be hard, but it was the only way to get what he wanted.

This wasn't about just patching things up with Becca so she no longer hated him and then parting ways as friends.

This was about getting back the future that should have always been his.

Would have been his if he hadn't messed it up.

Something brushed lightly against his hip, and he glanced down to see Becca's hand. She hadn't turned her head and was still staring up at the wide blue sky above them, but she'd reached out to him.

His heart soared as he moved one of his hands to claim hers.

For a long time, they lay like that, both watching the sky and the occasional white, fluffy cloud that drifted lazily across it, both lost in thought. The sun slowly dried their soaked clothes and wet hair, the wafting breeze kept them from getting too hot, and honestly, even if it was a thousand degrees out there, nothing was going to make him move and end this perfect moment.

"I still love watching the clouds, seeing what shapes they make." Becca's voice finally broke the comfortable silence.

Turning to look at her, Connor found she was watching him now. He didn't know for how long, but he liked that she was finally able to look at him with a peaceful expression, one free from the pain of his betrayal.

"You always loved that game when we were little," he said.

"And when we were not so little. I still remember the last date we went on before I was hurt. You took me out to the beach, we swam, we laughed, we made out, we lay on the sand watching the sky, and then we roasted marshmallows and made S'mores over a bonfire before you took me home and made love to me in our bed."

"I remember." It had been about ten days before Dylan had accosted her that night in her car and raped her.

"I never told you what I saw in the clouds that day."

"I think you told me about a dozen things you saw. There was a baby elephant, a train, a chicken, a seahorse, a—"

"Okay, okay," Becca said with a giggle. "So I told you *some* of the things I saw that day, but there was one I never mentioned. One I thought about a lot these last several years. At the time I thought ..."

"Thought what, moonlight?" he asked as his fingers stroked her wrist, soothing her because he sensed her increasing anxiety.

Her dark blue eyes met his directly as she spoke. "I could have sworn I saw a ring. Like an engagement ring. Right when I spotted it, the sun shone right through it, making the clouds seem like they were glowing, almost sparkling. It's silly but ... I wondered if it was kind of like a sign. That maybe you were almost ready to propose."

This time, he didn't resist the urge to tug her over so she was kneeling above him, her knees on either side of his hips. Retaining his grip on her hand, Becca's other splayed out on his chest, ironically right above his heart. His free hand gripped her thigh, holding onto her because he was half afraid that if he didn't, she'd disappear.

"I was ready to propose to you when we were six," he told her, making her smile. "I'm not joking, Becca. I told Cooper that you were going to be my wife when we were grown up, and he scrunched up his nose and told me girls were icky. I was six, I agreed. Girls were icky back then, but not you, because you weren't a girl. Well, you were, but really you were just mine. I bought you an engagement ring before we'd even slept together. I saved almost all of my money from my part-time job and bought you a ring. It was small, but I knew you wouldn't care."

"Why didn't you ever propose?"

"Because I thought it had to be perfect. I thought the timing mattered. I thought that I had to wait until we both graduated, got jobs, and then we could get married. I thought that we had to do things a certain way. I thought I had to plan something really special, romantic. Because I hadn't spent a lot on the ring, I was planning this amazing vacation to take you on after we graduated so everything would be perfect. Do you know what I realized after I lost you?"

"What?" she asked breathlessly, hanging on his every word.

"There's no such thing as perfect. You were perfect for me and there are no rules when it comes to life. I wish I'd proposed when I wanted to, which was right after high school. I wanted to get married that summer and start college as a proper married couple. It's another one of the mistakes I made." If they'd been married, he'd like to think he wouldn't have freaked that day, or if he had, that Becca would have waited for him to come back so they could talk.

"Connor, you want to know what I realized after we broke up?"

"What?"

"That happiness is what you make it. You're right, there is no such thing as perfect. While this world is full of so many beautiful things it's also full of darkness and a lot of bad things. You can't escape them, but you can survive them."

Was the damage he'd caused to their relationship one of those things you could survive?

Connor prayed with every fiber of his being that it was.

Because living out the rest of his life without Becca by his side was not.

~

August 22nd
2:38 P.M.

"Connor!"

"What?" he asked, freezing at her outburst as though something was poised and ready to attack them. Only what could attack them in the beautiful woods where she was finally finding the peace and tranquility she'd been chasing for twelve long years, she had no idea.

"A bridge," she said, tugging him over to stand on the small wooden bridge that curled above the river that flowed lazily beneath it.

"Oookkaaay," he said slowly, clearly having no idea what she was talking about.

"Don't tell me you've forgotten."

"All right, I won't tell you I've forgotten," he said with a smirk.

Becca rolled her eyes and then planted her hands on her hips. "I can't believe you'd forget something so important."

"You've lost me, babe. I have zero idea what you're talking about."

"Look around you," she instructed. Surely, he couldn't really have forgotten another of her favorite childhood games. Not when they were standing on a bridge.

Obediently he began to scan their surroundings. "Okay, I see a whole bunch of trees, lots of pretty flowers, I see clouds in the sky and the sun, there are some bees and butterflies, probably a whole bunch of other insects I can't see. There's the river, and this bridge, and the path we were following before you scared me half to death. What in particular am I supposed to be focusing on?"

With a sigh, she tugged her hand free of his, held up said hand to indicate he should stay right where he was, and then hurried off the bridge to scan the ground. Her gaze landed on what she needed, and she bent down to snatch up two sturdy-looking sticks and then scampered back to Connor.

"Well?" she asked as she held up the sticks.

His brow furrowed. "Sticks?" Then she could see it clicked together in his head. "Oh, sticks and we're on a bridge. My little Winnie the Pooh fan used to be obsessed with playing Poohsticks."

"Right! How could you have forgotten that?" she asked, beaming up at him, pleased he'd remembered even if she'd had to prompt him a little.

"I have no idea," he told her with another one of those charming smiles that had her having to squeeze her thighs together as heat zinged between her legs.

"I always used to win at Poohsticks," she said as she kept hold of the stick that looked like a Y and passed the other one to Connor.

"Actually, yeah you did. I have no idea how. The game is totally random and not even up to anything we do or don't do, yet you did always win."

"That's where you're wrong," she informed him. "There absolutely is something you can do to ensure you always win."

"Yeah? What's that then?"

"Pick the right stick," she said, holding up hers, which she was positive would indeed be the winner when they dropped them over one side of the bridge and then moved to the other side to see which one appeared first.

Connor's laugh rang out, so pure and full of joy that she froze. How could she have lived so many years without hearing that sound? Those last four months they'd been together were rough, and neither of them had had a lot to laugh about.

Hearing it now had tears stinging the backs of her eyes.

She'd missed it so much.

Missed him so much.

Just because she hadn't allowed herself to think about Connor because it was too painful didn't mean she hadn't been living her life with a part of herself missing.

"You okay?" Connor's hand swept down the length of her long

braid, then lifted to palm her cheek. His fingertips caressed her skin, and she sighed and nuzzled into his hand.

"I'm okay. I just ... I missed hearing you laugh," she admitted.

Sadness wiped away the last of his joy. "I'm sor—"

Lifting a hand, she pressed a finger to his lips to silence him. "No more apologies. I get it, Connor. And you've apologized repeatedly. I believe you and I believe in your sincerity. I accept your apology," she said the words she knew he needed to hear and was rewarded when something in Connor eased, like a weight had been lifted from his shoulders.

It wasn't quite a yes to his question about second chances, but it was a step in that direction.

"Thank you," he said softly. Leaning in, he pressed his lips to her forehead and held them there. "I don't deserve you, Becca."

"Why? Because you messed up? I hate to break it to you, Con, but even though you messed up, you were my rock those first four months. I would not have survived them without you. You gave me everything I needed even though you were hurting yourself in the process. You can't do that again, Connor. I mean it," she added when he opened his mouth and was about to say what she knew would be a protest. "You weren't taking care of you, and that's why you let everything build up and broke down like you did."

Taking a deep breath, Becca considered her words.

Wanted to get them just right.

"If I let myself lean on you again, you have to know that if you leave it will break me. I've survived a lot, but I can't survive losing you twice. If I allow myself to trust you and believe in you like I used to, then it has to be with the understanding that you aren't going to prioritize me to the exclusion of everything else. I needed you then, Connor, but I still could have supported you the way you supported me. If you'd needed a day off, I would have been okay. If you needed to scream and yell, I would have been okay. If you needed to cry, I would have been okay. Partners have each other's backs, it's not one person shouldering everything."

"You didn't need my pain on top of your own," he said, his fingers on her brow sweeping in soft circles.

Jutting her hip out she stared at him defiantly. "I could have handled it."

His brow furrowed like he was deep in thought, things occurring to him that hadn't before. "You're right," he finally agreed. "I was so focused on trying to protect you from everything, including myself and my feelings about your assault, that I forgot how strong you are. I swear, I won't make that mistake again."

She believed him.

Which was why she mentally took another step toward trusting him.

"Good. See that you don't. Now, are you ready to play?" she asked, pushing aside the heavy emotions that had dimmed the wood's peacefulness.

"Ready," Connor answered, his easy smile sliding back into place. Still, before he released her, he leaned in and dropped another featherlight kiss, this time to her lips.

It wasn't what she wanted, she wanted fiery and passionate, but for now she'd take it.

One step at a time.

Plus, she was already planning what was going to happen tonight. Last night, after learning about Connor abstaining from sex for over a decade she'd chickened out, back peddled, overcome she'd needed a little distance.

Tonight, she was getting what she craved.

What she knew they both craved.

When Connor finally let her go, she stepped up to the side of the bridge where the direction the water was flowing would carry the sticks to the other side. Connor came up beside her, one hand settling on the small of her back like it always used to, and she smiled.

Things were slowly returning to the way they used to be, and it felt right.

"One," she started, and they both held their sticks in the air, ready to drop them. "Two. Three."

Both sticks hit the water at the same time, and since the bridge was small and it would take only seconds for them to reach the other side, they both hurried across it, giggling like they used to when they were seven, and would play this game on lazy summer afternoons.

About two seconds after they leaned over the side of the cute wooden bridge the sticks appeared.

Hers in the lead.

"Victory!" Becca cheered, jumping up and down and pumping her fists in the air. "I keep my perfect score."

Connor groaned. "How do you manage to always do that?"

"Told you, it's all in the choice. You pick a winner, and you win, you pick a loser, and you lose. Simple as that."

Those words clicked something into place inside her.

You picked a loser, and you lost.

Picking Toby had been the wrong choice. Not because he was a bad man, he wasn't, not at all. He was just bad for her. The wrong choice for her.

If you'd asked her a month ago if picking Connor was the right choice or wrong, she would have readily said it was the wrong one.

But that would have been a lie.

Because Connor was never the wrong choice for her.

He was always the right one.

You picked a winner, and you won.

Becca was well and truly ready to do some winning for a change.

CHAPTER
Fifteen

August 22nd
8:36 P.M.

Something was different about Becca.

Connor couldn't put his finger on exactly what it was, but something had changed while they spent the day out in the woods.

Fresh air and sunshine were food for the soul.

That's what his mom used to say to him and his brothers when they hit those preteen years and started wanting to spend more time inside playing video games than they did outside riding bikes and playing.

At the time, he'd groaned and grumbled, as had the rest of his brothers, they wanted to do what their friends were doing, but their mom was tough. Tough but loving and always fair. She insisted that growing boys needed fresh air and sunshine to grow their souls just as much as they needed copious amounts of food to grow their bodies.

In the end, they always had fun after they finished complaining about how unfair life was and how Mom didn't understand that they weren't little kids anymore.

Thirteen had been too young to lose her.

Too young for him to realize the gifts she was giving them.

Too young to realize just what a great mom she was and how lucky he was to have her.

Sorry, Mom. I hope you know that even though the guys and I were so angry with you for getting married again so soon after Dad died, it was only because we didn't understand and not that we didn't love you. We did. We loved you a lot. So much.

Enough that none of us will ever stop fighting to prove you were inno- cent, that you never betrayed your husband, his team, or your country. No matter the cost, we owe you that for how we treated you and how we behaved those last six months.

"Connor?"

Blinking, he saw that Becca was looking over at him, concern on her face, and he realized he'd been standing at the sink, a plate in his hand, under the running water, lost in thought.

Was he really willing to prove his mother and stepfather's innocence no matter the cost, even if that cost was Becca's life?

Mom wouldn't want that.

She loved Becca like another daughter, and she'd always known he was going to make her his wife one day. It was going to happen a whole lot later than he'd originally planned, but ever since they talked on the bridge that afternoon, Connor had found a certainness settling inside him.

Becca was going to say yes.

It might take her a little more time, but she was going to give him a second chance and he had no plans on squandering it.

Would continuing to fight against the men who had already proved they would do whatever it took to silence them wind up having him squander that precious second chance? It was easy to say that nothing could make him back off when it wasn't the life of the woman he loved hanging on the line.

"You okay?" Becca asked.

Forcing a smile to his lips, Connor shoved away the negative thoughts. He and his brothers would keep Becca safe the same way they'd keep Cassandra, Willow, Susanna, Essie, and Gabriella safe. They were proving that not only were they a strong unit, but they also got stronger as they got bigger.

"I'm okay," he assured her.

She twisted her hands together and rocked from foot to foot, a sign that she was nervous. "You sure? Because I was going to suggest we light a fire in the firepit and make S'mores, but if you'd rather spend the evening alone, I can just go up to bed and leave you to it."

"No!" The word blurted out of him in a rush. No matter his doubts and concerns, any time Becca wanted to spend with him was time well spent. "No," he said again, calmer this time. "I don't want you to go up to bed, I don't want to be alone. S'mores and the firepit sound wonderful. Why don't you gather supplies, and I'll go get a fire started."

For a moment she studied him, but then she relaxed and smiled. "Okay. Meet you outside in a few minutes."

It still felt like she was up to something, but whatever it was couldn't be bad, so Connor didn't dwell on it. Instead, he set down the plate, turned off the water, and left the dishes to drip dry on the side of the sink. He'd worry about them in the morning because right now, he wanted to just focus on Becca.

The firepit was about twenty yards from the cabin on the left side, the river side, about halfway between the building and the dock where they'd laid in the sun earlier. Already some wood sat inside, and he'd grabbed a small lock box with matches on his way out.

By the time he heard Becca approaching, he had a nice little fire going and dropped down into one of the Adirondack chairs that circled the stone firepit. He watched as she came closer, she'd taken her hair out of its braid, letting it hang down her back in a mass of kinky, black waves, and she'd thrown on a sweater since the night air was getting chilly as the summer wound down.

Her long, lean legs ate up the distance between them, and even though she had the supplies to make S'mores in her arms, she dumped them in the chair beside his, then instead of finding her own chair she planted herself on his lap.

Surprise had him freezing.

What game was his moonlight intent on playing tonight?

It was clear she was determined to follow through on whatever plan she had brewing in that pretty head of hers because he recognized the glint in her eyes.

It was her Becca means business look.

"What are you up to?" he asked as his hands moved to grip her hips, keeping her in place in case she decided to change her mind. Holding her, even if this was all they did tonight, was more than worth it as far as he was concerned.

"I have something for you." She held up a sonogram picture, a photo of a tiny bundle wrapped in a blanket wearing a little blue cap, a card with the smallest footprints he'd ever seen, and a pair of knitted booties. "I needed something to do with my hands after you left so I took up knitting. I wanted to make something for the baby. He was already gone before he was born but was big enough to hold for a photo. I wanted to share these with you."

His heart ached at the knowledge he wasn't there the day Becca had gone into labor.

"This isn't to make you sad, Connor," she said softly.

"I know, baby. It makes me sad because it's a reminder of my failures. But I'm so grateful you shared these with me."

"Yeah?" Becca searched his gaze seeking the truth.

"Yes. Always yes. He was our son."

"Carter Marsden-Charleston."

Surprise had him tightening his hold on her hips. "You named him after my dad? And gave him my last name?"

"He was both of ours."

"Thank you." Tears blurred his vision, and he touched a kiss to her forehead. "Thank you for carrying my son inside you. Thank you for loving him even when you didn't know he was mine. Thank you for loving me even after I hurt you."

"Loving you is as easy as breathing."

"The most natural thing in the world," he agreed.

"I wanted you last night, Connor, but I was a coward. I'm not going to be a coward again tonight," she told him, her hands landing on his shoulders as she studied him, allowing him to see her eyes and the certainty in them.

That was way too open for interpretation for his liking.

Went against their rules, and she knew it.

"Words, Becca. I need you to use your words like a good girl," he murmured, his voice low as fire lit inside him. If she was asking for this, if she was sure it was what she wanted, then he wouldn't hesitate to give her everything. Everything her body could take and then some.

She shivered and a dreamy smile lit her face. "I always loved it when you called me a good girl."

"You are though, aren't you?" His hands shifted slightly, still holding her hips, but now his thumbs hovered on her soft skin, right at the edges of those tiny jean cut-off shorts she was wearing. So close to where he longed to touch her. "My good girl."

"Yours, Connor," she agreed, squirming a little.

"Then give me your words, baby. Tell me what you want. What you need."

"Everything," she answered without hesitation. "I need your hands on me, touching me, like you used to. I want your mouth driving me wild, sucking on me, licking me, making me come on your tongue. I don't think I can survive another day ending without feeling you inside me, making me complete again."

"Making *us* complete," he corrected. Because there was no Connor without Becca, just like there was no Becca without Connor. They were two halves of the same whole, and even though Becca said she forgave him for tearing them apart, he wasn't sure he would ever completely forgive himself.

"Making us complete," she agreed. "But first, before I let you touch me, I need to do this."

Shifting off his lap, Connor reluctantly uncurled his fingers and let her go because one thing was certain, and that was in any making out they did, Becca would always be in control. Becca knelt before him. Not in a submissive way, neither of them was into that, although, no shade to anyone who was, but it wasn't their thing. They were equals in every way including in the bedroom.

But this wasn't about submission, this was Becca reminding herself she was safe and in control, that only what she wanted would happen between them.

So even though he ached to touch her, bring her pleasure, he didn't move as she pulled his length free. Didn't move as the heat of her mouth enveloped him. Didn't grab her hair and begin to thrust into her mouth as she sucked on him, her hands joining in the fun, touching and stroking.

This was his girl's show, and when pleasure coiled tightly inside him, then exploded throughout him Connor watched in wonder as his beautiful, brave, strong, smart girl stared back at him with so much love in her eyes he felt like he was drowning in pleasure.

~

August 22nd
    8:57 P.M.

"My turn," Connor growled before she even finished swallowing.

His hands hooked under her armpits, and he lifted her up and onto his lap like she weighed nothing at all. While Becca knew she was small, only five foot two, and weighing in at just over a hundred pounds, Toby had never been able to lift her like that. Not that there was anything wrong with him being skinny and a little on the scrawny side, at the time it hadn't mattered, but there, with Connor, seeing how strong he was, she realized she'd missed it.

Maybe a part of her had been damaged when she was assaulted that liked knowing how big Connor was, how easily he could protect her.

"You ready for my fingers, babe?" Connor asked, a reflection of the firelight dancing in his eyes, giving her a literal representation of what she knew he was feeling inside.

"I'm ready," she said breathlessly.

Actually, she was more than ready.

She was ready to let go and move forward, ready to stop allowing the past to control her future, ready to hand her trust back to Connor and pray that this time he wouldn't wind up using it against her.

He wouldn't.

If she'd needed any more convincing, then the way he'd just

reminded her that he would only touch her if she expressly asked him to, using her words, as he called it, had pushed her over.

Connor had her best interests at heart, and this time, they both knew the cost of him ever shoving aside his own needs to prioritize hers. He had promised her he'd learned from that mistake and wouldn't repeat it, and she believed him.

"Touch me, Connor," she whispered and was rewarded by a kiss, exactly the kind she'd craved earlier. This one wasn't soft and gentle, it stoked the fires burning inside her and stole her ability to think because all she could do was feel.

When his fingers brushed against her soaked center she was almost caught by surprise.

She'd been too caught up in his mouth, his lips against hers, his tongue dueling with her own to realize anything else.

Now those fingers teased her through her panties, brushing featherlight touches along her center. She rocked her hips, trying to make him shove the thin material aside and push inside her, stroking deep, filling her up.

A moan tumbled from her lips, half pleading for more, half already reaching toward an orgasm.

Connor smiled against her lips, pulling back just enough to whisper, "Greedy tonight are we, moonlight?"

"Greedy," she agreed as his fingers finally slipped past the cotton of her panties, circling her entrance.

"Mmm, I love knowing how badly you want me," Connor whispered before his lips were on hers again.

While his mouth ravaged hers, his fingers brushed over her bud, then they were where she wanted them. She was already wet, and Connor slipped the first finger in with ease. It had been a long time since she was touched and there was a slight pinch as her body stretched to accommodate his finger, but it passed so quickly it was nothing more than a blip.

Another finger joined it, then a third, stretching her to perfection and getting her ready to take Connor's long, thick length later.

Now, though, she was content to rock on his fingers, enjoying the way they felt stroking deep, catching that special spot inside her with every thrust. Connor's large hand was easily able to reach her bundle of nerves at the same time and his thumb set up a steady pace, pressing with just the right amount of pressure as he circled it while relentlessly pumping his fingers in and out of her, working her higher, building the pleasure inside her.

When it grew too big to contain any longer it exploded.

Her scream was captured by his mouth as he refused to give up, working her through the orgasm, dragging it out, making it last forever until it consumed her body, mind, and soul.

By the time she floated back down to earth, he was already standing, carrying her back inside the cabin.

"Need a bed for this, baby," he whispered in her ear. His lips nibbled at the skin on her neck, and she tilted her head to the side to give him better access.

"My room," she said before he drew another moan from her as his tongue found the sensitive spot behind her ear. "I want you to do something for me tonight."

"Anything, moonlight. There isn't a single thing I wouldn't do for you," he assured her as he headed up the stairs.

She hoped that was true.

Because what she needed tonight wasn't something she'd ever asked of him before. Maybe wasn't even something she'd want to do again. But tonight, she needed it. Needed it to be able to take that final step in moving on from her past. Something she'd only realized in spending time with Connor that she hadn't completely done.

"What do you want, baby?" he asked as he set her on her feet and made quick work of stripping her out of her sweater, T-shirt, shorts, and sneakers. Leaving her naked and vulnerable before him.

Only she didn't feel vulnerable.

Not with Connor.

Connor would never hurt her.

As he stripped off his clothes she went to the nightstand where she'd left it earlier, when she'd devised this plan, knowing it was what she needed.

"Ribbons?" he asked, clearly confused when she held them out to him.

"To tie me up," she explained.

"No way in hell am I tying you up," Connor growled, tossing the ribbons onto the floor like they'd physically hurt him.

Stepping closer, she nestled her head against his chest, willing him to understand. "You always let me be in control, and I needed that, I know I did. But now, tonight, I need to know that I can let you take control."

"I'd never hurt you, Becca. I'd rather cut it off than cause you any pain."

Laughing softly, she circled his "it" and stroked it gently. "I know that. It's why I can do this with you. Only you. Teach me that it's okay not to be in control, Connor. Help me learn that again because it's exhausting trying to be in control of everything all the time. I don't want to do it anymore."

Hooking a finger under her chin, he nudged until she looked at him. "You sure?" he asked, searching her eyes.

"Positive."

"I won't tie you tight enough to hurt, not even tight enough to really hold you in place, just to give you the illusion that you're surrendering to me," he told her, and she knew there was no point in arguing, he'd made up his mind. It didn't matter, that was all she needed, it wasn't about pain, or even being tied up, it was just about allowing her mind to let go of its need to control because it knew she was safe.

"Okay," she agreed.

Picking her up, Connor laid her out on the bed, then scooped up the ribbons. With gentle fingers, he bound first one wrist to the bedpost, then the other. After tying her right leg to the bedpost, he held up the fourth ribbon. "Can I take your foot off, baby? I want to see all of you tonight."

"Yes." There was no need to hide from Connor. Besides, he'd seen the wounds when they were ugly and raw, they'd healed a lot over the last decade and looked a whole lot better than how he likely remembered them.

His smile was soft as he removed her prosthetic and set it on the floor. Then he knelt at the end of the bed and touched his lips so gently to her stump. It felt weird, her skin didn't feel normal there, not the way the rest of her skin did, but she felt the kiss, felt the love pouring from it, and when he moved on to find her next scar, tears burned her eyes.

By the time he'd kissed his way along every scar on her body, worshiping them with his lips and his tongue, she was crying.

Happy tears though.

Because he made her feel so accepted, so beautiful.

Just because she never acted self-conscious about the scars her ordeal had left behind didn't mean they never made her feel less beautiful.

They did.

Especially the way Toby used to pretend they didn't exist. Like she didn't have scars and a missing foot.

But Connor had never shied away from them, not even in the beginning when they were painful and so very obvious. He'd just accepted them as a part of her.

Now he touched kisses to her cheeks, catching her tears.

"Thank you," she whispered.

"Hey now, if I'm not allowed to say sorry for hurting you then you're not allowed to thank me for loving you. I couldn't not love you if I tried, Becca."

She believed those words.

With every fiber of her being.

Connor's dark head settled between her legs, and there was not an ounce of fear at her body bared and vulnerable before him. She was so secure in the knowledge that she was safe, that Becca was able to turn her brain off as his tongue swiped along her center.

Safe.

Safe to give up control and just feel.

Like his fingers had done by the firepit outside, his mouth worked her higher now. It teased her, alternating between plunging his tongue inside her and closing his lips around her bud, suckling hard as his tongue flicked at her, driving her wild.

Her fingers clutched the sheets, her head thrashed from side to side, her body squirmed as he worked her higher and higher, higher than she'd ever climbed before. It was going to be one heck of a fall when he had her tumbling over the edge.

Every time she was sure she'd reached the peak, Connor seemed to manage to push her higher still.

Then just when she thought she couldn't take a single second longer, it rushed through her. A wave of pleasure unlike anything she had ever experienced before tore through her as she screamed Connor's name. It touched every cell of her body, cleansing her of old fears, purging all the bad from her soul, and leaving her feeling fresh and clean again for the first time in over a decade.

There was a smug smile on Connor's face when she blinked open heavy eyes to find him kneeling between her legs.

"You look pretty pleased with yourself," she mumbled.

"You look thoroughly loved," he shot back.

"Not thoroughly, not yet. Hurry up and get inside me. I'm on birth control so you don't need a condom."

Nothing between them tonight.

Just the two of them getting back to where they belonged.

He was already hard, and he sheathed himself inside her in one smooth thrust, filling her to completion and giving her back the part of herself that had been missing ever since he left.

There would be time later for slow and sweet, now she just wanted to feel him come inside her. Connor seemed to feel that same urgency because his pace was almost desperate as he thrust into her. His fingers claimed her overstimulated bundle of nerves quickly pushing her toward her third orgasm in the space of a handful of minutes.

She cried out, her body trying to pull away from the too-strong sensations, but there was nowhere to go. Becca waited for panic that never came, and she stopped fighting against it and allowed the pleasure to sweep through her body once again. This orgasm wasn't as powerful as the last one, but it had a beautiful peace to it, and it seemed to go on and on forever, spurred on further when she felt Connor release himself inside her.

This was what had been missing.

Connor.

Her body and her soul craved him, and now she had him back she wasn't ever letting him go again. Those men hunting her and his family could try but they would never take the man she loved away from her.

CHAPTER
Sixteen

August 23rd
1:02 A.M.

The room was dark.

It shouldn't be.

The knowledge plucked Connor from sleep to find that the lights in the bedroom had indeed gone out.

After making love to Becca earlier they'd snuggled in one another's arms, basking in their love that felt renewed and reenergized, almost like it had been reborn. Then he'd taken her to the shower, cleaned her up, made love to her again, then not wanting her to miss out on her S'mores, he'd thrown his T-shirt on her, put his shorts back on, and they'd gone back to the firepit.

Around eleven, they'd headed to bed, and he couldn't not make love to her again, so they'd had another round of sex before exhausted, they'd fallen asleep in one another's arms.

Becca was still sound asleep, and he was pretty sure that if she'd woken up at some point and got up to use the bathroom, turning off the lights before returning to bed, he would have known. One thing he'd learned in his years as a SEAL and working for Prey was how to train his body to wake at the tiniest hint of movement or sound. In the field, it could mean the difference between life and death.

He prayed tonight it wouldn't.

As much as he didn't want to wake her and worry her, he needed Becca to be prepared if something was wrong. There was every chance that he was overreacting. Connor could hear a storm raging outside, it must have blown up quickly because it had still been clear and mild a couple of hours ago when they came back inside.

The storm could have knocked out the generator.

It was definitely the more logical answer.

Yet ...

Dangerous men were after him and his family, who would do anything to silence them, and who had already gone after Becca once before. It was nothing short of a miracle that he'd gotten her out of the camp without everyone waking up and realizing what was going on.

More than that, it was a miracle he'd proven himself to Becca enough that she was willing to give him a second chance. She'd never actually said the words, but her actions and what she had said were enough.

Nothing was going to ruin this chance.

Certainly not a bunch of powerful men who thought they could do whatever they pleased and then kill people to cover it up.

They weren't silencing him and his family, and they weren't taking Becca from him.

"Wake up, moonlight," he said softly, nudging Becca's shoulder.

She gave an indignant moan that made him smile and tucked her face tighter against his chest, which she was using as a pillow.

He'd worn his girl out with all the sex, but now he needed her awake and sharp. Just in case it was a worst-case scenario.

"Come on, babe, wake up for me," he urged. Even though the storm was the logical conclusion as to why the lights had gone out, he wasn't going to be able to relax until he'd proven it to himself. "You wake up now and I'll reward you with another orgasm as soon as I get the generator running again."

"Mmm, orgasm?" she asked sleepily, lifting her head and blinking open sleep-laden eyes.

"Knew that would do the trick," he teased, leaning down to kiss the tip of her nose.

"What's going on?" she asked, obviously picking up on his tension.

"Did you get up and go to the bathroom?" Just because he was pretty sure he would have woken if she climbed out of bed he had to check.

"No. Why?"

"Lights are out."

"You didn't get up to go?" A hint of fear crept into her voice.

"No. There's a storm, though," he rushed on to add, wanting to alleviate her fears before he knew if there was anything to be afraid of. "So that's probably what happened. The wind or the rain likely took out the generator. I just need to go out and check on it, get it up and running again."

"If there's a storm you shouldn't go outside," Becca protested. "We can do without the generator until morning. Then, if it's still storming or you can't fix it, we can just go back to the city. I can always stay with you until it's safe."

A growl warred with a smile at her words.

While he loved that she was willing to stay with him, it wasn't going to be until it was safe. Once he had her in the home he'd bought because it reminded him of Becca's dream house, he wasn't going to let her go.

"We can go back to the city if we have to, but I still need to check out the generator now."

"Why?"

"In case it's not the storm that took the generator out," he said gently, knowing she already knew this but was holding onto denial for as long as she possibly could.

She swallowed audibly. "You don't think it was the storm, do you?"

"I don't know," he assured her.

"But you suspect they found us."

"I don't want to think that, Becca, but I have to consider it as a possibility. If these men can contact a gang in remote Cambodia just because I hopped on a plane to go and see you then I don't think there's much they can't do. I won't take any chances with your safety. Which is why I want you to get dressed, get your prosthetic on, then take Cade's weapon and find somewhere to hide."

Because he knew if he didn't get out of bed he'd never leave her side, Connor stood and reached for his clothes. Hopefully, this would turn out to be nothing, and he'd be climbing back under those sheets and wrapping his naked body around Becca's in no time.

But if not ...

Then, he would do whatever was necessary to keep her safe.

"I should come with you, we can watch each other's backs," Becca said as she did as he told her and strapped her prosthetic back on.

"Absolutely not."

Not happening.

No way.

No how.

Not in a million lifetimes.

"But—"

"No, Becca," he said in a tone that brokered no arguments. "I won't put your life in danger. Don't ask me to. You'll stay in here, hide, keep a weapon and a cell phone in your hand, use it if you have to, and stay safe. Do you hear me?" Connor stalked around the bed until he reached her then dragged her into his arms. "I need you to be safe."

"Okay," she agreed, her voice muffled as her face was pressed against his chest.

"This is what I do. I'll be fine," he promised as he made himself release her and shoved his feet into a pair of sneakers.

"Okay," she said again, a slight wobble in her voice.

"I love you, moonlight." With his weapon in his hand and his cell phone in his pocket, Connor paused only long enough to crush his lips to hers in a far too brief kiss before he was stalking toward the door.

"I love you, too."

The whispered words followed him down the stairs. It was dark down there as well. Even though there had been no lights on when he locked up and took Becca back upstairs to bed, there should be the glow of the clock on the microwave and the one on the oven.

Both were dark.

Which meant there was definitely no power in the cabin.

One step outside was all it took for him to be completely drenched. The wind was horrendous, and he could hear thunder rumbling in the distance although he hadn't spotted a flash of lightning yet.

Since Cade had owned this cabin for years, and he'd taken the whole family out there on several occasions, Connor knew exactly where the generator was and it didn't take him long to get to it.

Once he did, his worst fears were confirmed.

This wasn't storm damage.

It looked like someone had gone to town on the thing with a baseball bat. It was broken beyond repair and would have to be replaced.

Someone had wanted to knock the power out, had done it deliberately, which meant he and Becca weren't alone. It had to be the people his family was hunting, there were no other logical conclusions to draw, but how had they found them? And so quickly. They'd only been there a matter of days and yet they'd already been found.

Whoever it was hadn't gone straight to the cabin after destroying the generator. Even if he'd woken as soon as the lights went out, it had taken him several minutes to wake Becca, get dressed, and get outside.

What were they waiting for?

Were they watching him right now?

Were they wanting to separate him and Becca? If they were, he'd just given them exactly what they were after.

What was the end goal? To kill them? To abduct them? To torture Becca in front of him until he agreed to back off? To torture him in front of her until her screams and pleas forced him to give in?

Whatever it was, he had to get to Becca, had to get her to the car and out of there.

Just as he turned to head back to the house, the sound of a gunshot roared above the howl of the wind, and pain stabbed through him.

~

August 23rd
    1:09 A.M.

. . .

That was a gunshot.

Wasn't it?

Becca froze, unsure what she was supposed to do.

Connor had insisted she stay inside, hide somewhere, remain armed, and call for help if they needed it.

They needed it.

Gunshots meant bad news.

It couldn't be anything else.

Wearing the same jean cut-offs, T-shirt, and sweater she'd been wearing yesterday, her prosthetic was back on, and she'd just finished shoving her feet into her sneakers when she'd heard the unmistakable crack of a bullet being fired.

It *was* a bullet being fired, wasn't it?

Had it been a crack of lightning instead?

Or maybe it was just her imagination working overtime.

The wind howled outside. If someone fired a weapon, would she be able to hear it from inside?

She wasn't sure.

Her legs shook so badly she could hardly walk, but she had to. Had to figure out what she was going to do. Connor had told her to hide, but where was she supposed to do that?

It was the same problem she'd had when he first arrived, and she hadn't known it was him and she'd panicked and armed herself. There had been nowhere to hide then and there was nowhere to hide now.

Especially given that the cabin was remote.

If Connor was right and someone had tracked them to the cabin, then sabotaged the generator to plunge them into darkness and even the playing field, or separate them or whatever the reason had been, no one was going to be able to get to them in time to help them.

And Connor could be hurt.

Could be ...

No.

She couldn't even allow herself to think that.

For all she knew, it was Connor shooting at someone. Maybe he needed her help and she was just standing in the bedroom frozen in fear.

Come on, Becca.

Pull it together.
Connor needs you.

Why hadn't she said the words she'd already decided on? She should have told him that she was giving him a second chance. It was true, and she thought her actions had shown it, there was no way she would have had sex with him if she wasn't willing to try to work things out and rebuild what they used to have, and she was sure Connor knew it.

Didn't he?

There was no way to be sure, and now, all she wished was that she'd said the words. She wanted Connor to know for certain, especially since he'd gone running out into danger to protect her.

Palming her cell phone as she crept down the stairs, she wished she could walk as silently as Connor did. It must have been some super skill he learned as part of his training because he hadn't been able to walk without making a sound back when she'd known him. With her prosthetic, she doubted she could ever do what he did, but she wished she could.

Because someone could already be in the cabin.

It had been at least three minutes since Connor left the bedroom, and close to a minute since she heard what she was still sure was a gunshot.

Whether she was right or wrong it didn't matter.

Calling for help was the smart thing to do. Whatever was happening someone needed to know, even if it was just the storm. Flooding from the river, the torrential rain, or the screaming wind could still wind up putting them in danger.

As she reached the main floor, she scanned the space, looking for any signs that someone was in there. The front and back doors were both closed, but it was hard to see much of anything because it was so dark.

Pitch black.

Because of the storm, there wasn't even any moonlight to filter in through the windows, and there certainly wasn't any light from neighbors. From what Cade had told her on the drive up there, the nearest neighbors were almost two miles away. Nowhere near close enough for her to easily reach in a storm.

When nothing moved and she didn't hear any other sounds than the wind, Becca crept over to the back door. The generator was around the back and off to the right a little. Cade had shown it to her just in case she needed to know where it was, although neither of them had thought she really would.

Since Connor was outside, there was no use calling him. She was close with all of his brothers, they'd all grown up together, but this was Cade's cabin so she brought up his number and hit call.

The phone rang three times before it was answered.

"Becca? What's wrong?" Cade asked without preamble. She appreciated him just jumping into the issue and not wasting time on small talk, after all, she wasn't going to be calling him in the middle of the night for small talk.

"There's a storm and the generator went out," she blurted out.

"Where's Connor?"

"He went out into the storm to check it out. He hasn't come back. It hasn't been that long, but I thought I heard a gunshot."

Silence met her.

"Cade?"

More silence.

Moving the phone from her ear she saw that the call had been disconnected.

Quickly redialing she waited.

And waited.

And waited.

Nothing.

The call wouldn't go through.

Had to be the storm messing with the reception. She was probably lucky she'd been able to get through to him at all, but had he heard what she'd said about Connor and the gunshot?

If he hadn't, he might just think she was letting him know about the storm and not worry about it until morning.

By morning it would be too late.

That she was certain of.

If it was just the storm taking out the generator, Connor would be back by now. He wouldn't leave her to worry about him, he'd come back and let her know and then go back to see if there was anything he could do to fix it, or they'd just wait out the storm together.

But he hadn't come back.

That meant he couldn't.

Because of the gunshot.

She couldn't stay in there if he was outside somewhere hurt, maybe even dying. What if the people who had taken out the generator had shot Connor and were now trying to kidnap him? They might have come to take him so they could use him to blackmail his brothers into backing off in their search for answers.

If there was a chance he was alive she had to try to go to him.

Mind made up, Becca put her hands out in front of her and worked her way through the cabin to where Cade had told her the emergency kit was stashed. There was a flashlight in there, and if she could get it, she could go looking for Connor.

It didn't take her long to locate it, and once she had the flashlight in her hand she felt marginally better. The cell phone was useless without reception, so she left it on the kitchen counter and switched on the flashlight.

The beam of light bolstered her and as she swung it around the cabin, searching for any other presence, she saw no puddles of water inside. Anyone coming in would be drenched so she knew for certain she was alone.

The question was, how many people were outside the cabin?

Only one way to find out.

For all she knew, it was only Connor, and he'd just been hurt somehow in the storm and it was his weapon that had gone off. Calling out to her and telling her he needed her.

After that first step out the back door, she was drenched.

Soaked to the skin.

Walking with her prosthetic across the muddy, slippery ground, with the rain beating down upon her was difficult, but she headed for the generator with the same determination that she had approached all the operations and therapy she'd faced after her assault.

When you put your mind to it you could do anything.

So she kept going, ducking her head, following the thin beam of light from her flashlight, steadfastly putting one foot in front of the other.

She was most of the way toward it when she saw something on the grass that made her stop.

Was that ...

No.

It couldn't be.

Yet it looked like ...

Blood.

It was dark red and a large puddle of it was only two yards away from the generator. The torrents of rain were quickly washing it away, but she would have bet anything that she was right and it was blood.

Bending down beside it, she set her weapon down on the ground and reached out a trembling hand toward it. Touching her fingers to the puddle, she lifted them to her face and sniffed.

The metallic smell of blood assaulted her nostrils.

She was right.

Someone had bled out there and recently.

Connor. Where was he? Had they already taken his body? Was he dead or alive?

Jerking to her feet, she spun in a circle, screaming his name over and over again. The beam of light danced around her, but it wasn't enough to cut through the utter darkness of the combination of the night and the storm.

Then she saw them.

Shadows.

Multiple shadows.

Moving through the dark.

Toward her.

Circling her.

Closing in on her.

A scream fell from her lips as they grabbed at her.

CHAPTER

Seventeen

August 23rd
1:14 A.M.

Pain throbbed in his shoulder as he hoisted himself up into a tree, but since he could move his arm, Connor didn't think the injury was life-threatening in any way.

Maybe a little more than a flesh wound but nothing that was going to hamper him.

Hell, even a life-threatening injury wasn't going to stop him from doing whatever it took to protect his girl.

Because once again Becca was his.

As far as he was concerned, there had never been a time when she wasn't, but for her things were different.

It had taken courage for her to put her trust in him again after he'd already decimated that trust once before, and it was a gift he would never squander.

Which meant whoever was out there had to die.

He wasn't sure how many of them there were, but after hitting the ground when the bullet striking his shoulder had him overbalancing in the wet and slippery grassy mud, he'd then used the dark to his advantage and slipped away into the trees. His plan had been to watch and set himself up in a position where he could pick them off as they approached the cabin. Of course, without night vision goggles, it wouldn't be easy, but it wasn't completely pitch black out there, and all he would need was a glimpse to make sure he hit his targets.

They needed one alive.

The chances that a random person was out there targeting them, going to this amount of trouble, was virtually non-existent.

Whoever was there had to have been sent by the people intent on silencing him and his family. Apparently, there had been four men involved, one of whom was Tarek Mahmoud. He was already dead, killed himself because he feared his co-conspirators so deeply. That left three men unidentified.

Three men with enough power to orchestrate attack after attack on his family and the people they loved.

Their last lead had also gone up in smoke while one of the men who had been involved had decided taking his own life was better than letting these men get their hands on him.

Another chance at intel couldn't slip through their fingers.

If they wanted to finally get ahead, get a name, something they could use, they needed information. Having Cassandra's DNA hadn't led them to her biological father but the men who had come after him and Becca at the cabin tonight might.

Just then, he spotted three shadows moving through the darkness close to where he'd tucked himself away. From what he could see, and it wasn't a lot, they didn't appear to be wearing NVGs.

Probably why he was still standing.

Not only did that substantially level the playing field, but it also told him these weren't highly trained men. Like the gang from Cambodia, these men were likely to be bloodthirsty and dangerous, but without the skill and training he'd gone through to become a SEAL they weren't going to have enough to measure up.

Numbers meant something but they didn't mean everything.

Unless there was an entire army of them, they wouldn't mean enough.

Another group of three men moved toward the group closer to him.

Six to one.

Connor liked those odds.

Especially with Becca tucked safely away in the cabin.

He was sure the men were coming up with a plan to find him, disable him, either by killing him or injuring him enough they could tie him up and either abduct him or force him to watch them torture Becca.

Not going to happen.

Only then the unthinkable did happen.

Light danced inside the cabin, spilling out through the windows.

There wasn't a chance in hell the six men didn't notice it.

Stay inside, Becca, please, moonlight. I need you to be safe.

While he hadn't had a front-row seat to her rape when they were in college, he'd been there for the aftermath. Through months of surgeries and therapy. He'd gotten a glimpse of what it would have been like to be there when she'd been hurt in Cambodia. Becca had been hit a few times and almost raped.

But if these men got their hands on her tonight, it would be so much worse.

Highly trained or not, they'd likely come with the same orders as the gang in Cambodia had been given. Do whatever they wanted with Becca and then kill her as a warning to his family, motivation to back off.

He had to kill the men before that could happen.

Although as soon as he fired his first shot, he'd give away his position.

In the dark and the rain, there was no way he'd be able to take down all six of them before they could return fire.

As he was debating if he should risk it or slip down, try to separate the men and take them out quietly one by one, his worst nightmare happened.

The door to the cabin opened and he saw Becca step out into the night.

Damn it.

She must have heard the gunshot, gone hunting for Cade's emergency kit to arm herself with a flashlight, and come looking for him.

His brave girl was going to get herself killed.

As the flashlight in her hand danced about, indicating her path, he saw the six men disperse into the trees.

While the dark was working to his advantage in one way, hiding him and protecting him from being spotted, it gave the enemy the same advantage.

"No, baby, stay inside," he whispered, his words caught by the wind and tossed away before they could reach anybody's ears.

But she didn't.

Tracking her progress was easy as she headed toward the generator. That flashlight was a beacon, showing anyone within sight exactly where she was.

He knew the moment she must have spotted whatever the rain was yet to wash away of the puddle of blood he was sure he'd shed when he hit the ground because she froze and then dropped to her knees.

Since all he could see of her was the flashlight and not her body, he couldn't see her expression, but nonetheless, he could feel her terror floating through the storm to his perch in the tree.

A moment later, she was back on her feet, and even across the screech of the wind, he could hear her screaming his name.

She was spinning wildly in a circle, no doubt looking for him, wanting some indication that he wasn't dead, that he hadn't been snatched away from her.

As much as he wanted to give her that reassurance, he couldn't.

In the dancing beam of her light, he could see the men approaching her.

They knew an easy target when they saw one, and whatever their orders, they weren't going to pass up a chance to get their hands on a beautiful and very vulnerable young woman.

Even from where he was, he knew the second Becca spotted them because she froze, and a scream tore from her lips as they pounced on her.

His finger twitched on the trigger. It would be so easy to start firing and make those men regret ever putting their hands on the woman he loved.

But shooting wildly, in the dark, in the middle of a storm, with his girl right in the line of fire, was a recipe for disaster. It was only going to make things worse, not better.

If he wanted to get Becca out of this alive, he had to keep his emotions in check and play this smart.

Right now, the men didn't know how badly they'd hit him. They knew he was alive, or at least that he had been, but they didn't know if they had incapacitated him or if he was still a threat.

That meant he had to leverage that and use it to his advantage.

For now, the men were dragging a kicking and screaming Becca back toward the cabin. They had abandoned their search for him, so he had a little time to try to set something up.

Becca wasn't going to be killed right away, and while his every cell urged him to go to her and protect her from any harm, he had to focus on the big picture. Getting Becca out alive was what mattered the most. Anything else they could survive together.

The light reached the cabin and moments later entered it, enclosing Becca inside with six men who would take great pleasure in inflicting pain.

Big picture.

Becca needs you to be strong right now.

You promised her you would never let her down again and that's a promise you have to hold onto.

Already forming a plan, Connor climbed down from the tree. Those men weren't going to know what hit them. One by one he was going to lead them to their deaths, give them the only fitting consequence for their actions, then he was going to get the answers he needed to keep his girl safe.

Hold on for me, Becca, be strong.

～

August 23rd

1:20 A.M.

She wasn't going down without a fight.

That was the one thing Becca was sure of right now.

When Dylan had raped her all those years ago, she'd fought. It hadn't done any good, he was bigger and stronger than her, his large hand around her neck, squeezing the life out of her had given him even more of an advantage.

But she *had* fought.

That fact had helped her in the weeks and months following her assault. It had given her strength when she'd felt broken, it was something she reminded herself of often, any time those bad thoughts came creeping in.

She wasn't weak.

She wasn't a coward.

She wasn't pathetic.

Just because she'd failed didn't mean she hadn't given it everything she had, and that mattered.

It did.

Just like it would matter now.

Six men were dragging her back toward the cabin. While it was dark other than the light from the flashlight she'd brought with her and she couldn't see just how big they were, there was more of them than there were of her. That alone meant she likely wasn't going to survive whatever they had planned for her.

But she would fight.

And if she died, she would take her final breath knowing she hadn't given up, hadn't surrendered, that she was as strong as she could be.

With the men dragging her along faster than she could walk across the wet, slippery ground she kept stumbling. Almost hitting the ground only for a set of rough hands to grab her, yank her up, and shove her forward.

Just hours ago, these peaceful woods had been a safe haven. A place to find comfort, to relax and recharge, to find the pieces of herself that had been missing since she was twenty and her life had changed forever.

Now they were like a wet, windy hellscape.

Was this going to be where her and Connor's story ended?

By the time they crossed the short distance from the generator where she'd found Connor's blood to the cabin, Becca was shaking badly. The freezing rain and howling winds whipped through her, but it was nothing compared to the gaping wound in her heart from not knowing if Connor was still alive.

Stepping inside gave relief from the storm, but she would much rather still be out there hunting for Connor than be protected from the worst of the weather.

There was no time for her to recover or even catch her breath before a hand between her shoulders shoved her down onto her knees.

Not content with her on her knees before them, someone kicked her, and she sprawled out on the floor. Pain flared through her body, and her palms slipped on the puddle she was creating as she tried to push herself back up.

Before she could, a foot planted itself on her back, holding her down, and laughter echoed over the raging storm outside.

She wasn't stupid, she knew what was going to happen to her.

Same thing that would have happened to her in Cambodia if Connor hadn't gotten them out of that camp before it could.

"Made it so easy for us," one of them taunted.

When she tilted her head as shoes stepped into her line of vision, she saw a man spinning the weapon she'd stupidly set on the ground when she found the blood and forgot to pick back up.

How could she do that? If she'd kept hold of it at least she might have stood a chance.

Connor would be so disappointed in her.

Tears of frustration burned the backs of her eyes. She knew better than to make such a silly mistake, and yet she'd been so focused on her fear for Connor, of losing him, that she hadn't been able to think of anything else.

Now Connor might die because of her stupidity.

If he was out there somewhere bleeding out and in need of first aid he wasn't going to get it. She was trapped, a captive of these men who had been sent after them, and he was all alone out there in the pouring rain.

I'm sorry, Connor.

"You're prettier in person than in your picture," another one told her as he knelt in front of her.

When he reached out toward her, Becca tried to shrink away, not wanting to feel more people touching her without her permission, but there was nowhere for her to go. The foot on her back held her in place, pressing hard enough that her healing ribs screamed for mercy.

Not that screaming or pleading for mercy would result in receiving any.

"Can you just wait one moment before you start drooling all over her," another of the men snapped irritably. "We have all the time in the world. She's not going anywhere, and neither is her boyfriend."

Boyfriend. She liked hearing someone call Connor hers, but right now her fear for him stole any joy it might have given.

The men said Connor wasn't going anywhere, but was that because he was dead? Because he was too badly injured to fight back? Or because they already had him restrained and tucked away somewhere?

"Put her in a chair, I want to get out of these wet clothes, then we can get started," another said, his tone lazy like he didn't have a care in the world.

Apparently, his word was law because the foot holding her down was suddenly gone and in its place were two sets of hands, grabbing her biceps and hauling her to her feet. Becca didn't even have a chance to get her bearings before she was shoved down into one of the solid wooden chairs that sat around the table. She'd sat in those chairs several times over the last couple of days, enjoying the smooth wood and rustic look. She'd even wondered if Cade, or one of his brothers, had made them by hand.

Now it felt too big, too strong, and as her wrists and ankle were firmly attached to the arms and leg of the chair, she knew there was no way she'd be able to fight her way out of them.

Upright again, she was able to get a better look at her captors. All six men prowling around the room were big, but not as big as Connor.

They were dressed all in black, and even if they hadn't lucked out with the timing of the storm they would have faded into the night.

Weapons hung from holsters on their hips, and the man who'd picked up the gun she had carelessly discarded was still spinning it on his finger even though she knew how dangerous that could be. He didn't seem to be worried about it, and when he saw she was looking at him he shot her a cocky grin.

"Can't wait to get my chance to play with you, beautiful," he taunted, stepping closer. Eyeing the weapon he was so carelessly playing with, his smile turned sinister. "Never played with a girl and a gun before." He snickered at his words. Then he shifted the weapon so it rested on the chair between her spread legs. "Could be fun," he added, nudging the gun closer until the muzzle brushed against her center.

"Would you knock that off," another of the men snapped, shoving the gun freak in the shoulder.

"Yeah," another added. "We're all supposed to get a turn before we hack her into pieces and have them delivered to the homes of her boyfriend's brothers. You keep that up and you're likely to kill her too soon."

Becca was still stuck on what was supposed to happen to her.

She was going to be viciously gang-raped, including with a gun if the sick look on the man's face was anything to go by, he was all in with his new idea. Then her body was going to be cut up and sent to Connor's family.

To Cade who had a little daughter who would be traumatized forever. To Cooper who had only just started a new relationship with a woman who had suffered at the hands of the people who had sent these men. To Cole who had likewise just started a relationship with another woman tormented by these men who thought they were untouchable. To Jake and Jax whose dad had been collateral damage and yet had never once backed away from supporting their stepbrothers in a hunt for answers.

That couldn't happen.

But how could she stop it?

She was tied up and helpless, surrounded by six big men who watched her like she was nothing more than prey they couldn't wait to pounce on, tear to pieces, and then devour. The storm raged outside, isolating her even further. No one would hear her screams when they were torn from her lips. And Connor was possibly dead, but at the very least, incapacitated in some way and wouldn't be swooping in to save her like he had in Cambodia.

Right as one of them reached out and palmed one of her breasts, an ear-shattering boom shook the cabin.

CHAPTER

Eighteen

August 23rd
1:26 A.M.

Kill.

That was the word that echoed through Connor's head as he ran through the torrent of rain pounding down around him.

Every single one of those men who had dared to put their hands on Becca, hurt her, scare her, they all deserved to die.

Slowly.

And painfully.

But since he wanted Becca safe more than he wanted those men to suffer, he'd suffice for just dead.

As badly as he wanted to run to one of the cabin windows, confirm that Becca was alive, and see what they were doing to her, he couldn't risk it. Not only would it waste time they didn't have, but if one of them caught sight of him before he was ready, it would ruin his plans.

So instead of following his instincts to creep up to the cabin, he bypassed it, circling it at a safe distance and heading for the small shed out the back.

Thankfully, when Cade and his then girlfriend had first bought this place it had been a wreck, about two steps up from dilapidated. The whole family had spent a lot of fun hours out there, rebuilding the cabin, crafting furniture to go inside it, sleeping under the stars at night, and cooking around an open fire. It had been wonderful, brought them all closer together, and even though he could never have foreseen how his life was going to turn out, that Becca would be back in it, and they'd both be there fighting for their lives, it meant that he knew every inch of the place.

Knew where the tools were. Was able to snatch up a hand saw without needing to be able to see where it was in the wall of tools inside the shed. It also meant he knew the perfect way to create a distraction that the men in the cabin couldn't attribute to him.

Once he had them outside, not only did it give him a clear shot at eliminating them, but it also lessened the threat to Becca.

With the saw in his hand, Connor barely noticed the rain, the screeching wind, or the throbbing pain in his shoulder as he ran for the tree closest to the cabin. When they'd been rebuilding the place, they'd debated for almost three weeks whether to leave it where it was or have it cut down. It was a beautiful old tree, and it provided shade for the cabin on hot summer days, but there was also the possibility that in a storm such as this, it could either topple over or lose a branch and damage the cabin.

Exactly his plan for tonight.

Well, he was going to do his best not to damage the cabin, but he also needed this to be real enough that it would get everybody's attention.

Climbing the tree in the middle of a raging storm with a saw in his hand and one of his shoulders messed up wasn't as easy as he would have liked, and he lost precious seconds. Once he was high enough that he could reach one of the branches that fanned out over the cabin, he sat, wrapped his legs around it, and shuffled his way along. When he was about halfway, he got to work.

The rain made everything slippery, and he almost lost his grip on the handle of the saw several times, but he was determined, which helped him fight back against the storm's advantages.

Becca was counting on him, and he wasn't going to let her down.

Not again.

Not ever again.

Nothing was going to stop him from saving her.

With a groan, the branch he sawed began to wobble, then with the most exhilarating sound, it broke off and slammed into the side of the cabin with a crash.

Because he hadn't cut off anything too big, damage to the cabin was minimal at best, not that Cade would care if he'd had to destroy the thing. Family. That was what was most important. The people you loved who loved you back, they were what life was all about. Raising his daughter alone after losing his wife meant Cade knew that better than most.

Fueled by adrenaline, Cade didn't bother climbing back down the tree, he simply jumped.

The landing was hard, but he barely felt the pain that ricocheted up his legs, and the now-soaked and muddy ground helped to cushion his landing, preventing him from breaking anything like he might have if he'd jumped that same distance twelve hours ago.

Just as he hit the ground, he saw the cabin door open, and four men came spilling out.

Four to his one.

Perfect odds.

Two of them ran for the branch that had just hit the cabin.

"Think it was the storm or him?" one of them yelled out, his voice getting carried by the wind so Connor could hear his every word.

"Probably the storm," another answered confidently.

"Where'd you hit him?" a third asked.

"Couldn't tell because it was so dark," the first man answered.

"If he'd given us the tools we needed, we could have finished this job properly," the fourth man huffed, clearly irritated.

"You know he said he didn't have time to pull everything together. Once he found out where they were he had to act right away," the confident man said.

"Yeah but we don't know if he's dead or alive."

"If he's alive he's plotting something."

"We all served, we have training," the confident man bragged.

"Yeah, but he's a SEAL, man, a freaking SEAL. You know those guys are trained way harder than we were," the man who had shot him said. "If I'd had the night vision goggles like I requested, he'd be dead, and we wouldn't be worried about it."

"Relax, dude. We have the girl. We have our fun with her like he told us we could, and then we kill her and cut up her body and send it to the family as a warning. If he's still alive, we at least know we hit him. When the storm lets up, we'll go looking for him," the confident man said like it was all that easy.

Rage burned inside him as he listened to their plans for Becca.

Not happening.

None of it.

"We should look for him now," one of the men insisted.

"Fine." The confident man sighed, long sufferingly. "Dingo and Mad, you two go looking for him, just in case it was him. Ridge and I will check the damage caused to the cabin, make sure it won't fall down or anything."

Perfect. They were going to split up and make his job so much easier than it would otherwise be.

Following the two men who peeled off from the cabin, he didn't even have to sacrifice speed for silence thanks to the storm.

The first man never knew what was happening.

One second, he was walking through the woods, the next, his hands were flying to his neck as Connor sliced the saw blade through his carotid artery.

Leaving the man to bleed out, he darted up to the one a few yards ahead of him. The man turned at the last second, probably to say something to his now-dying teammate.

"What the—?"

The man never got to finish his question. Connor plowed a fist into his solar plexus, shoving all the air from his lungs.

"Shouldn't have put your hands on my girl," he snarled as the other man sagged to his knees, attempting to gulp in oxygen. "The only easy day was yesterday. You'd know that if you were a SEAL, and you would have insisted on having the equipment you needed. Now you and your friends aren't going to be alive by the time the sun rises."

This time he used his weapon, firing a single bullet into the man's head, killing him instantly.

Echoing through the storm, he hoped the sound carried enough to reach the cabin.

Two men were outside and two inside, and while his SEAL training was indeed far superior to theirs, there was still the storm to consider.

A few seconds later he was rewarded by the sound of a voice.

"Was that a gunshot?"

"Just thunder," the confident man replied.

"Really? I know your nickname is Cocky but come on, dude," the other snapped irritably. "That was no thunder. Couldn't have been. Had to be a gunshot."

"Hey, you asked the question, so you don't know either," Cocky snapped back. "How the hell am I supposed to know anyway? It was supposed to be an easy job for a lot of money. Break the generator and kill the man when he came out to check. Then get the girl. This storm is ruining everything."

Actually, it was going to save his life, Connor thought.

Two shadowy figures came into view, and he dropped his saw and focused. At this distance, with the wind and the rain, it wasn't going to be an easy shot. He had to take out both before they could return fire.

Apparently, mother nature was on his side because right at that moment, a bolt of lightning lit up the night, and he took aim, going for the man called Ridge first since Cocky seemed too arrogant to be smart, Connor fired.

Then without wasting a single second, he fired again into the oppressive darkness right where he'd seen Cocky before the lightning had disappeared blanketing them in the dark again.

He'd hit them.

Neither of them had fired back which meant they were dead or dying.

As badly as he wanted to get to the cabin, he had to confirm though. He didn't want any nasty surprises popping back up.

Taking the saw with him in case it came in handy again, he closed the distance to where the two men were. Finding their bodies he confirmed both were deceased, then he took off at a dead run to the cabin.

I'm on my way, moonlight.

~

August 23rd
   1:31 A.M.

"What the hell was that?" one of the men asked, a hint of panic in his tone as though he feared the storm.

"Just the storm," the one who appeared to be the leader said in that lazy tone. He didn't seem fazed by whatever had just shaken the cabin. In fact, he'd taken off his wet shirt and tossed it carelessly onto the kitchen counter and was standing there eyeing her up like she was a piece of meat, and he was starving.

A gust of wind suddenly ripped through the cabin making her shiver as it made the wet clothes clinging to her feel like ice.

"Looks like a branch came down," someone called out from the door.

"See, just the storm," the leader drawled.

"Could be the guy," another countered. "We don't know how badly he was hit."

Please be Connor.

Please be Connor.

Please be Connor.

Becca chanted that over and over again. Because if Connor was responsible for a branch coming down and hitting the cabin and not the storm, it meant not only was he still alive, but he couldn't have been badly injured. Even if she was still consumed with anger toward Connor like she had been when he showed up in Cambodia, she still would have trusted him implicitly to get her out of this mess alive.

If anyone could do it, it was him.

Sitting tied to a chair, dripping wet, shaking uncontrollably, terrified of what these men were going to do to her, it finally sank in.

She trusted Connor.

Completely.

With everything.

Including her heart.

Despite everything else, Becca smiled. It felt so good to trust Connor again, to know that things were back to how they'd been before, how they were always supposed to be.

She would survive this.

She had to.

It didn't matter what the odds were, she had to survive because she had to say the words, had to tell Connor she trusted him again and she absolutely wanted to give him a second chance.

Determination flooded her system, and when the gun man stepped up close to her, nudging her chin, she met his eye squarely. She was still terrified, but she wasn't giving up and she wasn't giving in. Everything they took from her they were going to have to fight for.

"What are you smiling about, girl? You like the idea of playing with my gun as much as I do?" he taunted, dragging the tip of the weapon down her cheek and along her neck to her chest. He circled both her breasts and then pressed the muzzle above her heart.

While her heart rate increased, she maintained his gaze.

She wasn't backing down.

Connor was out there fighting for her, she was going to do the same in there.

"Cocky, Ridge, Mad, Dingo, go outside and check the damage, I don't want this cabin falling down around us, so we have to wait out the storm in the rain," the guy in charge ordered.

Please let the gun man be one of those he just mentioned.

Of all of the men in the cabin, gun man was the biggest threat to her because she absolutely didn't want to play his sick games and get raped by his weapon.

But he wasn't one of the men who headed out the door, he was still standing in front of her, still holding his weapon pressed to her chest, still leering at her with that expression that made her skin crawl.

The door slammed shut, taking the wind with it, but leaving behind that icy chill.

If it was Connor who had taken down that branch, she had no doubt he was going to kill the four men who had just headed back out into the stormy night. But that still left these two inside with her.

Did she have what it took to kill them if she got a chance?

When the man had attacked her in the camp she'd acted on instinct, stabbed him before he could hurt her.

This would be much more premeditated.

"Can I untie her?" gun man asked.

"She's scared, but she's got that determined glint in her eyes that says she's going to run if we give her a chance," the leader replied as he strolled over to her chair and studied her like she was a specimen under a microscope.

"So, I'll make it so she can't run," gun man said, and he lowered the weapon and knelt before her. "Don't think you'll be needing this." Removing her prosthetic, he flung it across the cabin, laughing when it hit the wall and bounced to the floor over by the fireplace.

Damn it.

He had stolen her ability to run.

She could hop on one leg, but she was easily catchable, and there was no way she could hop her way to safety outside in that storm with the ground so muddy and slippery.

"Problem solved," gun man sing-songed, and when the leader shrugged and drifted away to the kitchen, he made quick work of untying her other bonds.

Excitement danced through her blood.

He'd made a mistake.

Just because gun man didn't know it yet didn't change that fact.

She might not be as strong as Connor and didn't have his training or experience, she was a fighter and she wasn't going to give up.

Not when the future she'd always dreamed about was back within her grasp.

"I'm going to have fun with you, girl," gun man told her as his hands went to the hem of her sweater, and he tugged it over her head. In his eagerness to rid her of her clothes, her long, soaking wet hair tangled with the sopping wet top and she felt a sting in her scalp as he roughly yanked it free, tossing it aside.

The T-shirt she wore didn't do much to hide anything, it was plastered to her skin, and she was sure if the way gun man was practically drooling at her that it was half see-through as well.

His hardening length nudged against her knees, and then he was standing up, dragging her with him and lifting her onto the table. A hand on her breastbone shoved her back to lie against the smooth wood, and he wedged himself between her legs, forcing them open.

"So beautiful," he mumbled as his gaze drank her in, making her feel dirty as it lingered on the part of her that was only supposed to be touched with her permission.

But this man didn't care about permission.

In fact, he probably got off on the fact that he didn't have it.

"This is going to be fun." He grinned at her as he moved his weapon between her spread legs, dragging it along her center as though he thought that was going to turn her on.

There had to be something she could do to stop this. If she could just get her hands on that weapon, maybe she stood a chance. It wouldn't be easy, there were two of them, but she was going to try.

If nothing else, she was going to have to endure this sick man's games until Connor showed up and saved her.

Then gun man made a stupid move.

While he continued to stroke the weapon between her legs, he pressed his mouth to hers to kiss her.

Not happening.

Sinking her teeth into his bottom lip, Becca clamped her jaws together and didn't let go as he howled, and blood flooded into her mouth.

At the same time, the sound of gunshots echoed outside.

Knowing this was the opportunity she needed, Becca reached down and managed to grab the weapon, yanking on it as she shook her head from side-to-side, tearing through gun man's lip.

He howled again and backed up, his hands flying to his torn mouth as she lifted the weapon.

The other man stormed toward her so she aimed at him first and fired.

He dropped.

Without hesitation, she aimed at gun man. Realizing how stupid he'd been and the magnitude of his mistake, he charged at her, causing her to scuttle backward on the table and fall to the floor.

That was probably the only thing that saved her.

Pain darted up her back from the hard landing, but Becca shoved it away and lifted the weapon, firing at the man who had clambered up onto the table and was reaching down to try to grab hold of her.

He slumped down on the table, and she dragged in a breath, trying to calm her racing heart and refill her lungs with the oxygen panic and adrenaline had used up far too quickly.

Knowing she couldn't stay there in case the other men returned, Becca crawled to where her prosthetic had been thrown, and with trembling hands, put it back on. Then she shoved to her feet and ran for the door.

This time, she wasn't making the same mistake. She kept the weapon clutched in her hand as she threw open the door and stepped back out into the stormy night. With no idea where she was going, knowing only she wanted to put as much distance between herself and the cabin, Becca ran into the woods.

CHAPTER
Nineteen

August 23rd
   1:35 A.M.

Gunshots.

Connor could have sworn he'd just heard gunshots.

Over the roar of the storm, it was hard to be sure, but he thought that's what he'd just heard.

Since he'd killed four of the men who had come there tonight with the intent of killing him and Becca, only two were left behind. They would be watching over Becca, possibly hurting her although he couldn't allow himself to think too deeply about that right now.

The chances that Becca had gotten her hands on a weapon were slim to none.

That meant ...

As much as he didn't want to admit it, it likely meant that Becca was the one who had just been shot.

Twice.

Because he would have bet his life on the fact that he'd heard two gunshots.

Two gunshots meant two wounds.

Two wounds that could have either ended Becca's life or she was bleeding out from them right now.

He had to get to her.

Pushing himself harder, Connor ran full out through the storm. Several times he slipped, almost losing his balance. But he kept going. The need to get to Becca was too strong to be ignored. Nothing was going to get in his way. Nothing was going to stop him.

When he reached the bridge they'd played Poohsticks on just hours ago, Connor faltered for a moment. How had they gone from that perfect moment where they'd shared and taken another step to getting back what they'd had to this mess? To running through a raging storm, to fighting for their lives, to blood and death and pain?

Forcing himself to keep moving, Connor pushed harder, fought against the wind gusting against him, trying to push him backward, slow him down. The rain and the dark made it almost impossible to see more than a few yards ahead of him, but he didn't need to see. He knew where the cabin was, and he wasn't going to stop until he got there.

Finally, the cabin came into view.

Light still danced from the window so he knew that Becca and the other two men were inside.

Even though his heart urged him to keep running, to go bursting inside, to shoot anything that moved that wasn't Becca, Connor managed to cling to the last dregs of his self-control and slowed down.

Bursting in there could get Becca killed.

No way was he going to be responsible for her death.

If she was still alive.

Creeping up to the house, keeping to the shadows, approaching from the darker side of the house, Connor stopped when he reached the kitchen window.

There was no one in there.

The cabin stood empty.

Panic stole any remaining common sense he had left, and he bolted for the back door, flinging it open and stepping inside.

It looked pretty much the same as when he and Becca had gone up to bed before the storm rolled in and the generator went out. Except one of the chairs had been pulled away from the table and there were pieces of rope lying around it. Becca's sweater lay discarded on the floor, and as he scanned the room, he noticed the body lying on the ground.

Even in the thin light of the flashlight, he could tell it was too big to be hers.

That might have given him some relief if Becca was anywhere within sight.

The front door stood open, and other than the body, it didn't seem like anyone else was inside. Still, he hurried over to the body, crouched beside it, and reached out to touch his fingertips to the man's neck to confirm that he was indeed dead. He was. There was no pulse, and he could see that the man's chest wasn't rising and falling so he wasn't breathing. He was still warm, but it had only been a few minutes since he'd heard the gunshots.

The shot had hit him in the neck, and he'd bled out quickly. Who had fired the bullet?

Becca? If she had, how had she gotten her hands on a weapon?

The missing man? Had he shot his teammate and gone rogue?

Was that why Becca wasn't there now?

Shoving to his feet, Connor paced toward the stairs. He couldn't hear any sounds to indicate that someone was up there, but he intended to check. If they had fled out into the storm what did that mean? Where were they?

What the hell had gone on in this room?

Just as he passed the table, something caught his attention. A crack of lightning lit up the world outside, and some light filtered into the cabin. It illuminated the table, and he caught sight of something shimmering on the smooth wood.

It looked like something wet.

Blood.

There was a puddle of blood on the table.

Whose blood?

Becca's?

It was clear she'd been in the chair at some point, the men wouldn't have tied up one of their group, that made no sense. So she'd been the one in the chair and yet someone had cut her free. Why?

His gaze landed on the sweater.

It was soaked and lying in a puddle of water. He couldn't see Becca going out of her way to ask to take it off. She faced bigger problems than sitting in a wet sweater, and even if she had taken it off, her T-shirt and shorts would have been wet anyway.

Someone had taken it off her.

To rape her.

There was no other option.

It was the only thing that made sense, and he already knew what the men sent here had planned.

So one of the men had cut her free from her bonds with the intent of raping her only somehow she must have gotten away from him and gotten her hands on the weapon. She had to have been the one to shoot the other man because, otherwise, the two would have overpowered her together and she'd still be there.

She must have gotten another shot off as well, hit the man who'd been going to rape her. It had to be his blood on the table. With both out of commission, she must have taken her chance and run.

Out into the storm.

Only the second man wasn't dead.

And he wasn't in the cabin.

Connor's gaze shifted to the open front door. The other man must be out there hunting her, injured but still able to move, and now with a grudge against her.

Did Becca know she wasn't alone out there?

Did she know she was prey being hunted?

Locating the flashlight, Connor switched it off and pocketed it. If the man came back to the cabin, he didn't want to give him any advantage, and if he found Becca and she was hurt, he wanted to be able to attend to her.

Then he took off back into the storm.

It hadn't abated, if anything, it seemed to somehow be increasing in intensity. The wind was so strong even he was struggling to make progress against it, he couldn't imagine how much harder it was for Becca, who was not only so much smaller than him but had a prosthetic that would give her another disadvantage.

He ran through the woods, desperate for a sign of her, but there were none to track thanks to the rain. It felt like hours had passed since he woke to find the generator had gone out. In reality, it couldn't be more than an hour. Exhaustion hammered at him, though, the physical toll of running through the storm, along with the gunshot wound he'd gotten was getting to him.

Not that he had any plans of stopping.

The only thing that would stop him was finding his girl.

When he had her safe in his arms, they could sleep for a month.

Since he had no idea which direction Becca would most likely have gone, he was searching blind. She didn't know these woods like he did, she could be running closer to the road or away from it. She could be running toward the closest neighbor or further out into the woods. Or she could be running in circles.

Which was exactly what Connor felt like he was doing. He was trying to cover as much ground as he could in the shortest amount of time possible, so he was zig-zagging about, trying to find any sign that Becca had come this way.

He'd worked his way up a small mountain that he knew had a sheer cliff on the other side, a drop of around fifteen feet to the forest floor below and was about to turn around and work his way back down the mountain and head to the other side of the river when a crack of lightning lit up the night.

For one second, he saw her.

Becca. Standing on the edge of the cliff, looking away from him.

Unfortunately, he wasn't the only one to spot her right when she was at her most vulnerable.

One second, she was there, the next a body slammed into her, and she disappeared from view.

~

August 23rd
    2:02 A.M.

. . .

How long had she been running?

More importantly, how long could she keep going?

Becca trembled from cold and exhaustion. Her leg muscles were cramping, water had dribbled down her leg and gotten into the top of her prosthetic, making it slippery against her stump, and she kept losing her balance and hitting the ground hard.

Kept getting back up, though.

Now that she had this chance of freedom she wasn't going to waste it.

Only it felt like she *was* wasting it.

The storm had her all turned around, and by the time she'd run in a panic from the cabin and then calmed down a little, she was completely and utterly lost. She couldn't figure out which way led to the long, winding driveway that would get her to the road, and she couldn't remember which direction the closest neighbor was. She couldn't remember anything.

Which led to her just running wildly and hoping for the best.

Not a particularly smart plan, but what else did she have?

Even if she could find her way back to the cabin, it wasn't safe there. She was pretty sure she'd killed both the men, but she hadn't checked so there was a chance one of them was alive and waiting for her there. Connor had to be alive—she couldn't let herself think he was dead—and out here somewhere in the storm, but she had no idea how to find him.

All she could do was run and pray.

Those prayers came in pretty handy when she stumbled yet again, going down to her knees.

Only this time one of her hands landed on nothing but empty air.

Like it was happening in slow motion, Becca felt her body tip forward. Gravity and her body's momentum worked against her, and she was positive this was how she was going to die.

Her life flashed before her eyes.

Meaningful moments.

Shared with family and friends.

Laughter, joy, happiness.

Then darker ones.

Pain and loneliness.

Connor.

Her greatest love, her biggest betrayer, her hope for the future.

Her everything.

No.

She couldn't leave him.

Not like this.

Not when he could be out there somewhere needing her.

She couldn't give up now, she'd already done the hard part and escaped.

All that ran through her head in the half a second or so it took for her to shift her body weight so she could scramble backward away from the edge of the cliff.

Close.

Too close.

Ignoring her body, which was screaming at her to stay and rest, Becca instead shoved back to her feet. Through the dark, she looked down the side of the cliff she'd almost gone over. It was hard to see how steep the fall would have been, but she was glad she hadn't found out the hard way.

Right as she was about to turn and keep running in a different direction, a bolt of lightning lit up the sky and she got a clear look at what would have been her fate if she hadn't been able to pull herself back in time.

Becca gulped.

That had to be a fifteen-foot drop at least.

Possibly survivable, but not in good shape.

Certainly, not in good enough shape to find a way to get help for herself and Connor.

When something slammed into her, Becca was taken completely by surprise.

For a second, she thought it was just a gust of wind shoving her, then she thought it was a branch from a tree that had hit her.

It wasn't until she was falling that her brain finally clicked into place.

It wasn't the wind and it wasn't a branch.

It was a person.

A person who had shoved her right over the edge of the cliff she'd only just avoided falling over mere seconds earlier.

A scream was ripped from her lips. It was picked up by the wind and tossed about and she was sure that the only two people who heard it were her and whoever had just knocked her over.

Not that there was anyone else around to hear it anyway.

Neighbors were too far away. She had to believe that Connor had been able to kill the other men who had come after them, although she supposed there was a good chance that was just wishful thinking. They could be out there, hunting her, and Connor could be dead.

There was no conscious thought on her part to try to stop herself from hitting the ground.

Nothing more than instinct had her whipping out her hands, and when she found something to hang onto, her fingers curled around it of their own accord.

Her body jerked to a halt.

Stopping its descent abruptly.

Pain jerked through her shoulder, and the weight of another person hanging onto her almost made her let go.

Probably would have, but as she flailed wildly about, her feet were able to find some sort of purchase.

It wasn't much.

With all the rain, everything wasn't just wet, it was slippery to the point of barely being able to keep a grip on it. The wind only made it that much worse.

"Becca!"

Someone screamed her name, but it wasn't the man clinging to her stomach, his legs kicking wildly and almost making her lose her grip.

The voice came from somewhere above her.

"Becca!"

That sounded like … Connor?

All of a sudden, a bright light blinded her, and she cried out and quickly closed her eyes, so unprepared to be able to see anything that wasn't dark and rain and the odd glimpse of the woods that the sudden light sent pain stabbing through her skull.

"Connor?" she called out.

"Right here, moonlight," his soothing voice assured her.

Tears flooded down her cheeks, joining the steady stream of water. When she looked up, she could see his face as he'd adjusted the beam so it wasn't shining directly into her face.

"I thought you were ..." Becca trailed off unable to say the word.

"Ditto," he agreed.

"She's not going to live so say your goodbyes," a voice snarled right beside her ear, and she realized that whoever had knocked her off the cliff had shifted so he was pressed right against her back and reaching for the hand that clung to an old tree root.

It was the gun man.

She knew she'd shot him, thought he was dead, but he must have survived and come after her.

Now he had her.

She was too weak, too exhausted, and nowhere near strong enough to be able to stop him from taking her down with him.

Maybe she would survive the fall.

But maybe not.

And even if she did, she might wind up wishing she hadn't.

"You're not taking her away from me," Connor growled.

"Oh, I'm taking you down with us," gun man sneered, and she felt one of the hands wrapped around her waist like a vice move away.

Becca knew what he was going to do. He was going to grab the weapon that he almost definitely had on him, and he was going to shoot at Connor. Even though Connor was in a better position than either of them he wasn't going to move away from the edge so long as she was hanging there, seconds away from falling.

If she wanted to save the man she loved, she was going to have to sacrifice herself.

Something that, in the moment, Becca found easy to do.

She loved Connor and he'd been there for her through good times and bad. He'd made one mistake over a decade ago that had cost them the future they both wanted, but he'd never stopped loving her and she'd never stopped loving him.

If their positions were reversed, she knew he wouldn't hesitate to protect her.

She owed him nothing less.

By some absolute miracle, the weapon she'd left behind when she'd first spotted Connor's blood, but kept with her when she fled the cabin was still in her hand.

There was no time to worry about aiming. She couldn't see behind her, she could barely move without risking falling, and she could feel gun man moving, trying to get aim at Connor and take him out.

Not happening.

Shifting her arm behind her, Becca flinched when gun man fired his weapon at Connor. The sound was loud even though the wind stole most of it. Moving the gun until it pressed against the torso of the man intent on killing her, she fired.

A howl of pain tore through the night.

The arm around her waist tightened, almost making her lose her grip. She fired again.

The arm loosened a little.

She fired again, and again, and again until there were no bullets left.

Gun man was falling, the arm around her limp now.

"Becca!" Connor screamed and she saw him leaning over the edge just a couple of feet above her.

"I love you, and I want to give you—us—a second chance," she blurted out, just in case she did get taken down with gun man. If she was about to die, she needed Connor to hear those words.

But gun man drifted away, his hold on her disappeared, and just as she thought she had done the impossible and survived, she felt a tug on her prosthetic.

"Connor!" she cried out in panic.

The beam of the flashlight danced about. "Hold on, Becca. Don't let go. You hear me? Do not let go."

She wouldn't.

At least not if she could help it.

But the pull on her prosthetic was dragging her down.

Another shot fired, this one from Connor's weapon, and then gun man was gone, taking her prosthetic with him.

The smile filling her face died when she realized she was slipping too. His weight had been too much, and now with only one foot, she couldn't maintain her hold on the side of the cliff any longer.

CHAPTER Twenty

August 23rd
2:12 A.M.

Impulse.

It was the only thing that saved Becca's life.

Or at least gave her a fighting chance.

The man who had knocked her over the cliff, who had planned on taking her out with him, couldn't survive all the bullets she'd shot into him, and Connor's shot had merely finished what she'd started. But even in death, the man had tried to take her away from him.

Becca had lost her grip.

Been falling.

And purely on instinct he'd snatched out a hand and managed to grab hold of her wrist.

Now she was swinging wildly, dangling from his hand, and he'd dropped his grip on the flashlight, unable to hold it, his weapon, and Becca.

Of course, Becca was number one, the weapon was number two because even though all six men were dead, he didn't trust that more wouldn't come. He needed to be able to protect Becca against any threat and the only thing the flashlight provided was light.

So even though it had been a no-brainer to drop it in preference to his girl and his weapon it meant he couldn't see Becca very well. She was nothing more than the nickname he'd always called her, a pale shadowy circle, like faint moonlight, hanging below him.

Connor didn't need to be able to see her to know how scared she was.

He could feel her panic beating down on him as surely as the rain.

"Hold on, moonlight," he grunted out, struggling to maintain his grip. Not only was he holding her entire weight with the arm that had been shot, but she was swinging wildly, her fear making her panic, and the rain made everything, including her skin, slippery.

"I'm going to fall, I'm sorry," she babbled, her voice shrill above the howl of the storm.

"Why are you sorry, honey?" he asked as he stretched out on his stomach to stabilize himself better. Although it felt wrong to set his weapon down, safe was the last thing Connor felt right now, he knew he needed both hands to get Becca up on solid ground.

"Because I should have told you earlier that I wanted a second chance for us."

"You told me when you were ready," he assured her, reaching down with his now free hand.

"I was ready earlier, I just ... I couldn't say the words."

"Then you weren't really ready." Whether she'd been able to say the words or not, he'd known she was going to give him the chance he craved to rebuild what his stupid decision twelve years ago had cost them. He'd also been prepared to wait as long as it took for her to be in a place where she could say those words and mean them.

"I love you," she said with so much conviction that his heart felt like it was bursting.

"I love you, too, my beautiful, bright moonlight. Always and forever."

"Always and forever," she echoed.

"I won't let you fall, Becca, but I need you to help me, okay?" There was no time for him to work on soothing her, and the reality was, she wasn't going to calm down until she was no longer hanging over the edge of a cliff anyway.

"O-okay," she agreed.

"Reach up with your free hand and find mine. It should be about level with where I'm holding your wrist. When you feel it, I want you to grab onto me and not let go. I mean it, Becca. You don't let go for anything," he warned.

"What if ... what if I'm going to fall?"

"Then we fall together." It was that simple. As far as he was concerned, he didn't intend to live out the rest of his life without Becca being part of it. Either he got her up there with him and they both survived the night, or they both plunged over the edge, and their souls would be together in the next life.

"But—"

"No buts, Becca. Together. Always and forever."

"Always and forever," she echoed again.

A moment later, he felt her fingertips brushing against his hand and he quickly snagged a hold of them. After being out in the cold and the rain for so long, it was a wonder he could feel anything at all. His skin was a mixture of numb and aching, the pounding rain had been almost bruising in its strength, especially after spending so much time out in it.

"Got you," he told her, now holding her wrist and her hand securely. "I'm going to start moving backward, pulling you up with me."

"What do I do?"

"Nothing. If you try to help, you will only make your body swing more, making it harder. If you can get your foot braced firmly on the cliff face, let me know, and I'll tell you if I need you to do anything, otherwise your job is just to hang there."

Deadweight was, in fact, easier to maneuver than wriggling dead weight, so all he needed from Becca was for her to let him do all the work. Something he knew she would find difficult. She was strong and determined, but for this, all he needed was her trust.

Something that just a week ago he had been so sure he would never be able to regain.

But now, as he slowly worked his body backward on the slick, muddy ground, so very aware that at any moment he could slip and cause both himself and Becca to fall, he realized that he had it.

Completely.

She was doing everything he asked her to do, trusting that he would save her life.

Something he wouldn't fail at.

While it was unlikely the man who had taken her over the edge of the cliff would have been able to hit him, he'd seen the man raise a weapon, and Becca had shot him to save his life. His sweet girl who always wanted to see the best in people, had always looked for opportunities to help someone who needed it, and had dedicated her entire life to helping improve the quality of life for people in developing countries, had been willing to kill for him.

Never would he forget that.

It felt like it took him hours, but it couldn't have been more than a couple of minutes until Becca's head appeared over the top of the cliff.

Releasing his hold on her wrist, he grabbed her under the arm, then released his hold on her hand, hooked his other hand under her other arm, and pulled.

The next second, she was in his arms.

Nothing had ever felt as good as that moment. With Becca crushed against him, clinging to him, wrapped around him like an octopus, sobbing, her face buried against his neck, he'd never felt more in love with her. No matter how often he thought his love for her was already all-consuming, somehow, it managed to grow.

"I love you, Connor. So much. So much it hurts sometimes. I don't ever want us to be apart again. Not ever. Promise me." She sobbed, sounding borderline hysterical as she clutched at his face and held it between her hands. "Promise me we'll be together always and forever, just like you said."

No promise had ever been easier to make. "I promise you, moonlight. Always and forever. Nothing is ever going to make me leave you. Nothing. No matter how much life piles on top of us it's always me and you against the world. The way it's supposed to be."

With another sob, Becca crushed her mouth to his and kissed him, pouring into it everything she felt for him. He did the same, returning the kiss and not holding anything back. Every drop of love, respect, and passion for her came out until he felt like they were drowning in emotion.

It wasn't until he realized how badly Becca was shaking that he finally snapped to his senses. He had to get her back to the cabin, then he had to try to contact his brothers to let them know what had happened. Connor had no idea if there was any reception or if the storm had knocked it out, but if he couldn't call for help, he'd build a fire, bundle his girl in warm clothes and blankets, and they'd wait the storm out together.

Scooping her into his arms, he retrieved his weapon and then pushed to his feet.

"I can walk, Connor," Becca immediately protested, pushing lightly at his shoulders.

"I'm sure you could. I don't think there's anything you can't do. But you're missing your prosthetic, so you'd have to hop, and you're already exhausted. It would take too long, and you're already shaking from the cold. Besides, I like having you in my arms," he told her honestly.

With a content sigh, she stopped fighting him and snuggled into his embrace, nestling her head on his shoulder and allowing him to carry her.

Determination to get Becca safe and out of the storm fueled him, shoving aside the worst of his exhaustion, and he barely felt the pain in his shoulder, although he was sure once the adrenaline wore off it was going to hurt a lot. It didn't take him long to backtrack to the cabin, and he sighed in relief when it came into view.

Finally, safety, warmth, and rest were almost within his grasp.

At least that's what he thought until he stepped inside and heard a weapon cock as four shadowy figures appeared.

~

August 23rd
2:32 A.M.

. . .

No!

They were supposed to be safe.

Becca tightened her grip on Connor, so very aware that this could be the last time she ever got to touch him, as four men approached them.

"Sorry, moonlight, I should have scoped the place out first," Connor whispered against her ear, the warm puff of air against her chilled skin comforting. But it was a comfort that was going to be ripped away at any second.

"Not your fault," she whispered back. "I love you and I'm so glad we got to spend these last few days together. Thanks for coming to find me in Cambodia, and thanks for not leaving me at the cabin alone. I didn't realize how much healing I still had to do."

"Guess baby sister knew something after all," he said, and she felt the smile on his lips as he nuzzled her cheek. "I love you. I always have and I always will."

"Aww, isn't that sweet," a man mocked as hands grabbed at her ripping her away from the only man she would ever love.

If this was the end, Becca was truly grateful that the last of the wounds from her attack had finally healed and she'd gotten to spend her last days on Earth with the man who owned her heart. While she wished that things weren't going to end this way and she wasn't going to lose her chance at happiness for a second time, at least she'd forgiven Connor, and they'd worked through their issues.

This way she could die with a happy heart, at peace.

"It is sweet," she shot back, strength and determination that came from knowing she and Connor were one hundred percent in this together filled her up. Earlier, she'd fought for her life and won. As much as she was prepared not to win this time, she wasn't going to give up, and she knew Connor wasn't either. "It's something you won't ever understand because you don't know how to love so you can't know what it feels like to be in love."

"You got a big mouth for someone who's about to be dead soon," another man growled as she was manhandled over to the center of the room where the chair she'd been tied to earlier still sat.

"People have been trying to kill us all night, but we're still standing and they're not," she reminded him. This confident kick she was on would either get her killed quicker—more painfully—or it was going to provide them with an opportunity to strike back. Just because the odds were against them—and Becca wasn't pretending that they weren't—didn't mean she was counting Connor out.

After all, he'd somehow managed to convince her to forgive him, something she had spent twelve years being so certain could never happen.

Yet he'd done it in a matter of days by being open, honest, and giving her both the words and actions she needed to believe it.

If anyone could find a way to get them out of this, it was Connor.

A blow to the side of her face had her head snapping sideways and pain blooming, but what was new? She'd already been tossed about, threatened, and shoved off a cliff all in the space of a couple of hours. Adding more pain to that wasn't going to change their situation.

"You still got a big mouth, girly?" a different man asked, and even though she couldn't see anything more of him than a shadowy outline, she straightened and made sure she was looking right where she knew his face was.

"Nothing you do to us will change anything," she informed him.

"Becca," Connor admonished, and she could feel his fear for her. Fear that she was going to be hurt worse for speaking up, that she was drawing a larger target on her back, that seeing her assaulted might make him cave and give in.

But it wouldn't.

She wouldn't allow it.

"Sounds like your boyfriend has a different opinion," a man taunted.

"No, he doesn't," she said firmly, as much for Connor's benefit as these men. She and Connor were a team, they were in this together, and she loved his family as much as she loved her own. They deserved answers, they deserved to know who had been involved in raping their mom, Cassandra deserved to know the paternity of her sperm donor, and Carla Charleston deserved to have her name cleared.

She was afraid of the coming pain, no use pretending she wasn't, but so long as Connor had her back, she knew she could endure it. There wasn't anything she wouldn't endure for the people she loved.

"I don't care what they do to me, Connor. Don't let it sway you. They're bullies, they want our reactions, crave our fear, but I'm not giving it to them. We're not giving it to them. If they want to torture us, they can do that, but it's not going to change anything. It's not going to get you to agree to convince your brothers to back down. Just like our deaths aren't going to stop your brothers. If anything, it will only make them more determined. So do your worst," she told the men holding her arms. "But you should know that I bit the lip off the last man who put his hands on me, then killed his friend, and shot him when he tried to push me off a cliff."

Becca was proud of herself for not giving in to her fears tonight. She was fighting back, she was being someone she could be proud of, and if by some miracle she survived then knowing she hadn't given up would help her in the healing process.

"Let's see if you're still as mouthy after you get a little feel for the pain we're going to inflict," one of the men said as he grabbed her arm and bent it up behind her back.

"I was raped and dragged alongside the car when he shoved me out of it and drove off with me tangled in the seatbelt. I had skin ripped off, needed skin grafts, and wound up needing my foot amputated because they couldn't save it. Do you really think I don't know how to tolerate pain?"

"Maybe you can, but can he tolerate your pain?" the man holding her arm taunted Connor as he shoved it up higher and higher until she felt her shoulder joint pop out of its socket.

Being able to tolerate pain well didn't mean she was impervious to it, and she did cry out as her shoulder dislocated. But she was able to breathe through it and before the man could taunt Connor, she rushed to assure him.

"I'm okay. Don't give in, Connor. Please. I don't want to be the reason your family doesn't get answers. Whoever these men are, they're rich and powerful and if they hurt your mom they've done it to others as well. They have to be stopped, they deserve to be punished. I'm willing to sacrifice my life to make sure it happens. I don't want to, I wish we got the happy ending we deserve, but nothing is more important than family and doing the right thing. This is the right thing, it just sucks."

Connor let out a shaky breath, and she knew he was struggling to accept that he might have to stand by and not do anything to save her life. But she needed him to know that she wouldn't hold it against him, that she wanted him to do this, and she loved him even more because of his dedication to his family. They were her family, too, she loved every one of those men.

"I love you, Connor, and I don't blame you. Always and forever."

"Always and forever," he echoed just like she'd done when they were out in the woods, and he was trying to calm her down so he could get her back on solid ground.

"So sweet," the man who'd dislocated her shoulder snapped as he shoved her violently to the floor. Becca could tell they were getting annoyed because they weren't receiving the kind of reaction from her and Connor they wanted, that they'd expected.

"So stupid," another sneered.

A foot connected with her hip, sending pain spiraling through her body as she went skidding across the floor.

Something, and she wasn't sure what, some previously buried survival instinct, some ingrained self-defense mechanism, some deeply rooted desire to survive, had her reaching out and grabbing onto the foot that had kicked her. As she went skidding sideways she took the man down with her.

Like that was the domino that sent all the others tumbling down along with it, the cabin exploded into a flurry of activity.

People shouted.

Guns fired.

The storm continued to rage outside.

And Becca prayed that by some miracle she and Connor would survive.

CHAPTER
Twenty-One

August 23rd
2:38 A.M.

Chaos.

Pure bedlam erupted in the cabin when Becca fell to the floor and somehow managed to take one of the men down with her.

It was the chance that Connor had been waiting for, and he didn't hesitate to grab hold and run with it.

While he absolutely hated how mouthy Becca had been with the men, at the same time he was incredibly proud of her for refusing to cower and showing everyone how powerful and strong she was, his heart just couldn't handle the fear, she'd caused an unexpected consequence. The men had been so focused on her, so irritated that she wasn't cowering at their feet begging and pleading for her life that they hadn't been smart.

Not immediately restraining both him and Becca, but at the very least him if they wanted to taunt him with images of Becca being assaulted, was the biggest mistake they could have made.

Now they were paying for it.

Coming in low, using the fact that the cabin was still almost pitch black and the men didn't appear to be wearing any NVGs, to his advantage, Connor plowed his shoulder into the nearest man, taking them both down.

They tussled, but Connor had something the other man didn't.

Rage.

This was a job to these men. Nothing more, nothing less. They had likely been looking forward to it, enjoying the free rein to do whatever they wanted to a helpless woman, no rules, no holding back. It would feed their sick desires, but they weren't invested in this the way he was.

Connor wasn't just fighting for his life.

Wasn't even fighting just for Becca's life.

He was fighting for his future.

For everything he'd always wanted, everything he'd always dreamed about, everything he'd had and ruined by one moment of letting his emotions and fears get the best of him.

There was no way he could lose.

So he threw punch after punch, aware of the sounds of people scrambling around him. He had no idea where Becca had gone, but he sincerely hoped she'd managed to tuck herself away someplace where no one would be able to find her.

Arms locked around his neck, dragging him backward.

He was throbbing all over because the man he'd been beating had gotten in a few hits of his own, but none of it was enough to disable him.

Ramming his elbows backward into the man's stomach, shoving the air from his lungs, he slammed his head backward at the same time, and was rewarded with a pained yelp that told him he'd just broken the other man's nose.

Taking advantage of his momentary distraction, he broke free of the man's hold and slammed his fist into his assailant's neck, dropping him instantly.

The man he'd been beating on was still down, dead possibly, at the least disabled, and no longer a threat. That still left two other men in the cabin somewhere.

As much as it was helping him, the dark was still a hindrance, he could see shadowy figures moving about but it was more instincts than anything else that had him throwing himself sideways right before a bevy of bullets rained down on the spot he'd just been standing in.

Keeping low, he circled the cabin to where the shots had been fired from and heard muted whispers as the remaining two men obviously tried to figure out a plan where they didn't wind up dead along with everyone else.

Not happening.

None of them were leaving there alive.

"Where is he?" one man muttered.

"Has to be here somewhere," the other said.

"How did he take down Smoke and Roller so quickly?" the other asked.

"He's a SEAL, thinks he's better than us," the other replied.

"He *is* better than us," the first said, a thread of fear in his voice.

"No, he's not. Find the girl. We get the woman then we control the man."

Please be somewhere safe, moonlight.

As the two men shifted further away from him, Connor aimed for the closest one and pounced.

With the dark obscuring a clear view of anything, although he was able to deliver a blow to the man's head it wasn't enough to take him down, and he spun, raising his weapon.

Aiming for the man's arm, he grabbed his wrist and elbow and yanked both in the opposite directions, hearing the satisfying sound of bone snapping as the man howled in agony, the weapon clattering to the wooden floor, skidding off into the dark.

As Connor was about to finish him off, two shadowy figures moving toward him stopped him in his tracks.

"I wouldn't do that if I was you," the man who had been so confident that he had what it took to destroy Connor despite his superior training said in a sing-song voice. "Not unless you want me to blow the brains out of her pretty little head."

Despite the dark, he could make out Becca's much smaller frame angled in front of the man's larger one. He could also make out the outline of a weapon held pressed against her temple.

One shot was all it would take to end Becca's life.

To snatch her away from him and if that happened, he would much rather join her in death than live out the rest of his life without her.

Because he had no other choice he froze, holding himself perfectly still so that the man who had Becca in his grasp would see that he was complying and removing himself as a threat.

"Kill them, Connor. Go for the gun," Becca shouted, her voice so brave, so strong despite the fact there was a gun to her head, that his heart swelled with love for her.

"He can't, beautiful," the other man taunted. "He moves, you die."

"I don't care. So long as you die too then it's worth it," Becca spat back. "Besides, he already took down three of you. You really think he can't take down you as well?"

"Not if he wants to keep you breathing he won't," the man told her. "Deakin, you okay, man?"

A groan was the only response the man whose arm he'd just broken gave, but now he knew at least one of the other men in the room were still alive. He doubted that the man he'd struck in the neck was, and the man he'd been beating he'd give a fifty-fifty chance of still breathing.

"Okay, here's what's going to happen. You're going to get down on your knees, I'm going to throw you some handcuffs, and you're going to cuff your arms behind your back. Then you're going to stay on your knees while I tie up your girl. One wrong move and I shoot her. I'm thinking I'll start with her kneecaps and see where I go from there," the man with the gun informed him.

It went against everything he had been trained to do, but when the handcuffs clinked onto the floorboards in front of him, he picked them up.

He'd snapped one end around his left wrist when he felt it.

A change in the atmosphere.

Something he couldn't quite put his finger on, but as soon as he felt the shift a bullet whizzed through the air.

Fear for Becca had him lunging toward her despite the possible risk. Just as he snatched her into his arms, he realized it was the man who'd been holding a gun to her head who had been shot.

Was it deliberate or did someone hit the wrong target because of the lack of visibility?

He got his answer a moment later when light suddenly flooded the cabin as several torches lit up and multiple people came strolling in.

"You're welcome, bro," Cooper's voice called out and Connor relaxed.

"Guess it wasn't the storm that took out my generator," Cade grumbled as he no doubt took in the mess of blood and bodies littering his cute little cabin.

"I've got four dead but this one's still alive," Jax announced.

One alive.

Perfect.

That was exactly what they needed.

Relief was so strong it almost stole his breath. They were still alive, he hadn't lost Becca, hadn't lost the second chance she had gifted him.

"Moonlight?" he asked as he shifted his hold on her.

In the stark light of the flashlight beams, she looked much too pale, they were both still wet, and he could see lines of pain bracketing her mouth. But she was alive and that was a win as far as he was concerned.

"I'm okay," she assured him as her gaze roamed him, no doubt searching for additional injuries other than the gunshot wound she already knew about.

"We'll get your shoulder put back in for you, sweetheart," he said, stroking his hand down her wet hair then palming her cheek. "Cole, I need your help. Becca has a dislocated shoulder."

"Let me see, honey," Cole said as he hunkered down beside him.

"How'd you know we needed help?" Connor asked his little brother.

"Your girl here called Cade to tell him about the generator going out," Cole replied.

"I wasn't sure he heard me say that I didn't think it was the storm," Becca said.

"He got that and rallied the troops. We got here as soon as we could, but it seems you guys mostly had things under control. Mostly," Cole added in a teasing tone. "Still needed our help though."

"You guys saved Becca's life, I can't ever thank you enough for that,"

Connor said, finding it difficult to get the words out past the lump in his throat.

"Nah, no need for thanks. You all helped me with Susanna, and we all helped Coop with Willow. I'd say we're pretty even. All right, Bec, let's get this shoulder back in place for you, that should help a lot with the pain," Cole told her as he placed a hand on her shoulder and shifted so he would be able to manipulate it back into the socket. Connor moved too so that between the two of them they'd get it done quicker.

"Connor, wait!" Becca cried out, and he froze.

"What? What's wrong?" he demanded.

She chewed on her bottom lip in the most adorably uncertain way. "Before you ... put it back in, I need the penis."

August 23rd
2:44 A.M.

"You need the what?" Cade demanded, almost choking himself.

Becca felt her cheeks heat. Right. She hadn't thought how that would sound saying it out loud to a bunch of men who weren't aware—at least she didn't think they were—of her and Connor's little collection of penis stuffies.

Connor threw back his head and laughed. "She means my penis."

"Your what?" In the dim light of the torches, Cooper's eyes about bugged out of his head.

"You're incorrigible," she told Connor, swatting at his shoulder with her good hand. "He doesn't mean *his* penis." At least not yet, although she would for sure need it later when the adrenaline wore off and the fear settled in. "I meant the plushie that he brought me. It's upstairs in the bedroom, and I ... wouldn't mind holding onto it while you put my shoulder back in." It was a poor comparison to having the real thing in her mouth, but that wasn't appropriate when his brothers were in the room with them so she'd settle for the toy.

"I'll go get it," Cole offered, clearly trying not to laugh.

"Thank you," she whispered, a little mortified that she'd just blurted that out in front of men she considered brothers. Becca decided she'd blame it on the exhaustion that weighed heavily against her body, the throbbing pain that pounded through her, and the fact that she and Connor had almost died in this room.

Never would she forget the feel of the cold metal pressed to her temple.

It wasn't the first time she'd been close enough to death to feel it curl its fingers around her life, squeezing just enough for her to realize the strength of its power.

But it was the first time that Connor had been right there.

When Dylan Sanders had assaulted her, she'd been alone. When she'd been in the cabin earlier and threatened with rape and death she'd been alone, even when she'd gone over the edge of the cliff, she'd been alone even though Connor had been close by. But this, he would have gotten a front seat to every horrific second of torture and she couldn't seem to get over that.

Maybe because she knew how much she couldn't have coped with watching him be killed and she knew just what she'd been asking of him to not cave and give the men what they wanted no matter what they did to her.

"Here you go, Bec," Cole said as he pushed the penis plushie into her hand.

Immediately, she felt some of her tension recede. This really wasn't as good as having Connor's in her mouth, but it was better than nothing. Enough at least to get her through the next few unpleasant moments.

"Won't take long, moonlight," Connor assured her, and she managed a nod for him because the last thing she wanted to do was worry him when she knew he must be feeling as exhausted and emotionally strung out as she was.

Lifting the plushie to her face, she brushed it across her cheek and closed her eyes, doing her best to imagine the silly toy was really Connor. Trying to ignore it as Connor and Cole positioned themselves by her dislocated shoulder, it hurt, but somehow it was the fear of how badly it was going to hurt when it was put back into place that was worse.

It was over quicker than she would have thought.

A muted grunt of pain as they manipulated the joint and suddenly it was back in and the pressure in her shoulder was gone. It still hurt, but it wasn't the pulsing pain that had been there when it was popped out.

"You did amazing, baby girl," Connor whispered, nuzzling her cheek alongside the plushie while Cole slipped a sling around her neck and tucked her arm into it.

That helped ease the pressure in her shoulder even more and now wave after wave of exhaustion was buffeting against her. All she wanted was to change into dry clothes, crawl into a warm bed, feel Connor's body wrapped around her, and sleep for a week.

Soon, but not yet.

Fighting against the weariness weighing her down, Becca blinked open heavy eyes. "Connor got shot," she told his brothers.

"What?" Cole asked sharply.

"It's fine. Flesh wound. Becca was more important," Connor said like it was obvious.

"I'm all taken care of now," she told the man she loved. There were other wounds she was sure she had, bruises, scratches, she hurt all over, so it was hard to narrow anything down to any particular location. But she was okay. She wasn't going to die from any of those injuries and she was worried that Connor's gunshot wound was worse than he'd been letting on.

Just because he'd pulled her up the side of the cliff and carried her back to the cabin didn't mean that his wound wasn't serious. She knew there was nothing he wouldn't do for her, including downplaying an injury so she didn't worry.

"Can you check him out please?" she asked Cole.

"I'm fine," Connor insisted.

When she looked up at his face, dirt-streaked, hair still wet and sticking up at weird angles, lines of exhaustion bracketing his mouth, Becca found tears flooding her eyes. She could have lost him tonight. They'd been so close. If his brothers hadn't shown up when they did, she had no doubts she'd be dead by now. She'd pushed too hard, and the men were itching to take her out.

"Please," she whispered as she chewed on her bottom lip to hold in a sob even as a couple of tears rolled free.

"Okay, honey." His hand swept down from the top of her head, settling on her cheek where his fingers caressed her skin for a moment before he nodded to Cole.

With worried eyes, she watched as Cole probed Connor's shoulder, watching for signs that the man she loved was in more pain than he'd been letting on. But she didn't see any tightening of his mouth, and Connor didn't grunt or whimper in pain. Didn't do anything, just held her steady gaze until Cole finished his examination.

"He's good, Becca," Cole assured her. "You both need a hospital but he's okay."

"Just a flesh wound?" she checked.

"Just a flesh wound," Cole repeated.

"Cole, can you take her out to the car," Connor asked.

"Why can't you? Where are you going?" she demanded, panic making her voice shriller than she'd intended. But after the last few hours, the last thing she wanted was to be away from Connor for any reason for even a single second.

"There's something I have to do but I'll be with you in a moment," Connor told her, his gaze flitting over to where Jake and Jax were standing over the only man who had survived, and she knew what he wanted to do. He wanted to question the man, get answers any way he could, and he didn't want her to see it.

"Can't they do that?" she asked, hating to be needy now that it was all over when she'd been able to be confident and strong while in the middle of their ordeal, but she was crashing quickly. Everything was sinking in, what had happened, what could have happened, and she didn't want to be alone.

"I need to do this, moonlight. They were going to torture you and kill you. I won't be long, okay? Promise. And Cole and Cooper will go with you."

When she managed a small nod, Connor leaned in and kissed her, then nodded to Cole when he pulled back. Cole scooped her up, carrying her outside. It was still raining and even though the car was fairly close to the cabin, she was drenched all over again by the time Cooper opened the back door of the SUV and Cole slid her in.

While Cooper climbed in beside her, tucking a blanket around her, Cole got in the front and turned on the engine, blasting the heaters as high as they'd go. It didn't really help. A chill had settled inside her, and only Connor could warm it up.

Keeping the plushie clutched in her hands, stroking it against her cheek, Becca did her best to imagine it was really Connor. She needed him now, in a way she couldn't have him until they were alone, but at least she could curl into his side, reassure herself that he was alive, she was alive, and their second chance hadn't been stolen.

A scream ripped through the night, howling above the roar of the wind and she clenched her eyes closed.

Another followed and another.

Cooper turned her into his arms, and she burrowed into him. It wasn't that she didn't understand why Connor was trying to get answers any way he could, she did, his whole family wasn't safe while these men were still out there. The man deserved whatever he'd got as well, it was just there had been so much pain and blood tonight and she just wanted it to be over.

Could have been minutes could have been much longer, but eventually the door opened and Connor slid into the seat beside her.

Immediately, she was on his lap, wrapped up in his arms, and snuggled against him. "Did you get answers?"

"Said he didn't know who hired them," Connor replied.

"Do you believe him?"

"Yeah. He and his friends are all former military. All had trouble with the law since they got out and hung around together at a local bar. Someone paid them a lot of money to come here tonight and torture and kill you, then kill me but pretend they'd kidnapped me. Use sending your body to my brothers as a threat of what they'd do to me if they didn't back off."

"But they didn't," she reminded him, feeling the tension in his hard body.

"No, they didn't." His lips touched the top of her head, and his arms banded around her, and for the first time all night, she felt safe.

Safe with Connor.

Always.

All of her.

Even her heart.

CHAPTER
Twenty~Two

August 24th
12:44 A.M.

It was almost time to shut this down.

Connor knew his family wanted to rally around him and Becca, wanted to make sure they were doing okay physically and emotionally, and make sure they knew they were safe now and no one was getting to them, but it was reaching the point where Becca had had enough.

It had been a really long day.

While at the time it had felt like their ordeal had gone on for hours and hours, not quite two hours had passed from when he first woke up to find the room dark, to when his brothers had come bursting into the cabin saving his and Becca's lives. Even after they'd piled into the car and waited for cops and paramedics to arrive, there had been no time for rest.

Hour after hour of giving statements to the point where he was ready to start ripping throats out of any person who kept pushing Becca so hard, she was shaking and doing her best not to cry. He knew the cops weren't trying to upset her, they were trying to gather as much intel as they could to identify the men who were determined to see his family dead.

They had been checked over by medics and doctors at the hospital. Scans and poking and prodding he'd tolerated only because he knew that Becca wouldn't settle until a medical professional assured her that he was okay. And he was. The gunshot wound had been stitched closed, and he had no other injuries aside from bruises from his fights with the men who had attacked the cabin.

Likewise, Becca had bruises and a few scrapes and cuts from running through the woods, but her most serious injury was the dislocated shoulder. He and Cole had gotten it back into place so aside from resting the joint there wasn't much more to do for it.

They were okay, but he knew Becca needed some time just the two of them. The way her fingers twitched as they rested on his thigh, snuggled beside him on the couch. The way she clutched that silly penis plushie in her hand, raising it often to brush across her cheek. The way she kept sneaking gazes at his lap while trying to pretend she wasn't.

His girl had done amazing last night, he couldn't have asked her to do any more than she had. But she was human, that last couple of weeks had been trauma on top of trauma on top of trauma. From his reappearing in her life, to everything that happened in Cambodia, to what happened at Cade's cabin. It was a lot for her to shoulder, and she was trying to hold it together as best as she could, but he knew what she needed.

And for that they needed privacy.

"Okay, guys, I hate to kick you out at midnight, but ..." he trailed off, hoping his brothers would take the hint.

"But you and Becca want some alone time," Willow said, and he shot the woman a grateful smile. Both she and Susanna had fitted in so seamlessly with their family that it was hard to believe they hadn't been around forever.

"We appreciate you all hanging with us," Becca quickly added.

"It's okay, pipsqueak, we get it, you want time with my twin and his penis," Cooper teased with an exaggerated shudder.

"Cooper," Willow rebuked her boyfriend, swatting at him.

Although her cheeks were pink, Becca met his twin brother's gaze and gave him a lazy smile before looking over to Willow. "We'll have to trade stories one day, compare notes, see who got the better-endowed twin."

Everyone laughed and Cole slapped Cooper's back. "Burn, dude."

Cooper rolled his eyes but grinned at Becca. "All joking aside, you did awesome last night. You're a fighter and you've always been a part of this family. If my jerk of a twin messes up again, you let me know and I'll set him straight for you."

"I don't think he's going to mess up again," Becca said, and honestly no words she could have said would have meant more to him.

"He better not," Cade said, shooting him that big brother frown he'd gotten used to when they were growing up. As the oldest of all seven of him and his siblings, Cade had taken on a parent figure role even though he wasn't much older than them. Taking Cassandra out of the equation since she was six years younger than Cole, between Cole and Cade there were only four years, but back then it had felt like that was a bigger gap than it was, and Cade had stepped up and looked out for all of them.

"I won't," he assured his brothers.

"Good, because it would be stupid to mess up something like this," Jax told him.

"It would," Connor readily agreed.

"Here, let me take her," Cade said to Gabriella who had gathered up a sleeping Esther into her arms.

"Thanks, she's getting so big and heavy," Gabriella said, her gaze lingering on Cade as he lifted his daughter, settling her against his chest with her head using his shoulder as a pillow.

It was the worst-kept secret in the family that Gabriella was in love with her boss. Cade was either blind to it or it was unrequited love, but whatever wound up happening or not happening between the two of them, Gabriella had been Essie's nanny for years and she was a part of their family.

"Can't believe she's going to be starting kindergarten in just a few weeks," Cade murmured as he snuggled his daughter closer. It was a shame his big brother couldn't see what was staring him in the face. Just because he'd lost the wife he'd loved didn't mean he didn't have another chance at happiness standing right in front of him. All he had to do was get out of his own way and reach out and take it.

Something Connor, unfortunately, knew all too much about.

But he had stepped out of his own way, stopped letting his guilt and shame stand between him and Becca, and now he had the second chance he'd craved with the woman he loved.

"We'll keep her safe," Jake assured Cade, whose face had taken on a worried expression. "We'll keep all of us safe. They aren't getting to us again."

They were all taking precautions to make sure that happened. Bodyguards were hired for Willow, Susanna, Becca, Gabriella, and Esther. There were no other lost loves floating around out there for Jake or Jax that could be in danger. They were all going to try to distance themselves from any friends or neighbors they feared could be targeted, and they were doubling down their efforts to get answers.

It was all they could do for now and they had to pray it was enough.

Leaving Becca on the couch, Connor followed his brothers and their girlfriends to the front door so he could set the alarm. While he and Becca had been at the hospital and giving statements, he'd had his entire system upgraded, there were cameras everywhere, the system would send alerts to his brother and local law enforcement, and he had a whole stash of weapons. Becca was going to be living with him from here on out and he wasn't going to risk her safety for anything.

Becca was yawning when he headed back into the living room and his entire being softened at the sight of her, especially when she gave him a sleepy smile.

"You ready for bed, moonlight?" he asked as he went to her and gathered her into his arms.

"Mmm, yeah. Thought for a while I'd never get to curl up in a bed beside you again." Her face nuzzled his neck as he carried her upstairs.

So had he.

For a while, he'd thought he was never going to be able to touch her, hold her, kiss her, or make love to her. That the chance he'd worked hard to prove to Becca he was worthy of would have been for nothing.

"What do you want, baby? A bath, shower, sex, sleep?" he asked in his bedroom.

"You know what I want," she whispered, a distinct sleepy note to her voice.

"Okay, sweetheart." Setting her on her feet, Connor stripped off her clothes, and then his own, and pulled back the covers. Scooping Becca up again he laid her down then stretched out beside her.

As soon as he was lying down, she crawled down his body until she could take his length inside her mouth. Pulling the blankets up enough to cover Becca, leaving his torso exposed, Connor tangled his hand in her hair and began to massage her scalp.

Moments later she drifted off to sleep, her lips still around his length.

There was no better way to fall asleep after the events of the last day than in his bed, in the home he'd bought with Becca in mind, buried inside her hot mouth, and Connor couldn't be happier.

~

August 24th
9:27 A.M.

Becca grumbled when she woke up to find that Connor's length was no longer in her mouth.

This wasn't the first time she'd fallen asleep that way, so she knew that it always slipped out as soon as she drifted off but she missed the comforting and reassuring feel and taste of him between her lips.

She had a vague recollection of waking at some time during the night, grabbing the covers Connor had tucked up to her shoulders leaving his torso uncovered, and fixing that. She liked being completely cocooned under the soft blankets, the dark of it different than the dark at the cabin had been, warmer, cozier, safer.

Other than losing her hold on Connor, she hadn't shifted much, she was still curled in a ball against his leg, her cheek pillowed on his muscular thigh. One of his hands rested on her head, his fingers lightly tangled in her hair, the slight sting as reassuring as the warmth and strength in the leg she nuzzled her cheek against.

Her movement alerted Connor that she was awake. His fingers shifted, stroking along her scalp, and she moaned and reached out a hand to grasp his hardening length. She smoothed her fingers along him, enjoying the way he continued to harden at her touch. It was powerful feeling in control of who she touched and who got to touch her.

With Connor she was truly safe, and it was such a heady feeling that she opened her mouth and shifted so she was straddling his legs and took him between her lips, sucking long and hard, savoring the feel and taste of him, something she'd thought she would never have again.

"Mmm, baby, I could get used to waking up like this every morning," Connor moaned, his hands tangling in her loose locks.

Becca hummed her agreement around his length making him groan, his fingers tightening.

Power.

Control.

Both were important to her.

But equally as important was the fact that Connor loved her. He happily gave up power and control and handed them to her because he loved her, because he wanted her to know she was safe with him, and he only wanted what was best for her.

Warmth blossomed in her chest, unfurling throughout her and sending tendrils of pleasure to every inch of her body.

She really could get used to starting her days like this, and she could.

This reality wasn't just within her grasp, it was right here, right now. With the danger surrounding the Charleston Holloway family, and the fact that she didn't even have a place to stay since she lived in Cambodia, she'd already agreed to move in with Connor. She wouldn't risk taking that danger home to her family, and besides, she wanted to be with Connor.

They'd wasted enough time, no more.

No more.

With a growl, Connor suddenly reached under her arms and dragged her up his body, flipping them over in one smooth move so she was laid out beneath him, a hungry glint in his blue eyes.

"I'm not coming before my girl," he told her, crushing his mouth to hers in a steamy kiss.

"Connor," she whined, missing the taste of him already. "I wanted—"

"And you will. After. But first I'm going to make you come over and over again until you can't think, can barely breathe, then I'm going to come inside you, filling you up because even though you can't get pregnant at the moment, I can't wait until our baby is growing inside you."

"Connor," she whined again, breathily this time, her body squirming with the need to be filled, because the thought of carrying Connor's baby was everything she'd always wanted as a child and everything she'd lost when their son hadn't survived. She'd had a great family growing up, and before his parents' deaths, Connor had, too. It had always been her dream to start a family of their own and make it every bit as amazing. Just because they'd lost their first child didn't mean they still couldn't have that family, and when they did, she'd make sure they never forgot their tiny baby boy.

Part of her future was uncertain. She didn't know if she was going to go back to Cambodia or somewhere else or take a more managerial position and stay with Connor, but it didn't matter, they'd work it out.

"Shh, baby, I got you." Connor pressed another kiss to her lips and then he was trailing kisses down her body. He paused in his descent to lick and nip lightly at the pulse point on her neck, making it pound wildly as need coursed through her.

Next stop was her breasts. Featherlight kisses brushed against first one nipple and then the other. His mouth closed around one, sucking hard then pulling back and breathing out a puff of warm air causing her nipple to pebble. He repeated that with her other breast and then he was moving down her body again.

When he nudged her legs, she readily opened wide to him, loving the sight of his large body and dark head settled between her thighs.

His lips pressed the softest of kiss to her center, and light as it was it sent little shards of lighting zinging through her body, tiny bolts of pleasure, just a prelude of what was to come and already she was squirming with need.

Large hands grabbed her hips, holding her in place as Connor devoured her. His lips and tongue seemed to be everywhere at once, delving inside her, suckling on her greedy little bud that soaked up every drop of attention it was given.

Pleasure built steadily inside her, growing rapidly until it suddenly cascaded over her as she cried out Connor's name. There was no time to process it, no time to float back down because Connor wasn't letting up. He kept going as though she hadn't come, licking, sucking, flicking his tongue against her bundle of nerves, dragging a second orgasm out of her.

Then a third.

And a fourth.

Tears streamed down her cheeks, her fingers curled in his short hair, she was begging and pleading, only Becca wasn't quite sure if she was asking for more or asking him to stop because she was sure she couldn't possibly come again.

Only she did.

After wringing a fifth mind-blowing orgasm out of her, Connor shifted back up her body. His grin was both smug and tender, and he looked so satisfied with his efforts that she couldn't help but give a shaky laugh.

"You outdid yourself this morning," she said, tracing her fingertips along his stubbled jaw.

"Just going to get better from here on out, moonlight," he told her as he lined up and sank inside her in one smooth thrust.

She moaned as he filled her so perfectly and lifted her legs to hook her foot around his hips, drawing him deeper. If it was possible, Becca would be perfectly content to spend the rest of her life like this with Connor buried inside her, their bodies joined in the most intimate of ways.

Each thrust was slow and sensual, building something powerful inside her. It started low in her belly, tingling and sending fire along her already overstimulated nerves. While he thrusted in and out of her, Connor kissed her, every bit as slow and sensual as he moved his hips.

That feeling continued to build, and when Connor reached between them, touching her where their bodies were joined a sixth powerful orgasm rushed through her. It hit every part of her body, consuming her in a fiery ball of pleasure.

Aftershocks were still rippling through her when she met Connor's gaze, the love that shone from his eyes took her breath away. How had she ever believed, even for a moment, that this man didn't love her?

There was no way to get back the lost years, so there was no point in worrying over the fact that they should already be married with kids. Those years were gone, but there were still so many years stretched out before them.

Years where together they could make every one of their dreams come true.

They'd sort out what she was going to do with her job. They'd find the men who had raped Connor's mom and make sure they were punished. They'd get married and start the family they both longed for.

Then they'd enjoy every second of life, making sure they never took it for granted because they knew how easily things could change.

With a content sigh, Becca pulled on Connor until he lowered a little of his weight to rest against her, his length still nestled inside her. Not heavy enough to crush her, his weight cocooned her, making her feel loved and protected, both things she knew were true. Connor was her soulmate, and her life could never be complete without him in it.

Life didn't always give you second chances, but this time it had, and Becca was glad she'd grabbed hold of it and refused to let it go because now she got to make her dreams a reality.

CHAPTER
Twenty-Three

August 31st
5:39 P.M.

"Huh."

Connor looked over at Becca to find her glancing at her phone. There was something in her expression that he wasn't sure he liked.

It had been a great week. They'd taken things easy and spent time recovering, most of that time naked and in each other's arms. When they weren't doing that, they were working with his brothers, continuing to comb through any scrap of intel they could get their hands on in their search for answers.

Which is what they were doing right now.

Pizza boxes were strewn over his kitchen counters, and on his table. Surrounded by plates of pizza and cans of soda were papers, laptops, and tablets. The more the danger surrounding his family grew the more desperate for answers they all got.

He was ready to jump headlong into the future with Becca he'd always dreamed of. He wanted to be focused on that, on getting to know each other again, sorting out what Becca would do about her job, and making this home more both of theirs than just his. He wanted to be able to propose and start planning for their future, but instead, it felt like they were trapped in quicksand that little by little was pulling them all down.

It had to end, and they were all doing everything in their power to make it end and yet they were moving so slowly they may as well not be moving at all.

"What's wrong?" he asked, shoving his chair away from the table and crossing to where Becca stood in the kitchen. She'd gone to get herself another drink but obviously stopped when someone called her. "Who is it?"

Her dark blue eyes were confused when she looked up at him. "It's a guy that works for the charity. He was with us in Cambodia."

"I don't remember there being another worker in Cambodia. I thought it was just you and Isabella." When Becca winced at the mention of her missing best friend, Connor smoothed his hand up and down her arm and tugged her into an embrace. While Prey was working on doing everything they could to locate who had taken Bella and where she'd gone after being snatched from the village, so far they were yet to make any progress. She was doing her best not to let worry over her friend ruin this time of them reconnecting and repairing what had been damaged, but Connor knew Becca was struggling to allow herself to be happy while her best friend was in danger.

"Sorry, didn't mean to bring up Bella. But who is this guy and why didn't I meet him when I was in Cambodia?" He hadn't spent long in the village, but he would have known if there was another worker there.

"John was getting supplies that day," Becca replied.

"Getting supplies? So he was conveniently not in the village when it was attacked, Isabella was abducted, and you and Connor were taken and almost killed?" Cooper asked, clearly skeptical about the timing.

As was he.

It didn't feel right, although there was no evidence yet to suggest it was anything more than coincidence.

"Well, it wasn't convenient, at least I don't think it was," Becca told Cooper, but there was a thread of doubt in her tone.

Did she really doubt this John guy or had they planted seeds of doubt in her mind?

"One of us always did the supply run once a fortnight. Up to the nearest town. It usually took about a day. He left after you showed up, and ..." she trailed off then looked up at him with wide eyes. "I don't remember seeing him after we got back to the village, and we were gone for well over twenty-four hours. You didn't even know he existed so he mustn't have been there."

"What's his full name?" Jake asked, shifting his laptop to the kitchen counter and looking at Becca expectantly.

"It's John Jones," she replied. When he quirked a dark brow at her, she shrugged. "Okay, so the first and last names are kind of common, but it's not like it's John Smith or anything."

"How long has he worked for the charity?" Cole asked.

"Not long. Actually, not long at all." Becca lifted her hands and rubbed at her temples as though she were getting a headache.

Stress.

Too much of it.

His poor girl needed a break, so she could process everything she'd been through these last few weeks and begin to deal with it, but they weren't going to get a break until they could eliminate the people out to get them.

"How long is not long?" Cole pressed.

"Umm ... Bella and I had been in Cambodia for around two years. We had a guy working with us, older, almost seventy, really nice, had been in the Peace Corps when he was younger. Then his elderly dad got sick, and he left. We were supposed to get another guy as a replacement, but at the last minute, he pulled out and we got John instead. He'd been there for a little over a month I guess."

"So right around the time that I was in Egypt and met Willow and we took down Tarek Mahmoud," Cooper said, slinging an arm around his girlfriend.

"Not a coincidence," Willow added.

If it was possible, Becca's already wide eyes widened further. "You think that someone was already investigating you all and linking me to Connor because of our past, then somehow got the man who was supposed to come to back out so they could send their own person to ... what exactly?"

Tightening his hold on Becca, he tucked her head under his chin and without thinking, reached out to grab the penis plushie Becca had taken to carrying around with her like a security blanket and pressed it into her hand. Immediately, she began to stroke it almost compulsively along her cheek and he knew exactly what they'd be doing if they were alone right now.

If that was true, and that's what they'd done, then these men were truly diabolical.

It felt like they would never be safe again, but they couldn't back down. Not when they were finally making a little bit of progress toward proving their parents were not traitors.

"How did this guy act? How did he make you feel? Were you comfortable around him? Did you trust him?" Jax fired off questions at Becca, who shivered in his arms. No wonder knowing potentially she was being watched all this time. She'd been so vulnerable, and he hadn't even realized it.

"I ... didn't like him. Bella didn't either. She said he was creepy, and we didn't understand why he was there. He didn't seem to like Cambodia, or the people, or his job. We wondered why he'd even signed up for this kind of job if he didn't like it." Tilting her head up she gave him a worried look. "He asked me out a few times, but I always said no. It was Bella's turn to do the supply run, but he insisted it should be him after you showed up. Said I needed the support of my best friend. But, Connor. I didn't tell him anything about you. So how did he know I would need support? I mean, I guess I made it obvious we had a history, but ... I don't like it."

"Me either, moonlight," he said, holding her tighter and trying to convince himself she was there and she was safe.

"Why is he calling me now? Should I call him back?" Becca asked.

"Call him back," Cade answered.

Becca nodded but looked anxious about the idea, and Connor found he couldn't force her to do anything that upset her, especially after all she'd endured because of her connection to him.

"You don't have to if you don't want to," he assured her, ignoring his big brother's glower as he smoothed a lock of hair off Becca's face and tucked it behind her ear.

She looked up at him, gratefulness in her eyes, determination too. It grew as she took in the five other men and two women standing around them. Then she gave a decisive nod. "I can do it. We all need this to be over." Lifting her arm, she unlocked her phone and brought up the list of recent calls. After drawing in a deep breath, she clutched the penis plushie in one hand while pressing John's number with the other.

"Becca," a whispered voice answered on the second ring.

"John. Sorry I missed your call, what did you need? If it's about when things will get up and running in Cambodia again the answer is I'm not sure yet."

"No, it's ... I ... Connor Charleston, you know him?"

"Yes. Why?"

"I think his sister Cassandra is also my sister."

What will Cade Charleston sacrifice when his daughter is targeted? Find out in the fourth book in the action packed and emotionally charged Prey Security: Charlie Team series!

Vengeful Lies (Prey Security: Charlie Team #4)

Also by Jane Blythe

Detective Parker Bell Series

A SECRET TO THE GRAVE
WINTER WONDERLAND
DEAD OR ALIVE
LITTLE GIRL LOST
FORGOTTEN

Count to Ten Series

ONE
TWO
THREE
FOUR
FIVE
SIX
BURNING SECRETS
SEVEN
EIGHT
NINE
TEN

Broken Gems Series

CRACKED SAPPHIRE

CRUSHED RUBY

FRACTURED DIAMOND

SHATTERED AMETHYST

SPLINTERED EMERALD

SALVAGING MARIGOLD

River's End Rescues Series

COCKY SAVIOR

SOME REGRETS ARE FOREVER

SOME FEARS CAN CONTROL YOU

SOME LIES WILL HAUNT YOU

SOME QUESTIONS HAVE NO ANSWERS

SOME TRUTH CAN BE DISTORTED

SOME TRUST CAN BE REBUILT

SOME MISTAKES ARE UNFORGIVABLE

Candella Sisters' Heroes Series

LITTLE DOLLS

LITTLE HEARTS

LITTLE BALLERINA

Storybook Murders Series

NURSERY RHYME KILLER

FAIRYTALE KILLER

FABLE KILLER

Saving SEALs Series

SAVING RYDER

SAVING ERIC

SAVING OWEN

SAVING LOGAN

SAVING GRAYSON

SAVING CHARLIE

Prey Security Series

PROTECTING EAGLE

PROTECTING RAVEN

PROTECTING FALCON

PROTECTING SPARROW

PROTECTING HAWK

PROTECTING DOVE

Prey Security: Alpha Team Series

DEADLY RISK

LETHAL RISK

EXTREME RISK

FATAL RISK

COVERT RISK

SAVAGE RISK

Prey Security: Artemis Team Series

IVORY'S FIGHT

PEARL'S FIGHT

LACEY'S FIGHT

OPAL'S FIGHT

Prey Security: Bravo Team Series

VICIOUS SCARS

RUTHLESS SCARS

BRUTAL SCARS

CRUEL SCARS

BURIED SCARS

WICKED SCARS

Prey Security: Athena Team Series

FIGHTING FOR SCARLETT

FIGHTING FOR LUCY

FIGHTING FOR CASSIDY

FIGHTING FOR ELLA

Prey Security: Charlie Team Series

DECEPTIVE LIES

SHADOWED LIES

TACTICAL LIES

VENGEFUL LIES

Christmas Romantic Suspense Series

THE DIAMOND STAR

CHRISTMAS HOSTAGE

CHRISTMAS CAPTIVE

CHRISTMAS VICTIM

YULETIDE PROTECTOR

YULETIDE GUARD

YULETIDE HERO

HOLIDAY GRIEF

HOLIDAY LOSS

HOLIDAY SORROW

Conquering Fear Series (Co-written with Amanda Siegrist)

DROWNING IN YOU

OUT OF THE DARKNESS

CLOSING IN

About the Author

USA Today bestselling author Jane Blythe writes action-packed romantic suspense and military romance featuring protective heroes and heroines who are survivors. One of Jane's most popular series includes Prey Security, part of Susan Stoker's OPERATION ALPHA world! Writing in that world alongside authors such as Janie Crouch and Riley Edwards has been a blast, and she looks forward to bringing more books to this genre, both within and outside of Stoker's world. When Jane isn't binge-reading she's counting down to Christmas and adding to her 200+ teddy bear collection!

To connect and keep up to date please visit any of the following